THE MUSIC HAD TO GO . . .

"And it's not," said the Doom and Destruction Devil, familiarly known as Threedee, "as if we didn't have more important matters than that blasted banjo to attend to. I'm at my wits' end trying to keep peace from breaking out and all you people can do is worry about these silly songs."

"What do you think was responsible for the first peace threats?" the Chairdevil snapped. "But I see your point. Which brings me to mine. Basically, Debauchery Devil, since you volunteered, I think we'll leave the British end of the operation up to you. Contain these people and destroy them—or at least destroy that banjo they've been using against us."

"This book has just about every virtue one can reasonably expect in a contemporary fantasy tale, including a vivid portrait of the contemporary folk scene and a chilling emotional impact that makes many horror novels look pedestrian. Highly recommended."

—*Booklist*

Also by Elizabeth Scarborough

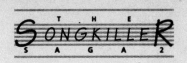

THE
SONGKILLER
SAGA 2

PICKING
THE
BALLAD'S
BONES

For Don
Picky picky
picky

ELIZABETH
SCARBOROUGH

▲▲▲

Elizabeth Ann
Scarborough

SPECTRA™

BANTAM BOOKS
NEW YORK · TORONTO · LONDON · SYDNEY · AUCKLAND

PICKING THE BALLAD'S BONES
A Bantam Spectra Book/December 1991

ISBN 0-553-29363-X

Published simultaneously in the United States and Canada

Bantam Books are published by Bantam Books, a division of Bantam Doubleday
Dell Publishing Group, Inc. Its trademark, consisting of the words "Bantam
Books" and the portrayal of a rooster, is Registered in U.S. Patent and
Trademark Office and in other countries. Marca Registrada. Bantam Books, 666
Fifth Avenue, New York, New York 10103.

PRINTED IN THE UNITED STATES OF AMERICA

OPM 0 9 8 7 6 5 4 3 2 1

For Linden Staciokas and Ted Sponsel, who showed me Scotland.

PICKING

THE

BALLAD'S
BONES

PART I

▲▲▲

Great Scott's
Ghost

CHAPTER I

The woman had promised in her ad to "Make a Spook-tacle" of herself for children's Halloween parties and was doing her best to keep her word. The children could tell the person in the black, hooded robe was a woman because of her voice, which was a very odd one, of a crackling, country quality such as a female of the jack-o'-lantern species might have. What would a female jack-o'-lantern be, a jane-o'-lantern? Seven-year-old Minda Maloney giggled at the thought and the flashlight she held in her lap jiggled in sympathy, so that the beam pointing toward her snub nose in order to cast demonic light on her cherubic features did a little shadow dance on the ceiling instead.

"Shut up," hissed third-grader Sass Pulaski, punching her remedially in the arm and sending his own flashlight beam gyrating wildly around the room.

All of the children sat in a circle on the floor, some of them seated on Minda's mother's sofa pillows, some merely sitting with the seats of their costumes on the cold tile floors. Each child had been provided at the request of the entertainer with a flashlight before all the lights had been turned out. The storyteller herself had then made her entrance, her robes flowing around her, her elongated shadow folding up over the wall and ceiling so that she looked twelve feet tall, and faceless.

Then she had glided to a halt, her long black robes spreading around her as she sat so it looked as if she were melting into the floor. She drew a candle, as if from no-

where, though of course it actually came from one of those big wide sleeves, from which her hands emerged white as a corpse's with long red nails that looked like a vampire's but probably came from the Pay 'n' Save cosmetics department just like the ones Minda's mom wore. The candle was a tall black column and already had squiggles of wax melting down from it. The woman lit it, making it look as if she had fire at the ends of her fingers.

"Well, now. Let's see," the voice from inside the hood said. "I'm supposed to tell you a love story. That right?"

"Yuck!" Sass Pulaski replied.

"No, it's Halloween," said Minda's younger sister, Sandy. "You're s'posed to tell scary stories."

"Oh, well, then. I guess I'll begin it the way all scary stories begin. Does anybody know how that is?"

"Once upon a time?" ventured Selena Anderson.

"Nope. That's for fairy tales. This one has fairies in it, sort of, but it should begin as all dread tales begin, 'It was a dark and stormy night . . .'

"It was a dark and stormy night when the airplane landed at Heathrow and all the barf bags were full."

"I like this story already," Sass said.

"The nine-hour flight from Seattle had started out pleasantly enough, with music all around. A very merry red-haired stewardess who wanted the passengers to call her Torchy danced impromptu jigs to the tunes played by the banjo accompanying the group. I say the banjo accompanied the group, rather than that it was played by one of them, you notice. The reason for that is that while it's true that all the passengers were musicians and singers who occasionally did pick a specific tune on the banjo, much of the time the instrument simply played itself, all by its lonesome. It was that kind of a banjo."

"What kind?" Sass wanted to know. "Was it like a keyboard that looked and sounded like a banjo?"

"Nope, it was like magic. It had been made by a luthier, which is what you call an instrument maker, who was a white witch from back in the Appalachian Mountains. He made it for a man named Sam Hawthorne who spent his life finding and singing special, important songs,

*songs that made a difference in people's lives and taught
them to look at things in new ways. Songs that made Certain Parties very uncomfortable. And it was these Certain
Parties who were after the magic banjo now, trying to destroy it and destroy all the people who protected it and who
were guided by it, the people who were the keepers of its
songs."*

"Well, who were they? The Certain Parties, I mean?"
Jason Collins asked.

"Music critics, dopey, who else?" Sass said.

"Well, son, you're only part right," the spooky lady
said. "Music critics at least need to listen to music before
they trash it. These particular parties couldn't bear to so
much as hear a single chorus, they hated it so bad. Of
course, sometimes they worked through music critics, but
basically, I believe you'd call them devils."

"Devils?" Selena asked suspiciously. "You aren't going
to start trying to preach religion here at our party, are you?
Because my mom doesn't like that and she would sue
Minda's mom."

"That so?"

"Yeah, and my mom doesn't want me to listen to stuff
about witches and demons and stuff either," Selena, sens-
ing she had the upper hand, added.

"No demons or witches or devils or religious stuff—I
suppose that means angels too?"

Selena nodded and said, unrepentantly, "Sor-ree."

"How about ghosts then?"

"Will they give me nightmares?"

"Oh, not intentionally. This is the ghost of a pretty nice
man. An interesting one anyway. And he's not anybody
you might run into around here. He's a Scottish ghost."

"That might be okay."

"Well, now, keeping in mind that we're talking about
old Scottish people here, who believed in such antediluvian
stuff as religion, talking purely about what they believed so
you understand I'm not preaching at you, do you suppose
your mama would have kittens if I told you first that there
is a Scottish prayer that this reminds me of? Sort of like
'Now I lay me down to sleep.'"

"Now I WHAT?" Selena asked haughtily.

" 'NowIlaymedowntosleepIpraytheLordmysoultokeepif IshoulddiebeforeIwakeIpraytheLordmysoultotake,' " said Minda. *"Honestly, you are so dumb. If you spoil this party I will never ever invite you again and I won't talk to you anymore either."*

"Me neither," said her brother.

" 'Oh, I guess it's okay just so she's not trying to convert me or preach creationism or anything like that."

"That's real nice of you, honey," the voice from deep in the cowl said. "Now then, there is this ancient Scottish prayer that says, and I quote, 'From ghosties and ghoulies and long-leggit beasties and things that go bump in the night may the Good Lord preserve us.' "

"Hey, I know, I know!" Minda's brother said, waving his hand wildly to be called on. "I bet it's not a prayer at all. I bet the Lord is like the KING lord and they're wanting him to save them from, you know, like the bad guys and all the animals that eat up dead people and mortars and nighttime artillery fire and stuff, huh?"

"Interesting theory," the spook in the hood said. "You should look into that sometime. But I'm talking a little more literally here. It is Halloween and this is a ghost story."

"Oh, okay. But I'd like a battle better."

"You know, you and the ghost I'm going to tell you about have a lot in common. You'll like him, I think."

The candle flame died down and the voice changed, so that the accent in it shifted shape, from southern to something with a's as soft and broad as the back of an old horse and r's that buzzed around the room like bees. And as the children stared into the candlelight, the story the woman told seemed to gain life within the flame, so that they could see the whole thing happening, all of it, and even the big words she used were easy to understand because the pictures they made were so clear, hanging over the candle's flickering flame.

Things were going bump in the night in the study at Abbotsford, which is a famous Scottish landmark, being the former home of Sir Walter Scott, who was a novelist, a folklorist, and, for his day job, a lawyer, what they call a barrister in Scotland. Sir Walter, who you might call the "ghostie" in this instance, heard the barking of the border collie who was the "long-leggit beastie" who guarded the house at night. The dog's carrying on was so loud it made poor Sir Walter turn right over in his grave. "My word," said Sir Walter, rolling onto his side to assume his favorite sleeping position from when he was alive, "strange sort of time for the National Trust to start renovations."

And the "ghoulie" who had been rifling through the library at the behest of Certain Parties paused for a moment, catching its breath, in a manner of speaking (since it is debatable whether or not ghouls, being deadish sorts, have need of respiration). The ghost of Sir Walter had been aroused by the disturbance the ghoul created in the ether when he manhandled Sir Walter's books and notes, which were as much a part of the great author's immortality as his immaterial self. The same ethereal disturbance rebounded to shake the ghoul to its rotting core as Sir Walter awoke and rotated in his resting place.

"Blimey," the ghoul said to himself. (He was not a very high-class sort of ghoul, merely the remnant of a burglar shot in the crossfire of a gun battle between his associates of similar low degree and the police. But he was the best Certain Parties could come up with on the spur of the moment. Besides, they hadn't reckoned that destroying part of a historic library required the assistance of a more refined thug, which showed a certain lack of respect for the material they wanted destroyed and its former owner.)

Mind you, Sir Walter Scott was not your typical sort of spirit. Not that his somewhat baroque field of interest had ever given him delusions of grandeur. When he invoked the common broad speech of the common Scot, he was not slumming, as some implied. Nor was he copying Robert Burns, as others would have it. His title might make him a toff, but it was part of his romanticism that Sir Walter was very proud to be not two generations removed from border raiders and brigands, and that the wife of a former Walter Scott had been known, when the larder was empty, to serve her lord husband his spurs on a plate as a not-too-subtle hint that it was time to take to horse and go rustle a head or two of cattle from the Sassenachs in Northumberland. The "refined" English speech had come later in the family's history. But the qualities of leadership needed in a brigand lord, more than manners and speech, remained even after the outlawry was duly legalized.

In Walter Scott the writer the leadership took a more imaginative and original turn than mere cattle thieving. In his lifetime he regained the right of the Scot to wear the tartan, even after it had been so thoroughly obliterated that clans, including those who had never affected Highland dress in the past, had to have whole new plaids invented to fit the fashion newly popularized by the English royalty. He found the lost crown jewels of Scotland, which you can see to this day in the treasure room at Edinburgh Castle. He wrote the most popular novels of his day. And, most important to our story, he preserved for posterity and in some cases restored and improved upon the folk ballads of Scotland, the great bloody romantic murder ballads, and the songs that encompassed the highly embroidered history of his land. And all that was in addition to holding down a respectable position in the Scottish superior court and being sheriff of the whole district to boot.

Scottish sheriffs were a little different from the ones in the cowboy movies, but they were lawmen all the same, and Sir Walter was a man of action just as much as anybody you'd see on the Late Show. And if there was one breach of conduct that had gotten him riled while he was alive, it was seeing somebody mistreat a book.

Now, Sir Walter had been an old fellow when he died, with lots of sickness and disappointment and grief to wear him down, just like most folks have. He didn't quite know what to think when he turned over in his grave and found he couldn't get back to sleep, except that he was a little irritated. He'd woke up a few times before to greet old friends now and then, welcome them to the fold, as it were, but mostly he just stayed dead and did whatever it is good dead people do when they aren't messing around with the living. But it dawned on him all of a sudden what that ornery low-class varmint of a ghoul was doing, and that he was doing it to Sir Walter's own beloved library. Sir Walter had paid a dear price for that library and for Abbotsford, had ruined himself putting it all together, and his spirit had been very relieved when the National Trust for Scotland took over the whole shebang. He'd gotten up special then to go to the ceremony and wandered around personally thanking the people, just the way he might have if he were having a birthday party while he was alive.

But he figured out all of a sudden that this ghoul was up to something no spirit with any gumption could just lie there and take, so Sir Walter's spirit, his mortal remains being long turned to dust, rose itself out of the grave at Dryburgh Abbey where he was buried and wished itself at Abbotsford. Without quite knowing what it was wishing, it also wished itself into a handy suit of armor loafing beside the entrance hall and wished itself down. The armor already had a sword conveniently clapped into its metal gloves.

So here you have this deserted mansion in the middle of the night, and Sir Walter's ghost, mad as a wet hen, clanking down that long tiled entranceway and into the study and to the library, *clank, clank, clank*, swinging that sword a little to get the rust out of the joints of the armor, ghost eyes glowing blue fire through the slit in the helmet, *clank, clank, clank*, bearing down on that ghoulish crook and demanding in a quavery Scots burr that chilled the ghoul to his own dead marrow, "Wha' the devil are ye aboot?" Of course, Sir Walter's ghost had no idea how close to being right it inadvertently was about the nature of the ghoul's bosses. Him sort of *knowing* about the devils well and truly spooked the ghoul, you should pardon the expression. The gruesome critter started to drop a first-edition copy of *Minstrelsy of the Scottish Borders* on the floor but a glare from the ghost froze the ghoul so it set the book nicely on the display case and slunk away, the ghost clanking behind it to see that it did so. When the ghoul was safely out the door, the border collie guardian beast came out from under the table and bowwowed bravely at the departing animated carcass, and even got so brave as to worry a piece of rotting finger bone it had left behind.

Sir Walter's ghost climbed back up onto the armor's niche, rearranged it into its original position, tsked-tsked at the trail of rust chips left on the tiles, and wafted back to the library. As long as he was up he thought he might wander through his beloved library again for a while. His hand itched for a pen. The ghost scene he had just enacted might seem corny to you and me with me telling it like this, but he considered it a classic and it gave him an idea for a story he wished he could write down.

CHAPTER II

▲▲▲

Meanwhile, at Heathrow airport, a certain redheaded hellraiser in a flight attendant's uniform watched a fellow flight attendant whose nametag said "R. McCorley" carry a wee little bomb off the plane in his carry-on luggage. McCorley shouldered his way into the cattle-pen maze barriers and walkways that herded people through the customs line, inserting himself between the musician, Willie MacKai, who was toting a banjo in a garment bag, and another musician named Brose Fairchild. They were bringing up the rear. The deaf girl, Julianne Martin, the dark growly-looking woman the others called Anna Mae but whose passport said "Mabel Gunn," the young Randolph couple, Faron and Ellie, and the chatty old gal named Gussie, who was much older than she had been a year ago but who was not yet as old as I am, were already being questioned.

The redhead, whose tag said "T. Burns," twirled her own flight bag from one finger and rocked one high heel idly from side to side, her mouth quirking in amusement as she ambled along behind Brose Fairchild and watched to see what McCorley would do next.

The Martin girl tried signing to the first customs officer but he didn't seem to understand, and when Gunn stepped forward to explain or possibly interpret, he warned her sternly to stay in line. Meanwhile, Fairchild, the old gal, and the Randolphs passed by another officer without much incident, but MacKai was stopped and ordered to unzip the garment bag.

"Anything to declare, miss?" the officer asked the redhead as she slung her flight bag up onto his counter.

"Just the usual," she said.

Up ahead, the customs officer was eyeing the banjo, which was softly playing a line from an old ballad that started, "Oh, let me in, the soldier cried. Cold haily windy night—"

"Does it always do this, sir?" the customs man demanded.

"Sure as hell does, buddy," MacKai was saying. "And you better believe it cost me a pretty penny to get that electronics engineer to rig it up this way."

"As you say, sir. However, we can't allow you to bring this into Britain."

"And just why would that be?" MacKai asked softly as anxiety welled up inside him that after coming so far, the devils were finding yet another way to separate him from the only key to reclaiming the music. At the same time, he knew that belligerence wouldn't get him far with the authorities so he tried to sound pleasant.

"We have a description of an instrument of this sort, self-frailing, I believe it said, as stolen goods, sir."

"That must be some other banjo they're talkin' about, officer. See this one here was given to me by . . ." MacKai tried to explain but the officer nodded to an armed man behind him who started forward.

"And what do you mean by the usual, miss?" T. Burns's official asked.

"You know, a lid of heroin, a few crystals of crack, and some new stuff—"

"I'm sorry, miss, we don't like joking about that sort of thing. You'll have to—"

Ordinarily, she would have delighted in choosing that moment to disappear from sight and memory, leaving the man with a loaded flight bag, a mountain of paperwork, and nobody to blame anything on, but McCorley had just opened his own bag. He pulled something from it and threw it to the floor behind the customs official. A thick cloud of acrid smoke billowed up from the floor as if cloaking some particularly bashful dragon.

"Shee-it!" Fairchild bellowed, and grabbed the redhead's hand, barreled into MacKai, and plowed the rest of his party before him with the exception of McCorley, who lobbed the wee little bomb far enough into the cattle-pen arrangement to give himself time to escape before the whole works blew sky-high.

Shouting, coughing, random gunfire, and an alarm siren mooing throughout the terminal added to the excitement. No security guards from inside the terminal tried to stop Willie and his friends from leaving the customs area, however, because of the nostril-burning day-old-corpse smell of the smoke that doubled everybody up with coughing. Out in the terminal, nobody tried to apprehend the fleeing group because plenty of other people were dancing around trying to find out what the excitement was all about, was it dangerous, and how to avoid being hurt by it while enjoying the spectacle as something to write home about.

Faintly tinkling in the background, the banjo, half-smothered by the garment bag, played the line from Loch Lomond that was sung as, "You take the high road and I'll take the low road."

"How the hell do you get out of here?" Willie demanded to nobody in particular.

"You heard the banjo," Gussie said. "They take subways around here. Torchy honey," she hollered back to the redhead, "You're the local. Which way is the subway?"

Torchy Burns, as she was sometimes called, occasionally liked to play by the rules just long enough to confuse everyone, so she led them to the nearest underground station.

▲▲▲

"Wait, wait, wait," Sass said. "What is it with this redheaded lady? Is she a spy or what?"

"Or what," the voice behind the candle and cowl drawled. "She's one of those Certain Parties I was telling

you about but I'm not supposed to say exactly who or what they are for fear of offending somebody's mother."

"But if she's one of the Certain Parties," Minda put in, "why is she helping them so much?"

"She's a little different from the other Certain Parties," the cowled voice said. "For one thing, she's not as reliable. She doesn't much care about right and wrong, just about doing whatever she feels like at the moment. Not much on long-range goals, doesn't care if she spreads disease, doesn't care if she doesn't, doesn't care if what she does kills folks, and doesn't care if it doesn't. She just likes to see what happens."

"Where'd she get all those drugs?" another kid wanted to know.

"Why, son, she's got all the drugs and all the booze and all the other mind-bending, weird-making stuff anybody'd ever think to look for. She's the source of all of it and the source of anybody wanting it. She makes any other drug dealer or vice lord look like an amateur."

"But she helped them," Minda said. "She helped them get away, didn't she?"

"In about the same way a cat lets a mouse scuttle out between its paws for a while. And she was still putting moves on ol' Willie, trying to charm the banjo away from him just to see if she could."

CHAPTER III

▲▲▲

The musicians followed the flight attendant blindly since they didn't have time to figure out the underground schedules. She herded them on and off the underground and onto a train bound for Scotland. Gussie nearly got a stiff neck from looking over her shoulder so much and she could tell that the rest of them were nervous wrecks too by the time they got settled into the little train compartment, which consisted of two long benches across from each other in a tiny little room with windows on one side and a door on the other. Their compartment was the last one in the car next to the sleeping car.

The train rolled away from the outskirts of London through all the ugliest, most industrial parts, dimly seen through growing daylight. How long had it been since they'd landed? It seemed like only a few minutes and Gussie's heart was still pitter-patting like mad, but when she asked Anna Mae Gunn and Anna Mae checked her wristwatch, a big old man's one on a black waterproof band buckled up to the last notch with the tip end hacked off with scissors so it wouldn't stick out over Anna Mae's knobby tanned wrist bones, the time was nearly six in the morning. Daylight swarmed in on them as they stopped for five minutes every ten minutes ·or so at some little podunk village with daub-and-wattle houses that looked a lot like the ones on the PBS mysteries Gussie used to like to watch on her nights off.

Brose Fairchild stared out at the villages backed by

rolling expanses of green and grunted, "Looks just like Missouri to me. Ain't much more than a Sunday stroll to get across the whole damn place." He rubbed his gray-black steel-wool hair with both Mississippi mud–colored fists and then rubbed his eyes as well.

"Don't knock it," Anna Mae Gunn told him. "We may be glad of it if we have to make a break. Not much cover though."

If it hadn't been for the events of the last few months, Gussie would have thought the former Native American rights activist was being a little overly paranoid, but in those same months Gussie's daughter and son-in-law had been wrongfully arrested for trying to help a Scottish musician enter the country, after which Gussie's own house was burglarized. When she had gone to a folk festival to raise support for the release of her children, she had been nearly electrocuted, shot, and arrested, in that order, before being personally hypnotized into driving God-only-knew how many miles into the traffic jam from hell from which she, Willie, Julianne, and a Texas lawman had barely escaped with the help of Brose, Anna Mae, the Randolphs, a chanteyman named Hawkins, and a few hints from that crazy banjo Willie MacKai carried. If that wasn't weird enough, Brose, Anna Mae, the Randolphs, and Hawkins claimed *they* had been prevented from getting killed or lost along the Oregon Trail by a series of apparitions Faron had started calling the Ghosts of the Pioneers, who steered the musicians into what was supposed to be a permanent and fatal traffic jam. If Gussie hadn't had almost positive proof that the self-playing banjo was in fact both bewitched and probably haunted by the ghost of the late great granddaddy of American folk music, Sam Hawthorne himself, she would have thought Faron was kidding about the ghosts. As it was, she took it for the literal truth and a part of the world as she now knew it. Unfortunately, she not only had to accept the helpful ghosts, but she also had to accept the insidious whoever-the-hell-it-was who made the phantom traffic jam. These insidious troublemakers, they had all come to believe, were responsible for a variety of circumstances that had virtually extinguished most music that could even remotely be called folk music from the United States. It was hard to say whether they'd been able to do the same thing in Canada since the borders were closed to musicians and there had been a postal strike for several months.

Anna Mae watched the land fall away behind them and fretted. "I was hoping we could split up again into teams and rent cars to investigate songs in the various areas of England, Ireland, Scotland, and Wales," Anna Mae said. "But I guess that's out of the question. They'd want ID to rent cars."

"I'm sick of drivin' anyway, after that mess out on the highway we got into on the way up to Washington State," Brose said. "Feels good to have somebody else do the drivin'." He glanced nervously over toward the banjo that leaned up against the seat beside Willie, who was having his chest hairs pulled by the redheaded stewardess. Brose was sure glad the banjo wasn't playing train wreck songs. Though sometimes the tunes or the lines it played were nothin' more than smart-alecky remarks about what was going on, sometimes the banjo warned them of danger—usually after they were already in it. Only once had it done something more and that was when it helped Willie MacKai and Julianne Martin write a song—kind of a riddle song.

"I hope to hell you all were right and that that song meant we was supposed to come all the way over here just to get ourselves in bad with the law."

"We have to reclaim the music, Brose, you know that," Anna Mae told him. "Don't pretend you don't. Without it we're helpless against whoever's behind this. You know the songs helped save Willie and the others—"

Willie yawned, too sleepy and too weary from the constant tension to be able to concentrate while circumstances seemed less than life-and-death urgent. Julianne Martin, trying to stay alert enough to guess what the others were saying that she could no longer hear, glanced over at him and quickly glanced away as Torchy Burns twined her legs around his knee and rubbed his shoulders long and hard with her hands, careful to make sure and draw herself up against him at every opportunity, her wild red hair screening them both. Julianne shrugged and looked out the window instead. She wasn't embarrassed particularly—years on the road with her late husband George, crashing and traveling with other musicians, would have cured her of prudishness, had she ever been inclined that way, which she hadn't been. But she did feel a little disappointed in Willie, that he seemed to be—well —too ready to fall into rather obvious distraction. Not that Torchy wasn't probably a perfectly nice person— although Juli thought there was something a little sly about her. It was just that although Juli had known of Willie for years and had run across him several times, only since they had been traveling together had she really begun to realize that there was something very special about him and she thought maybe he didn't realize it himself. She had hoped the business with the banjo and the music might help him to realize his potential. Her spiritual counselor, Lucien Santos, was very big on potential and had made Juli see that everybody had been given a lot of it and most people were just too foolish to spend the money to go to a wise counselor like Lucien to learn how to develop it. Juli thought Willie would probably have to try to develop his on his own—not with Lucien certainly. She didn't think Willie and Lucien would get along at all although she didn't go quite so far in her sizing up of the two of them to admit that the reason they wouldn't get along is they would each see through the other one's brand of horse-manure charm. On the other hand, whatever Torchy Burns was going to help Willie develop, Juli was pretty sure it wasn't his potential.

But then, maybe she was just jealous. Not that she had designs on Willie but seeing other people snuggling made her miss George, wish for him back to rub her shoulders or to be able to play the spoons along his back, which had made them both laugh and had usually led to other activities. She sent out a mental call for George's spirit, but got no answer. He probably couldn't hear her all the way over here in England, although with Lucien's guidance she had been able to have a number of illuminating conversations with George since he'd passed to the other side. George was the one who had told her that music was not to be her way. That she should study with Lucien to fully develop her psychic gifts instead. But since she had never felt inclined to blindly follow George's advice while he was alive (nor would he have expected her to), she certainly didn't see why she ought to now that he was dead, so she disregarded what George, Lucien, and the whole universe (as Lucien claimed) were telling her and had insisted on going to one last folk festival to try to gain everybody *else's* approval by performing again. She wished she could be strong and sure of herself and not *be* such an approval junkie—just charge right in there and do whatever she thought was best. Well, she did, actually, except that she never was really *sure* that it was best until it was over with. It seemed like if she took a poll first, even if nobody agreed with her, it was easier to decide what she ought to do.

The folk festival was a good example. If she hadn't gone, she would never have come into contact with the spirit of Sam Hawthorne inhabiting the magic banjo Lazarus, nor would she have known about the plot to wipe out folk music. That part of it was positive, surely, that and meeting Willie, Gussie, Anna Mae, and the others. She always tried to think of the positive first. Lucien had taught her that. And although she couldn't ever really forget it, when she brought the down side to the front of her mind, her eyes filled and she grew quivery and faint with the fear that she wouldn't hear again, would never be able to make physical music. So she didn't dwell too long on the fact that if she hadn't gone to the festival, she would not have been standing in front of the microphone when lightning struck it, deafening her. The deafness was probably only temporary, she told herself as the panic threatened to choke her and she fought her way back down to calmness and reasonableness by trying to concentrate on her mantra.

It couldn't be, couldn't be, couldn't be, *was not* permanent.

This was, like, her destiny, coming on this trip and somehow her being here would help reverse the evil that had fallen upon all of them. Surely her deafness wasn't retribution for continuing to yearn for music when all of the portents told her it no longer had a place in her life. Well, not all the portents.

Lazarus, Hawthorne's banjo, had spoken to her not just as a psychic but as a psychic musician whose deafness the banjo's magic had simply ignored when it gave her and Willie MacKai the song that would surely save them all. The song that would lift the evil from them, from the music and musicians all over the States. So surely, surely, please, God, please, goddess, please, collective unconscious and all the powers that be, it must be the evil that had made her deaf and if she helped reverse it—she stopped thinking then because Lucien had told her she had a regrettable tendency to believe in fairy-tale endings and she realized that her hope for her hearing involved one. So she turned her attention to Willie again.

Darn him. He was the keeper of the banjo and if they were going to beat their enemy—whatever it was—he was going to have to be strong and true and a real spiritual warrior, as Lucien would have said, and that was *not* going to happen while he was carrying on with redheaded bimbos.

"Can't we just take the train someplace? Ireland maybe?" Willie asked nobody in particular as he languidly wiped a strand of Torchy's hair away from his face. "Lots of songs in Ireland."

"There'd be too many ID checks along the way," Anna Mae said, frowning.

"Scotland then," Gussie suggested. "I've always wanted to see Scotland, ever since I read Rob Roy when I was a little girl."

Faron, who had been quietly conferring with his wife, said, "That's a great idea. The Child Ballads were from Scotland as much as England and we ought to be able to find a copy of *Minstrelsy of the Scottish Border* somewhere in Sir Walter Scott country, I'd think. The library at Edinburgh University is supposed to be great too."

"Oh, and they've some lovely pubs in Scotland," Torchy Burns purred, cuddling up even closer, though it hardly seemed possible, to Willie. "And these rail compartments are very nice, aren't they? Quite a pleasant trip this could be." In Willie's ear she whispered, "How about it, luv? There's a vacant compartment next car over. I peeked when I went to the loo. Who'd be the wiser?"

Julianne didn't need her hearing to figure out what *that* little exchange was all about. Willie was cozying up to the woman, buying into it.

Anna Mae Gunn didn't care much for the way the flight attendant was behaving either. She seemed entirely too nonchalant about their whole predicament. Why hadn't she tried to stop the terrorist? Wasn't she worried about losing her job? Anna Mae couldn't quite believe the woman was so impervious to everything but Willie's renowned fatal charm that she forgot everything. Little Torchy didn't seem like the kind of woman to let anything about anybody else make her oblivious to her own welfare.

Of course, what none of them knew about Torchy was that she had another career quite a bit more exotic than the one she had as a flight attendant, and it was in danger too.

As Willie MacKai would have told you in a New York minute, it wasn't that he was anybody's fool, in particular. And he certainly did not make a habit of making a fool of himself over women. Somewhat to his surprise, it had almost always been the other way around. He wasn't exactly handsome—in fact, if you looked at him carefully, you'd see that he most exactly was *not* handsome. Kinda ordinary-looking with a big nose and crooked teeth and a head of hair that in certain spots was, well, just a head. But he was generally lean and even when he wasn't he gave the impression of a particularly appealing coyote who had just benefited from a handout and would revert to rib-ridged skinniness in a couple of days. He had the same kind of animal magnetism as that famous trickster of Indian tales too, and could be wily in the woods or when he noticed enough of what was going on around

him to watch his tail. Mostly, though, he got so purely
wound up inside himself he just didn't notice, and if he
didn't have any special idea of what to do, he was content
to drift along with whoever did have. And Torchy Burns
was, more than anybody he'd ever been with, a critter
with an agenda.

In the sleeping car where she was all snuggled up with
Willie, Torchy pulled out a flask, took a swig, and
grinned to herself. She had plans that involved Willie
MacKai, oh, yes, she did. And his little banjo too. But
she wanted to have some fun first. At times, the other
devils could be as dull as saints and they didn't understand that a being could get bored unless she varied her
routine a little. One big smashing evil after another
wasn't as interesting as stringing people along, letting
them think they were going to make it, then hitting them
with something to wipe the self-congratulations right out
of them and scare them too. She would—

Her thought was sliced in half by the rude summoning
of the Chairdevil, who jerked her spirit right out of the
flight attendant's body and back to the boardroom. It
took her half of one of Willie's heartbeats to reassemble
herself in front of the devil board.

And Willie, who was so tired he couldn't do much
more than murmur sweet nothings in his sleep, didn't see
his playmate's hand stop with the flask halfway to her
mouth, drop limply to her side instead, and spill the perfectly good contents of the flask all over the floor of the
compartment. The woman's whole body sagged to still-
ness, the eyes wide open and starey as a baby doll's, as
the ornery spirit who was the animating force of that
body was yanked back to headquarters to be called on the
carpet by her boss.

"Just what do you think you're doing now, DD?" the
Chairdevil demanded in front of the whole board of devils meeting. They were all sitting around the big long
table looking as sanctimonious as if they worked for the
Opposition. The devil in the shape of the redheaded
woman didn't have a whole lot of use for her colleagues
and the feeling was mutual.

So the Debauchery Devil, since that was who the red-headed devil was, answered the Chairdevil in the voice of her Texas persona, Lulubelle Baker, talking right back to him just as saucy as good barbecue, "Why, boss, I was just fixin' to pass on a little somethin' to my buddy Willie MacKai."

"Isn't that closing the barn door after the horses got out?" the Chairdevil asked. "Wasn't that terrorist minion supposed to have blown up the plane in midair? What did you do about that, DD? You blew it, didn't you?"

She manifested herself a big wad of Beelzebubblegum and blew a huge, sticky bubble of it so fat it touched his nose before she popped it with a sassy grin and said, "Now, boss, you know I did no such thing. All I blew was this bubble and that is what's rilin' you, now isn't it? After all, I didn't pick the terrorist minion. Can I help it if he's a sweet, old-fashioned IRA type who gets all mushy over rebel songs instead of heavy metal?"

The Chairdevil puffed himself up like a cobra snake and said, "What I can't understand, DD, is how you came to be among these people anyway."

"I thought someone should keep an eye on them," she said vaguely, bouncing the high-heeled shoe on her left foot up and down on her toe. "Keep them in trouble."

"Hmph," he said. "It wouldn't have anything to do with the sneaking admiration you have for that Willie MacKai, now, would it?"

"A mortal? Boss! My interest is purely professional, I assure you."

"Well, as long as you're on the job, I think we'll just have to make it your responsibility," the Chairdevil said, eliciting groans and moans from the other devils.

"I object," said the Expediency Devil. "You know very well, boss, that if there's anything DD is not, it's responsible."

"Yeah," she grinned. "Being irresponsible is part of what I do. But what did you have in mind? I thought you didn't want to deal with the MacKai group directly anyway because of the banjo. I thought I'd just get old Willie drunk enough to shed the banjo along with his pants and then we could work our evil will on them all." She smacked her lips lasciviously.

"Aw, just let the cops get them," the Stupidity and Ignorance Devil said. "They'll throw 'em in the pokey for the mess that mick made of the airport."

"How many times do I have to tell you, I don't want them in jail?" the Chairdevil said.

"We know, we know," the other devils said. "They enjoy jail."

"But, boss, I don't see how else we're going to control them," the Superstition Devil said, whining a little. "That blasted banjo defeats all of our schemes and I just got a report that my ghoul minion has had to leave one library of that—well, you know, that material we don't talk about—untouched because one of the dead actually rose up to protect it. I don't like it when dead people I don't control start interfering."

"It's that banjo again, I'll bet you anything," the Expediency Devil said. "Old Wizard Hawthorne reaching out from the grave to foil us again with that spell on that blasted instrument. We have to destroy it and all of those songs but we're spreading ourselves pretty thin as it is. There's still work to be done in the United States, and Canada is presenting a real problem. The bureaucracy and big business aren't as firmly entrenched there and so the minions aren't as helpful. More amateur singing goes on up there too, so the resistance to us is stronger."

"And it's not," said the Doom and Destruction Devil, sometimes called D&D but more familiarly known as Threedee, "as if we didn't have more important matters to attend to. I'm at my wit's end trying to keep peace from breaking out and all you people can do is worry about these silly songs."

"What do you think was responsible for the first peace threats?" the Chairdevil snapped. "But I see your point. Which brings me to mine. Basically, DD, since you volunteered, I think we'll leave the British end of the operation up to you. Contain these people and destroy them— or at least destroy that *thing* they've been using against us. We've already used the minions to take out the libraries and collections and the major living receptacles of the material and it made so little difference to the living it didn't even create a stir. But the dead may cause you some problems."

"Maybe," she said. "But then, maybe I can talk to the lab and promote better dying through chemistry too. Trust me, boss," she said with a wolfish grin and another large bubble that grew and grew and grew until it obscured her whole form, which seemed to shrink as the bubble grew larger until, when the bubble popped, DD was no longer behind it.

Back in the sleeping compartment, Torchy Burns stretched. Oh, well, maybe she'd have to forgo most of the fun and wrap this up more quickly than she'd planned. That would require minions. She sent out feelers into the ether and way up at Abbotsford Walter Scott's ghost felt her sending. She'd overdone it a little, however. It just so happened she had the *most* appropriate people nearby. Use show business to fight show business, she chuckled to herself, and wrapped her arms around Willie MacKai, running the open neck of a flask under his nose. "Wake up, Willie, luv. Time for your medicine," she said. The banjo, abandoned in a corner, twanged "Whiskey in the Jar."

CHAPTER IV

▲▲▲

The train made a short sighing stop and hooked on to three private cars gaudily decorated like Gypsy wagons. One held the machinery of carousels and tilt-a-whirls, one held tents and caravans, and from one boxcar came the roars of big cats and the trumpetings of elephants. A sign on the side of the car proclaimed it Circus Rom.

In Carlisle the train stopped again. Emerging from the WC, in the back of the car, Juli looked out the window and saw uniformed policemen lurking near every car, trying hard to look nonchalant. Hurrying back to her own compartment, she pointed out the trap to the others. Anna Mae swore roundly and pounded on the wall separating their compartment from the one containing Willie and Torchy.

She was too slow. Willie and Torchy flashed by the compartment door, heading toward the back of the train. The banjo alone could have been arrested for disturbing the peace, so loudly did it continue to twang "Whiskey in the Jar."

"Where's he goin' now?" Gussie mumbled, waking from a fitful sleep crammed up against the window casing.

"The police are waiting for us," Julianne said, pointing out the window.

"Well, nice of Willie to let the rest of us know," Gussie said angrily. "I've got a notion to go give that young man a piece of my mind."

"You go right ahead and do that little thing," Brose said. "But as for me, I got an urgent appointment anyplace else but here."

▲▲▲

Although he had been dead for a couple hundred years (which was long experience compared to that of the living and a mere trifle compared to others he had encountered), Walter Scott had been a pretty good man and so he had not hung around in the ghost realm much before but had gone straight to heaven. He was a little baffled to find himself back in the ghost realm now. He was fairly sure heaven had been where he'd been keeping himself these last few years, and thought that probably the rumors were true that said paradise was so wonderful that nobody was ever granted memory of it for fear their other existences would be so filled with longing for it that they wouldn't be able to do what was necessary elsewhere.

He didn't find it difficult to determine the current date, because there was a guest book in the front hall where the Trust set up its information booth. He was very pleased with how they'd kept his home, approved of the minor alterations they had made to turn it into a visitors' attraction. He had promised Abbotsford to the trustees when he died, in expiation of that last bundle of debt he'd been trying to work his way out of when he died. Curious to learn how long he'd been away, he decided to go see how the outside world had changed. The moment he set foot outside the door however, he found himself back in his grave, which was a very dreary place for a conscious entity, even one with no body. No notepad or pen or books for company. Totally unsatisfactory. He tried to rise from the grave once more and found himself back at Abbotsford. So. He could come and go between two points—that which most concerned him while he lived and that which most concerned him while dead, but no other points in between. A nuisance, of course, but he supposed it made sense. Couldn't have a lot of dead folk indiscriminately disturbing the living. The thought of it made him feel very lonely, a condition remedied as soon as day broke, the custodians opened the hall, and tourists came pouring in, clutching maps and guidebooks, wearing extremely strange and sometimes indecorous garments, and chattering among themselves with varying degrees of interest or boredom. The energy of the most road-weary among them made him feel drained and diminished, and a part of him understood that this was probably why ghosts were not seen by day. The vitality of the living was such a contrast that he was like the moon in broad daylight, of no use or consequence and scarcely noticeable.

He also found, to his interest, that the spirit world was not quite like the world of the living. It bore some resemblance to life underwater. He felt intimations of persons and events and fluctuations in the—ether, he supposed some would call it—a great confusing babble of stuff from the very old to the very new. It was somewhat like the inside of his head, bits of history, biographies of personages, scraps of legend, glimpses of places he had not visited but which preoccupied his imagination. Underlying it all he sensed the continuous babble of sad stories, cries for help, emanations of anguish and anxiety and resignation and anger. And dominating every other impression was a compulsion for urgency as demanding as the tattoo of a war drum.

And this puzzled Walter Scott most of all, for he was not sure what on earth had called him back to it. The attempted desecration of his library, of course, had caught his otherworldly attention. But that thug was well and truly driven away, as he thought, for good, and the urgency remained, crying for attention. The resident border collie whined up at him, and the custodian, thinking the animal wished to relieve itself, put it out.

And so the only other being, besides the ghoul, who seemed to perceive Sir Walter departed for a time, and the ghost sorely wished he had chains to rattle or some other supernatural occupation—since it seemed the natural ones were denied him. Really, he had always fancied the supernatural without being particularly good at invoking or explaining it in his own literature. Everyone said his ghosts were quite thin though not as thin as he himself felt at the moment. He wished he had someone to advise him, someone knowledgeable in the ways of otherwordly activity. Now, his ancestor, Michael Scott the Wizard, would be an admirable advisor, but unfortunately, even if the old necromancer was still cavorting about on the plane nearest earth (and Walter had never particularly fancied that the Wizard had been around even during Walter's own lifetime), he was presumably under the same geographical-spiritual restrictions that bound Sir Walter and could not go beyond his grave and perhaps the tower where he had spent much of his life in Scotland. Unfortunately, Sir Walter's Haliburton blood had entitled him to be buried at the ruin of Dryburgh Abbey while his ancestor's resting place was Melrose. Bloody inconvenient.

The night returned and with it a growing sense of what occurred around him, though he still had great trouble telling if the occurrences were in the living world or the other. One fairly persistent noise that came to his ear was the keening of some musical instrument, playing now one tune, then another. He wished he could hear the words. He dearly loved music and it had always been a great disappointment to him that he was virtually tone-deaf, though that had never spoiled his enjoyment of a good song. He was, of course, a word man basically, and it was lyrics that spoke to him most, though a catchy tune never hurt. He caught familiar snatches of some of the tunes the instrument played, although he didn't recognize other pieces. Focusing his attention on the sound, he seemed to have a waking dream of a band of weary and desperate people, among them a beautiful melancholy lady, a woman with golden hair like so many damsels in distress he had once agitated heroes on behalf of. Her sadness particularly caught his attention, but whether she was near or far he could not tell and he passed the day in a state of perturbation. What was the point of coming back to watch strangely dressed people making rude remarks about the home he had built with such love and care if he was to be impotent to do anything, or even to discover what it was he was supposed to do? Or had his anger at finding his library disturbed been somehow a test, his pride having called him from heaven to intervene on behalf of his books and, having called him forth, trapped him in this realm? What a sad pass that would be!

For the last two nights now, the living music that haunted him from afar had kept him company, first with a mournful tune, then with a wild and reckless one. He dimly envisioned the band of travelers again, and tried to pay special attention to the fair-tressed lady, thinking that if he could perceive her and the music near her, perhaps she could perceive him and the otherworldly comfort he had to offer, which he imagined might possibly be somehow more potent than comfort of the worldly kind, since when he was living, people always had seemed to set great store by anything that came from beyond the pale.

But instead of the woman he sought, suddenly, as if someone had lit a fire, another image came to him, of a flame-haired woman with a strumpet's laugh and a wild eye. She wore trousers and a loose shirt, like many of the women who invaded his home during the day, but he held her image longer than any of the others. She seemed to be searching for something, calling something, and once her questing intelligence caused her, he could have sworn, to look directly into his mind's eye and wink. And at that moment he saw that her hair was not the orange color he had first perceived, but the red-gold of autumn, and noticed that her trousers were of a subtle cut that sometimes appeared to be a long, gray-green skirt, and that the loose shirt was of a velvet material. When she at last seemed to find what she sought, she laughed, and her laugh was not purely whorish but contained merry undertones like the ringing of silver bells as the mighty steed on which she rode carried her, the damsel, and others he had not yet differentiated from the ether toward something that amused her.

CHAPTER V

▲▲▲

"Where we headed, darlin'?" Willie MacKai mumbled
sleepily as he let himself be tugged past the compartment
where his compadres lay sprawled together like a litter of
hound pups, sleeping off the long trip and the excitement
afterward. It did occur to him that maybe he ought to let
them know where he was going, since he had Lazarus,
the banjo, which had gotten them all out of several jams
already. He should warn them—warn them—he couldn't
remember what he was supposed to warn them *about*.
His head was full of fuzz. Well, hell, they knew as much
about this as he did. Maybe they already knew about
whatever it was Torchy was going to show him. He saw
Julianne, still peakedy and peeling from her burns with
her eyebrows growing back a hair at a time and so pale
she looked like a forties movie star without her makeup.
She and Gussie looked up at him as he passed and he
shrugged and waved a feeble little wave and allowed himself to be towed. Whatever Torchy was going to show
him, he hoped it would be worth the strain of being woke
out of a sound sleep. He was a little tired of running all
over creation. That Torchy was a strong-willed woman
though—strong in other ways too. He wasn't sure he
would have been able to resist the tug of her hand if he'd
wanted to. He admitted to himself that he was somewhat
under the influence. Thoroughly gerzoggled, if you
wanted to know the truth. That was some whiskey that
woman had fed him.

He sobered up considerably, however, when Torchy answered, pulling him into another car, "Why, we're hiding, Willie luv. Didn't you see the coppers hanging about outside the car as we passed the windows?"

"Wait, wait, hold it right there," Selena Anderson commanded, waving her flashlight for emphasis. "You're telling us a story about a drunk person? You make it sound funny. That's really disgusting."

"Are you always this much of a pain in the tail or is this just special party manners?" the figure in the cowl asked. Then said, "Never mind. Maybe you're right. This part isn't right for kids." And with that, she blew out the candle and rose to her feet and started to glide away.

"Hey, wait," Sass Pulaski called. "Aren't you going to tell us the rest? How about the ghost? Does it meet Willie? What kind of a story is it that we don't know how it ends?"

"The usual kind," the voice drifted behind the woman as she opened the French doors and her black robes billowed behind her, along with the curtains. "The kind where you'll find out later, when you're older and maybe more ready for it, or if you're never ready for it, maybe you won't."

She hated to stop like that but the little Anderson girl was a problem. Minda Maloney's parents were okay; they were part of the underground that supported the activities of the storyteller, but the Anderson kid could get them all in hot water. Minda's parents would have to think of something to tell the kids. It had been agreed that the storyteller would simply leave if there was any trouble.

Between the condos, in the narrow path that led to the parking lot, she removed the robe and cowl and stuck them into an Adidas bag she had concealed under her robe. Now, as a small woman with a mop of gray curls, wearing a pink jogging suit and running shoes, she strode purposefully by moonlight and lamp light toward the ferry dock. The ferry would take her back to Seattle, and from there she could catch a bus to the airport. The hotels were always needing temporary bartenders to fill in during conventions.

She slept on the ferry going over, made a phone call to

one of her connections, and hiked up to meet the airport
shuttle, sleeping on the bus. Her connection, an old friend
from before the trouble, put her up for the night and
played her some of the bootlegged recordings she'd made
of the first of the clandestine concerts. The next morning,
the airport Red Lion hired the storyteller/bartender for a
postal employees' convention. She was glad she'd hung on
to the robe and cowl. There were sure to be a few private
Halloween parties where a likely-looking spook could find
a small audience.

▲▲▲

"Down in Carlisle there was a lady . . ." the banjo
frailed the melody line and Willie recalled the words as
Torchy pulled him behind her. The cars were all dark
back there, with no seats. If it hadn't been for the cops,
Willie would have insisted that Torchy stop and let him
rest. He could hardly walk. Good thing the train wasn't
moving.

These last dark cars smelled different from the rest of
the train. The smell was one he hadn't smelled for years
and yet it was very familiar—shit. That's what it was.
That and a wild and gamey musk but mostly just plain
shit—animal shit. Not horseshit or cow manure however.
This was exotic-smelling crap. The smell reminded him
of peanuts in the shell, of walking a lot on concrete, of
sticks with inflatable gorillas tied to them—the zoo. That
was it. It smelled like the zoo. Aw. That was nice. They
were going to the zoo. Who'd have thought Torchy was
the sentimental type?

She swung open the door of the car ahead of them. A
sign said No Admittance. He passed a door leading to the
outside as he slid in behind her. Willie stumbled again,
against some bars this time, and heard the clank of metal
against metal. He turned toward Torchy and saw for the
first time that her eyes glowed in the dark. Then she
turned away from him calling, "Come on, luv. This
way."

He followed slowly, banging himself and the banjo as

he tried to follow her. "Where are you?" he asked. "Turn toward my voice so I can find you."

"Sorry, luv, I seem to have dropped my hankie. *Do* come and help me look." He blundered toward her voice that seemed to be off to the left and slightly fainter. "Come on, where are you? Oh, I can't find that hankie anywhere and it's one my dear old granny give me." Her voice was so faint now it was hard to make it out and he took two more quick steps and banged into a wall, causing something to clang shut behind him.

"Torchy? Torchy, where are you, darlin'?" he called and something very warm and hairy brushed against his hand. He was thinking that Torchy had the most incredible case of morning mouth he had ever smelled as a hot gust of moist and smelly breath washed over him. Then the mouth behind the bad breath yawned with a sound like a burning house collapsing and Willie knew, if he should be lucky enough to survive, that that sound would echo in all of his nightmares ever afterward.

The big mouth with the bad breath swallowed the sound and as if from a great distance he heard the banjo frailing away at "The Lady of Carlisle" and he remembered that the song was the one in which the lady in question was such a twit she couldn't make up her pea-brain which of two men she wanted so she tried to figure out which one was stupid enough to climb into a cage of lions to pick up her fan. Oops.

Only in the song the choice the woman had given to the two men was to risk dying or risk not getting laid and since he, personally, knew how many fish were in the sea (or approximately) he much preferred those fish to the lions. He took several steps backward, ready to run back the way he'd come and let old Torchy handle the situation however she thought was fitting. However, he hadn't taken three edgy little sideways baby steps back the way he came when iron bars slammed against his face and old hairy sent a blast of hot, smelly breath down the back of his neck. He thought he heard the tinkle of feminine laughter fairly close by.

The banjo, leaning halfway through the bars, began

frailing frantically. Willie's memory was busy replaying all of the juiciest scenes of his life so he couldn't recall what the song might be but it made Old Hairy back off a pace or two. About that time a long staff of dim light glowed from a side door. Torchy's silvery giggle faded, and the light grew, only to be blocked out by somebody standing in front of it. A flashlight beam blossomed in the darkness and the lion or lions, as the case was (Willie was not anxious to find out), gave rather anemic little roars, then settled back to merely making noises like industrial-strength lawnmowers.

▲▲▲

"Now where do you suppose those two are going?" Gussie had asked as Torchy jetted past them, dragging a be-wildered-looking Willie in her path.

Julianne couldn't make out what she was saying and for want of a better answer turned her back on the corridor and stared out the window again. The uniformed policemen waiting outside the Carlisle station were not being the least bit subtle, standing there waiting for people to deboard, searching faces and referring to a pad once in a while. James Bond they were not. Juli grabbed Gussie's arm and pointed.

Gussie shook Anna Mae, Faron, and Ellie, saying to each in turn, "Get up. We got to hide. The cops are here. I'll be back in a jiffy." Then she set off down the corridor after Willie and Torchy to warn them. At first she'd thought maybe they had gone up to the lounge car to find Brose Fairchild, then remembered that the lounge car was in the opposite direction, seven cars up toward the head of the train. She'd never be able to warn Brose in time but she could maybe reach Willie and Torchy.

Anna Mae and Julianne scrambled down the side of the platform where the steps weren't, on the far side of the tracks, where other tracks ran alongside and they were in danger of being hit by other trains. Anna Mae, thinking Juli was right behind her, sprinted across the tracks and set off in the direction of the city.

Julianne had been right behind her until, with her eyes

straight ahead and her hearing gone, she neglected to see a switch engine until it almost ran her down. She flattened herself back against the side of the train and wondered what to do next. None of the others had followed Anna Mae and Juli personally didn't want to be separated from them.

She was relieved when Torchy Burns showed up. "Gussie caught you and warned you?" Juli asked, her tongue feeling thick from disuse.

Torchy nodded, grabbed her hand, and towed her as she had towed Willie down the tracks toward the last car, where she opened the door and waved to the occupants, then nodded to Juli and shoved her in. Juli, expecting to see the rest of her friends hidden perhaps in a car that had already been searched, found herself in a car that contained no seats and was in fact a big open rectangle bristling with the conflicting energies of several whole families.

One woman was cooking on a camp stove while two small children clung to her skirts and a baby sat on her hip. Two boys were tossing juggling clubs back and forth. Most people were sleeping on foam mattresses and cushions pushed up against the walls.

A man in jeans that were worn out at the knees and a scruffy-looking polyester knit shirt in paisley that looked as if it was left over from the 1960s came to stand spraddle-legged in front of her. She blinked her stubbly lids at him, feeling stupid and disoriented and wondering how in the world she was going to communicate with these people. The man leered at her and put his fingers under her chin, grinning at its peeling reddened skin and flicking the cropped remains of her bangs with the backs of grimy, very smelly fingers. Then he shoved her to the side of the car where she almost sat on a sleeping child. At that moment the people who were awake jerked to attention, however, and the man made a gesture and a woman near her handed Juli a soiled bandanna and motioned for her to tie it over her hair, which she did. The woman also handed her a moth-eaten sweater and motioned her to put it on and pretend to sleep, which she also did. She peeked only once as the policemen inspected the car, and wondered if she shouldn't give herself up then and there.

▲▲▲

Faron and Ellie Randolph simply disembarked with the rest of the passengers and walked over to the station, right past the policemen who were busy looking for clandestine departures of several members of a desperate gang and were paying no attention to a normal-looking tourist couple.

"Wait," Ellie said. "Shouldn't we stick around and see what happens to the others? Look over there! Isn't that Brose—"

"Shhh. Keep your eyes forward and try lookin' like you're late for work or something," Faron said. "And watch for a phone booth."

"Good idea. Only do you have enough change to call home?"

"I wasn't going to do that right away. Remember the last Silver Dollar Days when that Brit group was playing?"

" 'Old Hag You Have Killed Me'?" Ellie asked.

"Yeah, them. I remember talkin' to Terry Pruitt about how they ought to play 'Lady of Carlisle' since she lived here. Hope she still does."

"I don't think it's such a hot idea to involve other people with the cops after us and everything."

"Maybe not. But if this thing is what it sure seems to be, I bet any musician who's still trying to play traditional music is going to be involved whether they want to or not."

▲▲▲

The ghost of Sir Walter Scott was dimly aware of all of these goings on, as if seeing a play from a great distance, through a crowd of other conversations and street scenes. He heard Julianne Martin's silent prayers, which she would have called drawing on the collective unconscious, as she lay huddled in the midst of a bunch of Gypsies. Across the ether he also heard the wild beating of Anna

Mae Gunn's heart as she dodged and ducked her way from the station and into the town, heard the coin drop into the telephone with a little jingle as Faron Randolph placed his call, and heard the phone ring on the other end, at Terry Pruitt's house, on and on, ring after ring as she played her electric guitar with the sound going into headphones. And he heard the train pull out, pick up steam, and, as night came on, squeal and scream down the tracks.

▲▲▲

The troubles of the living in Carlisle, a ride of several days by horseback, came to the ghost no more sharply than a daydream, for now, during the day, when his house was filled with visitors, he was much less able to find distant vibrations than he was at night when there was little activity to mask such subtle emanations. The daylight diminished him, as he supposed it was proper that ghosts be diminished by the sun, and even on the gloomiest day he could scarcely see his hand in front of his face for the light. The banjo songs tolled in his ears like the knell of church bells, however, and as day carmined to dusk and the lady of the moon flung her tow-colored tresses across the carpet in his study, the events within the banjo's ken became his own dreams, sometimes vague and filled with symbol and portent, but other times as clear as if the people were staging a play for his benefit.

▲▲▲

The Shriners sprawled around the hotel room long after the party was over and the bartender had cleaned up. They were still listening to her story. She was a good bartender and quite the little entertainer too. Wally Haskell hadn't even had a chance to tell her the one about the Fuller brush saleslady and the Avon man and he was still keeping quiet, listening to her. Probably his vocal cords were paralyzed from those margaritas she'd been making.

"Screw the ghost," Harry Latimer said. "What happened to the little blond gal with all the foreigners? I

*mean, the redhead set her up, right? So those guys were
more than a circus, I'll bet. Probably white slavers or drug
runners or something, huh?"*

*"Boy, I can't surprise you with anything!" the bar-
tender said admiringly.*

▲▲▲

As soon as the policeman backed out of the car, Julianne
sat up and jerked the scarf off of her head but the man
she had first met came to stand spraddle-legged, looming
over her.

"Thanks for hiding me," she said, hoping that her
voice sounded calm. "But I need to go now. My friends
will be worried." The man shook his head slowly and
knelt over her knees, reaching his hand forward to stroke
her chin. He said something and for the first time since
the explosion had stolen her hearing she was glad she
couldn't hear what it was.

Others in the room were less fortunate, however, and
the woman who had been cooking dragged the two kids
who clung to her skirts closer to him. Juli noticed the
kids bailed out pretty quickly, releasing the skirt to stand
off to one side. One of them who must have been at least
six stuck his thumb in his mouth and stared with large
dark eyes. The little girl, probably three or so, danced
from one foot to the other with agitation. The woman
waved her free hand in the man's face and gestured angrily at Juli, making a slit throat sign across her own
neck. The man reached up wearily and shoved the
woman away with such force that she staggered backward several feet with no furniture to break her fall or to
injure her.

Julianne scooted her feet up under her, put her back
against the wall, and took a careful survey of who was
between her and the door. The Gypsy woman struck,
cuffing her man on the ear, and he turned in his crouch
and backhanded her, following, still not completely up-
right, to strike her again. The woman opened her mouth
to an ugly snarl, her eyes showing white all around the
irises, and she must have called a name, for a young girl

reached out and plucked the baby away just before the man struck again, and the woman, who first staggered back, half fell on him with her hands extended clawlike, her mouth open in what seemed to Juli a silent scream.

Her deafness gave Julianne a detachment from the scene that she was not unhappy to have, as if she had been able to cut the volume on some sordid soap opera that was being enacted in front of her. She had to remind herself that she was the focus of this particular soap, the girl most likely to end up tied to the railroad tracks. She decided she would rather deal with the police. The train was still moving but in the cars beyond were other, less crazed people. If only she hadn't listened to that damned redhead. Juli knew that woman was trouble and now it looked as if she'd fed Juli to white slavers. The guy who kept invading her personal space looked as if he definitely had a fate worse than death in mind for her.

As the Gypsy woman dragged the man to the floor, Juli bounded across the legs of two spectators and three sleeping children and grabbed for the door handle. She shoved but the door stayed resolutely closed for a moment. Then she saw the metal plate on the outer edge of the door and the sign that said PUSH. She pushed, lurched forward through the door as someone else wedged in behind her, her fingers frantically outstretched to push the metal panel on the door to the next car. Hands clung to her waist but she twisted aside and flung herself against the door, which gave, spilling her forward, into a dark void full of wild and gamey odors.

CHAPTER VI

▲▲▲

"You in there, Willie MacKai?" a female voice somewhat less seductive than Torchy's and much safer-sounding demanded. "You come out of there right now."

"Yes, ma'am," Willie said very softly. "Only please keep your voice down and come and get me out of this cage without unduly disturbing these—" The flashlight beam fell on moth-eaten furry golden backs and droopy-lipped furry faces. "Lions," he finished, gulping. The lions lay like pussycats with their chins on their massive paws, snoring. Underneath all the animal noises, and Gussie's questions, the banjo continued plinking, and as Willie scooped it up he remembered that the tune it was still frailing at for all it was worth was "Wimoweh (The Lion Sleeps Tonight)," probably the best-known African lullaby in the whole United States.

Gussie had seen the lions too, and as soon as she had Willie free of the cage, which locked from the outside with a big old-fashioned key that must have turned itself when the door slammed shut, she let Willie have it, asking him what he meant by running off with redheads and messing around with mangy old circus animals where he might get the banjo damaged or even get hurt himself.

Willie agreed with everything she said without paying any attention to any of it and concentrated on walking. He was walking kind of funny because by then his pants were a little messy.

He only started breathing again when they left the

41

stench of the circus car and the dark metal corridors of the cars between and stepped into the soft light of the passenger car.

The lions had produced what you could call a sobering effect on Willie and belatedly he realized that it was entirely possible that sweet little Torchy might have deliberately led him into the lions' den. (The woman did have a warped sense of humor. She always seemed to be laughing about something. He'd thought she was just good-natured. You never could tell.) She might also have been mixed up with the bomber at the airport and might, therefore, have something to do with the predicament Willie and his friends now found themselves in. He said as much aloud to Gussie who told him with a patronizing little schoolmarm smile that he was catching on okay, nothing got by *him*.

The banjo continued a medley of "Whiskey in the Jar," "Lady of Carlisle," and "Wimoweh" as the train screamed and screeched down the tracks, leaning into the curves, its metal straining and the wheels rumbling, jerking Gussie back and forth as she tried to sleep, or, rather, tried not to. Willie was sleeping like a baby. He had hardly been able to keep his eyes open long enough to sit down and Gussie supposed his lassitude was the aftermath of being scared half to death. If only they didn't have to keep still about being *on* this train, she would have told the conductor a thing or two about letting wild animals on board where they could scare the pee out of innocent bystanders. That was the trouble with not being exactly innocent anymore. Not that they were guilty of anything, really, but they'd been made to feel as if they were since Anna Mae Gunn's ill-fated folk festival two months before. Gussie rested her cheek on the rough fabric of her Mexican basket bag and stared out the window, watching the darkness roll past. Without the others here to remind her, she began to doubt what she'd been through. If only there'd been time to make plans before they'd gotten separated.

The conductor's voice woke her to watery sunlight wavering through the cracks between the shades and the windows. "Now arrivin' Edinburgh," he said with a lot more r's than it normally took to say such a thing. Willie still slept, his bare legs covered up by the blanket the railroad loaned people. Sometime while she slept he seemed to have gotten up and washed his jeans out—they were hung on the coat hook by the window nearest him.

Lots of soot-stained chimneys and the back ends of stone houses and factory buildings hemmed the tracks as the train puffed its way into the station.

She shook Willie. "This is our stop," she told him. He looked about as bad as she'd ever seen him and muttered that he felt worse. She had to help him put his jeans on because he said it hurt his head to bend over. They were halfway down the steps to the platform when she noticed he didn't have the banjo and she had to rush back and get it.

So she could tell right off he wasn't going to be much help the way he was. Probably be more trouble when he got to feeling better too. Willie MacKai was a good man but for all his easy drawl he was a jumpy sort of man and not a bit easy to keep track of, according to former girl-friends who had cried in their beer over him to Gussie in years past. Once he was fully awake again, she figured herding cockroaches at a garbage dump would be a cinch compared to trying to hang on to Willie. So possibly she should be grateful that he was still stupefied and take the bull by the horns and *do* something herself.

What she wanted to do was find the others and make a plan, but since she had no idea how to do that, the best thing to do would be to make a plan on her own and try to get Willie MacKai to help her. He stood in the light drizzly rain, looking around him blankly. Down at the end of the train, two cars were being unloaded into trucks.

Gussie sighed and tucked the banjo head into her basket bag so it wouldn't get wet. Lord only knew what had become of the garment bag Willie had wrapped it in when he came through customs. The banjo thrummed as she shifted it, its strings muted by the roar of disgruntled animals from the cages being unloaded down the track.

This must be some rich circus to have railroad cars *and* trucks to haul their equipment. The banjo twanged a little tune now and it sank into Gussie's consciousness. She could hear who?—Doc Watson?—singing that song "The Gypsy Davey." That song was one widely sung in the United States but it originally came from the British Isles —hard to tell which place, which figured, since Gypsies by definition tended to get around.

The sign on the side of the trucks said Circus Rom, plain as the nose on your face. Rom meant Gypsy in their own language, Gussie knew from her reading. As in Romany. And the people dodging around in the half-light were mostly dark as Indians, black-haired and very tan. But weren't the Gypsies hereabouts supposed to look like other folks? She could clearly remember from old Ewan MacColl songs and one sung by the Clancy Brothers lines about tinkers, as they called the Gypsies here. Tinkers, according to the liner notes, weren't dark, mostly, but red-haired and blond and as purely mixed up as other folks. Most of the ethnic-looking Gypsies, or an awful lot of them, had been killed off by the Nazis in concentration camps along with the Jewish people and everybody else Hitler wanted to get rid of. And mostly, she'd always thought, the Gypsies didn't run big operations like this one. But what the hell did she know about it? Her only contact with Gypsies at home had been seeing the palm-reading signs out in front of otherwise abandoned buildings in South Tacoma. She never had run into any of them at all while living in West Texas. Well, not that she knew of. If she had seen them, she probably took them for Mexicans.

All of that would have absolutely fascinated her a few months ago, back before this trouble first started, before the fire at Anna Mae's folk festival and the long drive Gussie had made with Willie, Julianne, and that cute little Texas Ranger smack into a death trap. Before everyone she knew or cared about seemed to be getting killed or hurt or in danger of it. Before Lettie and Mic had gotten themselves thrown into jail for trying to bring Hy

MacDonald back across the Canadian border. Folk-singers seemed to be contraband these days.

But—well, *damn*. She *was* tired. She *could* call Mac-Donald, couldn't she? He'd been deported back here to Scotland and she remembered that he lived near Edinburgh someplace. If she hadn't been so strung out she'd have thought of it a long time ago.

"Come on, Willie," she said, taking him by the arm and firmly leading him toward the station.

"What's wrong with this picture?" he asked suddenly, holding up his hands to make a frame, putting the whole sentence in quotes.

"What do you mean?" she asked blearily.

"Where are the cops?" he asked. "They were thick as crabgrass at that last stop. You s'pect we've been cleared since then? Or maybe they only do terrorists on alternate Thursdays and this is the day everybody goes after bank-robbers or kidnappers instead?"

Well, wasn't that Willie MacKai all over? You'd swear he was dead between the ears and find out he was way ahead of you. And he was right, of course. Not a single uniform was in sight except for a cluster of soldier boys standing next to the station. She tugged a little on his arm. "Let's just count our blessings."

▲▲▲

Brose Fairchild didn't even see the cops through the haze of smoke in the lounge car until they were almost on top of him. Since the car had no exit, he wouldn't have been able to escape anyway. The cops spotted him with no difficulty. Willie had the banjo, but Brose, as the only largish, freckled, red-haired black man on the train, was easily the most conspicuous. The cops had been perfectly polite, but he heard them say "nigger" every time they said "sir" and when they started questioning him, he wondered if the police were as careful not to be overtly accused of brutality over here as they were in the States. Of course, all that meant was they shouldn't leave scars, but the whole affair had him sweating up a storm even without the help of the traditional bright lights.

The hell of it was that he was entirely innocent of any crime he could think of except declining to aid the lawmen with their "inquiries," which he would be delighted to do. If circumstances were a little different, he would have given them the truth, the whole truth, and nothing but the truth, but they'd think he was fuckin' nuts if he told them that and he couldn't think up any real good lies that wouldn't get him busted in the mouth. Things being the way they were, he shrugged a lot and kept quiet.

That strategy did not exactly endear him to the police either. "Are you deaf, sir?" the woman officer, who looked as if she'd be hell on the soccer field, asked him politely.

"No, ma'am. That's the Widah Martin," he said without thinking about it.

"And who is she? Is this Julianne Martin you're referring to? One of the other passengers who arrived with you on flight ninety-one twenty-two?"

"Yeah. That's her. Listen, do I get a phone call?" Brose asked, remembering what all the crooks on TV said (right after saying "ya can't pin nothin' on me") when faced with police harassment.

The woman cop raised a sandy eyebrow at him. "And just whom would you like to call, sir?"

Brose didn't know, exactly, though the SPCA naturally came to mind. Brose had devoted his scrubby ranch to caring for animal dropouts from the local humane society shelter where he worked. He wished some Lassie dog, Flipper, or Flicka would come break him out now. "I'll think of somebody," he grunted to the woman, and urgently wished he could.

▲▲▲

"DD?"

"What is it now, boss?"

"What have I been telling you all along about these people?"

"Oops. I forgot. No jail."

"That's right."

"Shit. Okay, okay. I'll take care of it."

▲▲▲

As Brose was trying to decide who he could phone who might help him—maybe the American embassy? he doubted if they'd be any big help, but it was worth a try —someone knocked on the frosted pane of the door to the interrogation room. The woman officer flicked her eyes to one side like she'd been watching way too many reruns of *Miami Vice*. Her partner, who looked as if he should still be driving a skateboard, answered the knock. There was a little intense whispering back and forth, then the fellow stepped outside the door. After a moment, he stepped back inside the door and motioned for the woman, who joined them.

When she returned they put Brose in a cell. About fifteen minutes later, they took him out again.

"What the hell's going on?"

"You're being released," the skateboard jockey told him. "But the attorney from the American embassy understands that you are not to leave Britain. We'll require your testimony against the terrorist."

"You mean, you know I ain't him?"

"That's right, sir. He turned himself in in London a few moments ago. We received a telephone call and shortly after the embassy's attorney arrived demanding your release. If you get in touch with your friends, we would appreciate it if you enlisted their cooperation as well."

"Uh-huh," Brose said. "Sure."

As he collected his belongings, he spied a strangely familiar blonde, all done up in a little gray suit with a white blouse and a pussycat bow. She smiled a cold, prissy smile at him as the barred door clanged behind him and followed him when he stepped once more onto the street.

"How do you do," she said in a la-di-da accent, extending her hand. "I'm Miss Firestone, the solicitor from the embassy."

"Uh-huh," Brose said, ambling away from the police station. "Thanks a lot. See ya 'round—"

Miss Firestone caught up with him, hooking her arm through his and bumping her gray-suited hip against him. "Whatsa matter, Yank? Don't you want to buy a girl a drink?" she asked, sounding very familiar indeed now. "You could be a little friendlier, surely, after I've gone and done one of me best impersonations for your benefit?"

"Torchy?" he asked.

She tipped her blond Princess Di wig at him and several long red tendrils of her own hair snaked around her face. "At yer service," she said.

He looked from her back to the police station, expecting pursuit. "How did you get them to buy it?"

"Easy, ducks. I told you. I'm an actress. And some of my best friends are lawyers. Now come along, why don't you, and I'll show you a real English pub."

Since he didn't have a clue where the others had gone, Brose figured Torchy's idea was as good as any.

"So—did that Irish guy turn himself in really?" he asked loudly when they were sitting in front of a couple of pints. The rock music was so loud it hurt his stomach but the place wasn't crowded. Torchy had explained that the older, quainter places would be full of London yuppies at this hour so she took him to a newer pub, a former petrol station called The Plastic Card.

"Yes, he did. *Very* sorry he was, once he'd been given time to think about it," she said.

CHAPTER VII

▲▲▲

Anna Mae Gunn was not one to stay lost for long. As an activist, she knew the value of connections. As an organizer of several now-defunct folk festivals, she knew at least a few people in most parts of the world, including an American woman, Terry Pruitt, one of the friendlier members of a British folk-rock group, who lived in Carlisle and made a point of singing about it and who had invited Anna Mae to visit her if she had the chance. Anna Mae found the number in the phone book easily.

"Terry?"

"No, this is Dan," said a warm male voice. "Terry's in the shower. You're not another lady from America, are you?"

"Another?"

"Yeah, two of Terry's other—" and in the background Anna Mae heard a voice that sounded like Ellie's say urgently, "Shh, Dan. Careful."

"Oops, sorry. I mean, who may I say is calling?"

"Tell Terry and Ellie—that is who I hear, isn't it?—that this is Anna Mae Gunn."

"Anna Mae? Didn't you help Sam Hawkins organize—"

But at that moment, Ellie Randolph came on the line. "Where *are* you?"

"In a phone booth outside what appears to be a bar. Have you seen any of the others?"

"We saw Brose Fairchild being hauled away by the cops. We never saw where Willie or the others went."

"Can you meet me here? And ask Terry if she knows of any good lawyers."

"Terry and Dan are getting ready to take a train to Heathrow to fly to Norway for an African Music Conference."

"Oh, great."

"But they say if we'll drive the van back from the train station we can borrow their van."

A sudden chill ran down Anna Mae's back, as if someone was watching her, which, of course, someone could be. "Look, I'd better get off the street. I'll meet you inside this bar. Here's the name and address."

Anna Mae entered the pub, whose walls winked with neon beer signs glowing through a whirl of smoke. Above the bar was a particularly prominent specimen, one which appeared to have once hung outside. The illustration that had once graced it was now quite faded and a rock had been thrown through the neon legend so that the first letter was illegible. The rest of the sign said HELL OIL.

Anna Mae scooted in next to a blonde who looked like the Princess of Wales and started to order a drink from a cadaverous-looking bartender.

"Hello, ducky," the Princess said. "We've been wondering where you were, 'aven't we, Brose luv?"

One seat down from her at the bar, Brose Fairchild grunted a greeting. The Princess lifted her blond wig and stuck it in her briefcase, shaking out her long red hair. Anna Mae suppressed an expression of disgust. Here she'd been worrying how they were going to get Brose out of jail, thinking about staging a protest or some kind of media event, and he was sitting in this bar with this— this bimbo, Anna Mae thought, then promptly felt ashamed of herself. Torchy had been nothing but helpful so far and there was something very charming about her —she was as charismatic as the best performer Anna Mae had ever seen, with her elfish grin and those fascinating eyes that were at times mischievous and at times deep and unfathomable, changing like some weird hologram from bright green to dark brown. And in the dim light of the bar, with the neon flashing off them they glittered with red. You couldn't help liking Torchy, and she had been friendly enough—very friendly with Willie, which made Anna Mae wonder how they came to be separated and where Willie *was* anyway. Nevertheless, Torchy was clearly trouble if Anna Mae had ever seen it.

The music was too loud for conversation and Brose looked as relieved as Anna Mae when Ellie and Faron arrived with a tall gray-haired man and a slender dark-haired woman Anna Mae remembered as Terry Pruitt. Both of them looked a little like elves too, come to think of it. Maybe it was just the influence of being in Celt country. But everything about Terry Pruitt was slightly elongated—long-boned legs and arms, long face framed by long brown hair, and hands whose fingers were twice the length of Anna Mae's. The man had a floppy, beseeching expression that made Anna Mae think he could be a were-puppy. Elkhound maybe.

The seating in the van was limited and Torchy ended up on Brose's lap. Surprise surprise.

"Where do you suggest we look for the ballads around here, Terry?" Faron asked.

"I'm not at all sure," she answered. "The folk scare is over. The folk-rock scare is over. The pubs that used to do that sort of thing are into rock and country, sometimes jazz nowadays. There are several archival collections scattered about—one on Iona that I've heard about, and then, of course, I'm sure there's something or other in Edinburgh at the university library."

"Seems logical," Faron said, "With both Burns and Scott being from around there. And the Borders were a great source of ballads."

"I'd think the Highlands were more interesting," Torchy said.

"Only if you speak Gaelic," the were-elkhound, Dan, told her. "And that trip got kind of overdone around here. That's one reason we're doing African music now. Besides getting to learn about people from other places, there's always little gatherings going on and people do like something different now and then."

"Good luck," Terry said, and she and Dan dragged a hammered dulcimer, a fiddle, guitar, octave mandolin, several drums of various shapes, and a mountain dulcimer from the back of the van.

"We'll give you a hand," Faron offered, but as he reached for Terry's guitar, he stumbled and fell. He felt the neck of the guitar in the lightly padded traveling case smash as it caught between his knee and the side of the van, and when he stepped back he put his other foot through a drum. As Brose reached out to help him on one side and Ellie on the other, the fiddle became caught between them.

"Cor," Torchy simpered with sugary sympathy. "What rotten luck!"

Terry opened her guitar case gently and pulled out the instrument, its neck hanging by its strings. "I see what you mean about that curse on music," she said tightly, referring to the story they had told her earlier of their misadventures back in the States, "but are you quite sure you weren't the cause of the curse?"

Faron just gulped, his Adam's apple taking a long plunge into the neck of his T-shirt and back up again. "Sorry," he said miserably.

Ellie dug in her purse and pulled out an American Express card. "Here. Buy new ones. We'll worry about the bill later. Don't worry about the signatures. They never check."

"Can we get a new van too if you wreck Terry's?" Dan asked eagerly.

If they hadn't been late for their train, Terry would undoubtedly have changed her mind about letting them use the van. But the fact was, she too had become aware of strange things happening regarding the music she used to play, and she did believe Faron. The only thing that made her mad was the way Torchy Burns kept smiling a little half smile when she thought nobody was looking, as if the whole thing was funny. They loaded the broken instruments back into the van. Terry was glad the van was very old and her insurance recently paid up.

"What an understanding sort of gel," Torchy cooed as they watched the train depart with Terry and Dan. " 'Scuse me. Back in a mo. Have t'use the facility." Ellie Randolph, who also had to use the facility, was surprised at how quick Torchy was to beat her into a stall. Actually, Torchy had just dipped around the corner, pulled a cellular phone from her lawyer's briefcase, and dialed the number that would refuse any charge made on Randolph's American Express card. Since she wasn't sure of the number, she had the computer refuse the charges on the card of anybody named Randolph. She sighed happily thinking of all the purely gratuitous disruption that would cause, a sort of a bonus. Ah, yes, bombs and such were all very well but, she reflected, little things *do* mean a lot.

CHAPTER VIII

▲▲▲

Julianne heard the banjo playing her song and ran straight for it, away from the hidey-hole she'd made for herself. Since she was a little bit of a thing, she had been able to hide behind some shit-shoveling equipment stored between the cages. The big cats had reached their paws back for her, dabbing at her like she was a catnip mouse but she had shovels and a garbage can lid to shield herself and they got tired of the game after a while and settled back to sleep.

The Gypsies naturally thought she'd just passed on through and the lions were upset because they were having so much company that evening. But the fact was that Julianne was so plain scared, she couldn't move much farther and she was afraid, once she wedged herself between the cages, that if she tried to move away, when she stood up one of those lions would reach out and sweep her foot out from under her and have lady toes for breakfast.

So she had not had a very good night, to put it mildly. She had sat there feeling the floor tremble when the lions roared, feeling the pad of their paws when they paced, feeling the vacuum created by their mighty yawns, feeling the generator-throb of their sleeping breath. She had a pain in the small of her back from sitting hunched up, and the backs of her thighs burned like she'd been doing six Jane Fonda tapes all in a row. Her hair was all tangled and she had a couple of long, deep scratches still leaking blood. Her clothes were bloody, torn, and dirty, and she smelled to high heaven of lion shit. But she was alive, the banjo was tinkling at her, and even though she couldn't hear another blessed thing, she heard it in her mind— "Fare thee well, Julianna, you know. Hoo row, hoo row, hoo row, my boys . . ."

She could hear not only the frailing of the banjo, but her mind replayed a memory of her and George singing that song, a modern sea chantey sung by men who fished from motorized boats that 'didn't require the rhythmic chanting quality of the older chanteys. It was a slow, rolling song that could be heard on shore when sung by a crew still far away, telling of the catch and if all were safely still aboard, and from whence they came. "Here we're comin' with blackfish and men" was one verse she remembered. But now it seemed to her the message was, "Here is Laz'rus with Willie and Gus, goodbye, fare thee well, goodbye, fare thee well." Leaving? Leaving her? No way!

And with that thought, the spell was broken for the lions were not nearly as fearsome to her as the terror of being left behind, deaf and alone in a foreign country. Besides, fortunately, the lions already had their moth-eaten furry knickers in a twist over having forklifts scooted under their cages to haul them off the train and onto the truck.

So Julianne jumped up, stumbled, since her feet were mostly asleep, and flung herself out from between the cages before the cats could finish airing their displeasure at the men and machines that were moving them out of the railroad car and onto the trucks. She half fell out of that railroad car and onto the ground beside the tracks. The forklift operator, who was the man who had been giving her a hard time back in the Gypsy car, sat there with his mouth open, then jumped down and started to chase her.

She kept the sound of the banjo in her head and although she felt the vibrations of the machines rumbling and the man's heavy running through the soles of her feet, she paid it no mind and ran on until she ran blindly into the door that Willie MacKai, Gussie Turner, and the banjo had just gone through. She wrenched it open, feeling the Gypsy man's breath on her scalp, and squeezed inside, pulling the door hard after her with one hand while groping toward Willie and Gussie with the other.

Willie MacKai turned around to see what was happening and was both relieved and aggravated to see the Widah Martin literally throwing herself at him. He'd honestly thought she had more class than that.

He stepped aside and she crashed into Gussie instead, and Gussie put her arms around her and petted her while her breathing calmed. The Gypsy man, who was starting to come through the door, got a load of Willie MacKai with his bloodshot eyes and his two days' worth of beard and his sweaty T-shirt and dirty blue jeans and his arms all corded up from playing the guitar most of his life. Not to mention his expression, which was mostly compounded of not yet having had enough coffee to be awake and also being peeved at all the noise that was threatening to shake him awake. Willie was a lover not a fighter. He didn't want to get the voice strangled out of him or his hands busted up fighting, not to mention getting his nose mashed or his teeth knocked out and him without insurance. But years on the stage had given him the trick of making anything he felt that he wanted to show look ten times more intense than it really was and he watched a *lot* of Clint Eastwood movies, so he did ferocious anger-on-a-leash very effectively. He projected his attitude at the Gypsy with a little half snarl he practiced in the mirror. He looked so dangerous that it occurred to the Gypsy that maybe the girl he was after belonged to this guy. The Gypsy decided that maybe he would a lot rather face his wife in a fair fight, and that there would be other chances to get the girl back later if that was still what the redheaded witch who kept his tribe supplied wanted him to do. So he smiled an ingratiating, gold-toothed smile and backed away.

An hour later Juli, Willie, and Gus were sitting in Hy MacDonald's bare living room. Hy's wife had left him two months before and he was down in the mulligrubs. A man like Hy, who was usually cheerful and full of noise, could be seriously depressed when he was so inclined, full of anger, black, self-deprecating jokes, and vicious attacks on his ex-wife's character and lineage. He told them much more than they wanted to know about all of that until Gussie put a halt to it, asking him where he thought they could go to find ballads and what was the best way of getting in contact with or leaving a message for the remnants of their group and could they, by the way, talk him into taking them around?

Far from resenting her intrusion, he actually looked relieved—tired, but relieved at having the flow of acid that had been eating him shut off for a while, and to be distracted by other people's problems that he could, of course, treat as if they were small matters he could handle easily. Other people's problems tend to be that way. Willie helped him finish a bottle or two of scotch and Gussie took a glass for herself and one for Juli too, strictly for medicinal purposes.

▲▲▲

"I'll drive," Brose said firmly to Faron.

"It wasn't *his* fault about the instruments," Ellie objected. "If you hadn't all been crowding him and been in such a hurry, he wouldn't have stumbled. He knows what he's doing."

"Uh-huh," Brose said skeptically, climbing behind the wheel and holding out his hand for the keys.

Faron handed them over with a shrug and pretended to curl up for a nap.

Anna Mae said, "Don't let's all be macho and infantile over this. We need to think up a plan."

"Goddammit, woman, we know we need to think up a plan," Brose said. "And don't start any of that women's lib crap on me now."

"Pardon me, but it seems to me that if your good buddy Willie MacKai was a little less into the old lone wolf act he and the banjo might be here right now and we'd know what to do. Not to mention if he hadn't separated from the group to begin with to go off with *her*."

She turned to Torchy, who was snuggling in as close to Faron on the other side as she could, to Ellie's consternation. "Just where *did* he go, anyway?"

"Don't frown at me so, ducky, just because he didn't come your way. I know he's attractive but it isn't *my* fault he preferred me. And later, he simply preferred someone else. For all I know he's still on the train."

"And he's not the only one missin', don't forget," Brose said belligerently. "There's Julianne too. I thought you two was together. If you're so damn smart, why didn't you keep an eye on her?"

"Look, I've lost my home, my land, and my job over this mess you people got me into," Anna Mae said. "Don't expect me to play nursemaid to you too."

Torchy smiled. "Wake me at the next petrol station, there's a love," she said to Faron. "I need to use the facility again."

"Do we even know where we're *going*?" Ellie asked.

"Faron mentioned Sir Walter Scott's estate and Gussie seemed to think that was a good idea," Anna Mae said. "And there's bound to be some border lore there someplace—maybe the guide can give us some idea where to look further."

"Okay, we'll drop you off there," Brose said. "And the Randolphs can go to the library, and do what college kids are good at. And I'll go talk to people, hang out in the clubs, see what I can turn up."

"I'm sure you'll just love that," Anna Mae sniffed.

Torchy passed out cold with the top of her red head snuggled against Faron's leg.

▲▲▲

"You're supposed to beat 'em, DD, not join 'em," the Chairdevil told her when the Debauchery Devil had resumed her seat at the board.

"I thought you said this was to be my operation, boss? I'm handling it my own way. After all, I've done the hardest part. Willie MacKai and the banjo have been eliminated and the girl—"

"Idiot!" the Chairdevil thundered. "Your job is to lie

to everyone else, not to me. Do you think I don't have ways of checking up?"

The Debauchery Devil raised an inquisitive brow.

"The two women, MacKai, and the banjo are all alive and well. Your minions failed and you didn't even check up. And now those—*musicians*"—he spat the word as if he were saying "cannibals" except that *that* word was one he tended to say with a sentimental smile—"are where they can actually locate some of those songs."

"Do tell?" she asked mildly.

"Your problem, Debauchery, is that you do sloppy work," the Expediency Devil told her. "You don't check up on things. You don't cover all your bases. You leave things to chance."

"Yeah," said the Stupidity and Ignorance Devil, "and we're in *charge* of chance."

DD, in the Torchy Burns guise, gave the other devils her very best ingratiating smile, the one they liked with a little hint of a death's-head grin, and said, "Thanks for the tip, ducks. Now, if you'll 'scuse me, I'll get my people right on this."

A few minutes later she kicked Giorgio in the tight ass of his counterfeit designer jeans. He had been changing a tire. Now he changed his expression as he caught a glimpse of her ethereally thundering countenance. She looked like his wife in a bad mood. But the witch's bad moods were something to fear.

"Diabla! How good it is to see you."

"What's the matter, Giorgio. Didn't you like my little present?" she pouted, a mockery of a normal woman. "You threw her back. And even those mangy beasts of yours thought they were too good to eat the tidbit I gave them."

"Diabla, I swear to you—"

"Save it for your wife, luv," she said, still smiling.

"You won't cut off our supply?"

"Oh, no, Giorgio. I wouldn't do *that*. But I think I'll start giving away samples to the kids and ease the old folks' pain along, how would you like that? And maybe

get you to do a lid or two with me but not your wife. Just
our little arrangement. Wouldn't that be nice?"

He had already been sweating but now streams of salt
water ran down him like the tears of all the grief he'd
ever caused. He had seen what the drugs he acquired
from Diabla and sold to his profit did to others. He knew
in the pit of his black heart that he was of the lowest
creatures of creation, but he was not yet that low. And
for the children and the elders of his tribe to succumb, for
he himself to be infected while leaving his wife in control.
No. He would have to kill her. His world would fall
apart. He would have no power any longer and no will to
wield it if he did. "It was not my fault, Diabla. My stupid
sow of a wife became jealous and attacked me and the
gadje woman escaped. As for the lions, I will shoot them
myself."

"Oh, Giorgio, would you really do that for *me*?" the
witch cried with the glee of a carrion bird finding flesh,
and transformed herself as she twined cold-bone limbs
about his neck, filling his nostrils with the stench of lime
and decomposing bodies, the stench he had smelled as a
boy when he and other boys had been on grave detail in
the camps. The gold in his own tooth was from gold he
hoarded from stripping those bodies. He would have been
killed if the Nazis had learned of his treachery, but he
learned treachery well and early. From the time Diabla
first came to him when he was no more than a feral-eyed
child, he had been able to most satisfactorily avenge himself on the world for the wrongs it had done him. And
had he not saved this small band of his people too? And
did he not care for them and provide them a good living?
The terror they felt of him was far less than the terror of
the camps. The thing they did to live they did only to
outsiders to appease their patroness. Even his wife, who
was crazy, was less afraid of him, less afraid of Diabla,
than of the outside world.

He spit on the outside world, but he could not bear to
look directly at the witch and said to the front of her
decaying dress, "I will get the woman back again and kill
the man with my own two hands."

"That would be so sweet of you, Giorgio," she said. "But what I want you to do first involves all of your people. I want you to bring me something."

"Anything, Diabla."

"It's easy, really, for such talented folk. Just some old books. I'll tell you which ones and where to find them and how to get them. But you must bring them to me, show me the titles, and burn them in my presence, then give me the ashes as evidence I can show my friends that the job is done and I've taken care of them, just as you take such good care of your people. Do you understand?"

He nodded, still sweating, still not daring to pull away from her charnel-house breath and fog-cold embrace.

CHAPTER IX

▲▲▲

Julianne took a hot bath at Hy MacDonald's house, or as much of one as she could get for the ten pence the heater took. She emerged from the tub wearing a T-shirt and jeans that belonged to Hy, the jeans a little big and held up with a woven band he'd bought at a crafts fair and thought might come in handy as a guitar strap. "Willie," she said, "I just wanted to thank you for—you know—helping me get away from that guy."

Willie waved his hand negligently and looked uncomfortable. He thought it was all very well that she thought he was good wolf-scaring material, but he actually much preferred the role of the wolf. Why should she need protecting anyway? She was a grown woman and had been away from her mama for quite a while.

She saw his impatient expression and added, "I was caught off-guard. I thought those folks would be fine since Torchy took me to them. I know you're getting close to her, Willie, but she's got really strange energy, y'know?"

He did know. Maybe he was mad at Juli partially because he was mad at Torchy, trying to make lion food out of him when he thought they had been getting along so well. Damn, it always seemed to be something with women, and sometimes he wasn't sure which kind griped him more, the ones like Torchy who were wild and sexy but treacherous as rattlers or the kind like Julianne who said they were independent and wanted to make up their own minds but still expected a guy to risk his neck defending them. He missed the fact that Juli had just been warning him about Torchy, not realizing that the redhead had already betrayed Willie. Juli thought that in warning him she was paying him back, somehow protecting *him*.

When Willie didn't respond, she smiled uncertainly at Hy MacDonald, who came out of the kitchen with a tray full of fresh drinks. Hy hadn't heard her. He was preoccupied with an entirely different issue.

"I wish I could be of more help," Hy was saying. "It's been very good to see you. I needed someone to keep me from drinkin' alone, y'know. But the timin' is a wee bit awkward as ah've got this new job. Taxes have hit me very hard and my brother has pulled quite a few strings to get me on the North Sea oil rigs. I'm hoping, of course, to pick up a bit of change entertaining on the side but we'll see how that goes."

"But don't you see?" Gussie asked him. "It's the same thing that was happening to us at home. It's these—these critters trying to run you folks away from the music just like they did us."

The banjo, propped up in the corner, played a tune Gussie recognized as some old Irish exile song, one of those with the general theme of "the landlord wants his rent, the tatties have gone bad, you're pregnant once again, and I'm outta here, my lassie-o."

"Yes, I do see," Hy said. "But I don't much fancy bein' one of the first casualties, like Hawthorne and Nedra and them, d'ye see? I can let you look through my record collection and books if that will be any help atall, and take you 'round to Sir Walter Scott's old place, since that's where you said the Randolph couple planned to go. There's tour buses in and out all the time so I'm sure you could pop back up here on one of them. You might find it all very interesting anyway. Sir Walter built his estate from the lands once roamed by Thomas the Rhymer—his turf, I suppose you could call it. And there's all the auld lit'rary places from the books thereabouts, and the Wizard's grave over at Melrose." He cast a rather nervous glance at the banjo mumbling to itself in the corner of the living room. "Perhaps your instrument could get old Michael Scott to exhume his magic book for you and give you a wee hand, eh?"

▲▲▲

Gussie Turner stepped into the entrance hall at Abbotsford as reverently as if she were entering a church. She stared up at the wooden ceiling and the carved wooden rafters with the little coats of arms in the middle and the miniature shields on either side where the rafters connected to the walls. She looked beneath her feet at the pretty octagonal tiles in five different colors of stone. She studied the carved wooden walls and the suits of armor and more little shields all around her. She peered closely at all of the doodads Sir Walter had placed very carefully around his house: the bust on the pretty shiny carved table, which she saw was of William Wordsworth himself, the fancy clock, and the two skulls on either side of it on the mantel above the very elaborately carved fireplace that had a genuine brass grate all backed by blue and white tiles that looked like those Dutch dishes, the kind with willow trees on them. The carvings above the fireplace looked like the naughty ones from temples in India and a row of uncomfortable-looking but very grand chairs that might have come from some ritzy church's business office ranked along one wall.

A lady about her own age with an expression that tried to be friendly but didn't succeed very well was sitting behind a desk. Her clothes, which looked like what high-school girls used to wear in the winter before the schools changed the rules to let them wear blue jeans, were a matched beige sweater set—short-sleeved sweater and a cardigan with little pearl buttons, and a red tartan skirt with pleats. Gussie wanted to ask her if that was the Scott tartan but felt shy because she figured the lady probably got asked that all the time and Gussie didn't want to seem so much like a tourist.

"My, this is a nice place you got here," she said instead.

The lady showed her teeth. "That'll be two pounds,

mum. And please sign the buke and be sure to visit the gift shop in the old stable."

Gussie was glad Hy MacDonald had let them stop at a bank. She forked over her two pounds and was signing the guest book when Willie strode in with his air of everything-can-start-now-that-I'm-here, clutching the banjo. Julianne wandered in beside him. In this setting, in Hy MacDonald's oversize T-shirt, she looked so wan that she could have gone drifting through the garden and passed for the lady in white in her nightgown.

Must be the setting, Gussie decided. Everybody looked like they belonged in a Gothic novel.

"Ah'm afraid ye canna bring yon instrumunt in he-er, sir," the lady said. "Might scratch the polish or bump somethin' ov-air, y'see."

Willie looked like he was going to tell her off for a moment, then he turned on the charm and said sweetly, "Why, ma'am, I promise to be real careful, but this is a special sort of an instrument you see."

"Can ye no leave it locked in yer auto?" the lady asked.

"Our ride just went back to Edinburgh," Gussie put in.

The banjo began frailing "Wassailing" in a minor key. Gussie remembered the words that went, "Oh, Master and Mrs. da da da da da Pray open the door and let us come in. Oh, Master and Mrs. who sit by the fire pray think of the traveler who walks through the mire."

"You see that, ma'am?" Willie asked, turning around to show the banjo playing itself to her. "I never touched fret or string. Have you ever seen a banjo do that before? Why, not only would I be careful not to let the banjo scratch your furniture or knock anything over, but I would be certain not to knock any of that stuff against this very valuable instrument."

"Ah'm sorry, sir. I dinna mak t'rules."

"I'll take it with me, Willie, while you look around," Gussie said. "I need to go find postcards to send Lettie and Mic and Craig Lee to let them know we're okay."

He gave it to her and she walked back out the big

heavy front door and back into the yard. The banjo began thrumming "Stewball" as she turned toward the direction the lady—a docent, they called people who watched museums and such—where the docent had showed her the old stables were.

The truth was, she was glad to be alone and just have some time to think her own thoughts. She had always wanted to come and see England and especially Scotland and now that she was here she was rushing around so much that she hadn't had any time to think about what she was seeing. She whirled around and leaned back on her heels and shaded her eyes, looking way up and all around at the cobbled-together mansion that had belonged to Walter Scott. It wasn't a very tall house, only a couple of stories, but it had two castlelike towers, one with a cone roof, one with those square toothy things, crenellations she thought they were called, and little bitty towers flanking the main entrance door. A whole raft of chimneys jutted above the main building, with more chimneys all around, and all of the gables and such had serrated fronts. The whole thing was done mostly in one color of brick with stone trimmings around the sides and windows and it had a castle-type wall around what would have been the driveway anywhere else but she guessed was a kind of courtyard here. She went beyond the wall to find the stable beside a couple of churchy-looking buildings.

The brick and stone all looked as cold and wet as only those materials can look on a dismal day, and she was glad to be able to stop in at the little tourist shop, and the song the banjo was humming very softly in her hand made her think she could still smell the horse manure.

There were warm-looking wool plaid scarves that said they were Scott and Douglas tartans, ruler-sized strips of color slides of the local sights, postcards of every tourist attraction in the Scottish Borders.

She lingered over some of these. On the road, the van had passed signs advertising these sights on the way from Edinburgh but Hy MacDonald had been in too big of a hurry to play tour guide.

But nearby there was Lintithgow Castle where Mary Queen of Scots was born and Hermitage Castle where she nearly died riding to find her lover. All around were the Eildon Hills where True Thomas met the Fairy Queen. There were battlefields like Falkirk and Bannockburn and coming up from Carlisle they'd passed by Flodden Field—she remembered songs about all of them, victories and defeats. The banjo, as if it had somehow been looking through the cards with her, would do a soft bar or two of each as she picked it up to look at it. The lady in the shop looked around as if searching for a radio but she was behind a counter and Gussie carried the banjo low, her hand circling its neck above the fifth tuning peg.

Shoot, they hadn't even gotten to see Edinburgh Castle where they kept the crown jewels of Scotland Sir Walter had rescued from their basement hiding place, nor Mons Meg the cannon that he had also brought out of obscurity. This place actually didn't look much different from other farmland she'd seen except there were more stone houses than any place she'd ever been except maybe New Braunfels, Texas, and most of the houses there weren't so big. In Missouri there were lots of stone fences just like here. They didn't have anything else to do with the rocks they dug up from the pasture. But this place was so crammed with history that it seemed like something important had happened three layers down on every scrap of dirt. It boggled the mind.

If she was going to see that fancy house, she decided, she had better get her postcards and go. But beside the coffee mugs that said Abbotsford, Home of Sir Walter Scott in tasteful rust against cream with a little drawing in rust-colored paint, there was a rack of books, paperbacks of the Waverly novels, which she had read a long time ago, and something called *The Lay of the Last Minstrel*. Seeing the word "minstrel," she snagged it and paid for it and rushed out to show the others the ballad book she had found.

Out in the open air she cracked it open to peek at it, as if afraid the songs would leak out, and saw to her disappointment that it was not a collection of ballads but one

long poem by Sir Walter Scott. Oh, well. It would give
her something to read during future traipsings around.

She took a step toward the main entrance door and
then remembered that the old dragon in the hall wasn't
any more likely to let her in with the banjo than she
would Willie. Gussie didn't figure once Willie got to
looking around in that fascinating old place he'd remember to stop anytime soon to come out and take charge of
the banjo.

She sighed and started to find herself a bench in the
garden to sit down and look at her book, and noticed that
one of the other doors was a little ajar. That wouldn't be
very honest, now would it, sneaking in like that?

She thumbed through the first part of her book but a
breeze came up, whipping up the rose petals shed by the
bushes nearby, and riffled the pages forward. When she
returned to the book, she found herself staring at a pas-
sage that said, "Now slow and faint, he led the way/
Where, cloistered round, the garden lay/The pillared
arches were over their head/And beneath their feet were
the bones of the dead." My, my, she couldn't have put it
better herself, she thought, shivering in the breeze and
resisting the temptation to lift her feet up lest she be
walking on anybody's grave. The open door creaked and
waggled back and forth as if beckoning her. The banjo
nudged her with "Onward, Christian Soldiers."

Well, what the hell, she *had* paid her money, hadn't
she? And she would be careful not to bump the banjo
against any of the fine furnishings. Like Willie said, it
wasn't only to avoid hurting Sir Walter's treasures, but
because if she wrecked the banjo they'd all be up the
creek without a paddle.

▲▲▲

The ghost held the door open until the older lady with
the banjo had entered then bowed her in with a playful
flourish. Guests! He was entertaining again. Not the
crude gawkers who came daily to his hall but people who
felt like old friends—almost as if they could have been his

characters, many of whom he freely admitted had been based on friends.

The golden-haired lass was clearly a tragic heroine if ever he had seen one, more than a little fey and quite charming. The man was roguish and venturesome and reminded him in bearing and attitude of his old friend James Hogg. But it was with the older woman, the one carrying the banjo, that he felt a most peculiar affinity. He had always done a good job portraying her type. He didn't do very well with women by and large, according to his critics, except for his peasant women, the mothers, the witches, the midwives and widows. This woman was of that sort—he fancied her a slightly aged version of Jeannie Deans, his heroine in *The Heart of MidLothian,* who had walked in a day and a night to London to save her sister's life. But, he saw with approval, this was no mere ignorant peasant crone but an educated woman. She carried one of his books in her hand—one of his first, by gar! Perhaps she would like him to sign it?

He could feel the emotions of these people and to some degree read their thoughts, as he had not wished to do with the tourists. He had known at once that these were the people whose journey had caught his attention across time and space—the instrument the woman carried had harped him from the dead. He liked the look of them. They seemed to him worthy wights. Noble ladies and gentlemen, if a bit on the scruffy side, on a noble quest. He wasn't sure exactly what it was—they were tired and their thoughts and feelings were not particularly congruous—but he was sure their cause was a good one.

As he held up his hand to bow Gussie in he fretted to see how the light pierced clean through his fingers, even on this drizzly chilly day when the wind worried the petals from his roses and rhododendrons into a mosaic of pink, violet, and white that the gardeners for the Trust would all too soon tidy away.

In his lifetime there had been a great deal of gruesome fascination with the subject of how contact could be made with the dead, but he couldn't recall that anyone had ever addressed the problem that perplexed him now, which was how to directly contact the living.

▲▲▲

Julianne Martin was wondering about making contact too. The longer her deafness continued, the more it became disorienting instead of merely inconvenient. Of course, the others remembered to look at her and make themselves clear when they were speaking directly to her. But it dawned on her now how much conversation is not face-to-face but casual, remarks thrown over the shoulder, overheard conversations between two other people not meant to exclude her specifically but simply not remembering that she could no longer choose whether to enter into the exchange or not. The absence of sound, which had always been her most important sense, made her feel as if she had become a ghost herself—or as if others had become ghosts, or television images with the volume turned off.

She felt half ashamed and half angry at the irritation she had seen in Willie's face when she thanked him for helping her with the Gypsy. She really *had* been betrayed by Torchy, whether intentionally or not. Maybe those people were great friends of Torchy's and she got along fine with them, but they were rougher than Julianne was used to, even when her hearing had been intact. Surely that was easy enough for Willie to understand. It couldn't be *that* hard for him to put himself in her place.

She had always been able to handle all but the most drunken and belligerent advances by herself, sometimes even making the guy see her as a person, even a friend, but Torchy *must* be a little twisted, judging from the company she kept, because that business with the Gypsies had been a whole other kind of scene. Juli had felt so panicky—so suddenly aware of all the nuances, all the signals she was missing that meant the difference between defusing the situation and escalating it to violence.

Under normal circumstances, if she had to, if she should remain deaf . . . (No, she wasn't going to think about that. She wasn't going to put that energy out there and manifest that reality.) But *if* she had to, she would eventually learn to do something else and become one of those differently abled people who become so remarkable that they have miniseries made about them. If she lived through this or didn't get abducted and sold to white slavers or spend the rest of her life in prison or something. After all, if she had a friend who was going through this, she'd tell them that they were expecting a little too much of themselves to think they could run away from the law and contend with lecherous lion-handlers *and* save folk music for posterity while they were like, in their adaptation phase. Oh, well. This was probably just another one of those profound experiences Lucien talked about where the universe was trying to teach you something. She just hoped it wasn't teaching her that in loosening her hold on what mattered most to her it was preparing her to leave this plane of existence.

Perish the thought, my dear! a reassuring little voice echoed inside of her in the way that her late husband George's always did. That gave her courage. She missed George and wished his spirit had been able to hitch a ride with Sam's in the banjo. She had heard those superstitions about ghosts not being able to cross flowing water and supposed it might apply to the ocean too. Probably the banjo making a corporeal body for the spirit to inhabit had enabled Sam's successful crossing. Whatever. The little voice encouraged her and she skipped forward, and passed Willie as he paused to pantomine looking thoughtfully at the book-lined walls of Sir Walter Scott's study.

The plush seat of the wingback chair at the writing desk made from the wood of ships from the Spanish Armada sank with a sigh.

▲▲▲

The Debauchery Devil felt picked on. Really, the way the other devils delighted in spoiling her fun, you'd have thought Torchy was a mortal instead of one of them. They resented her glamorous past and all the perks of her particular specialty, she'd always known they did. But that was no reason to go spoiling a whole long car trip. She had planned some really special stuff for the Randolphs, the big mocha man, and the half-breed bitch. But with Julianne loose and spreading goodness-only-knew-what stories, Willie MacKai alive and unlionized, and the banjo still functioning, little Torchy Burns really needed the lot in the van to assist in raising her credibility level.

"So, Torchy, just where *did* you take Willie anyhow?" Anna Mae asked.

"Oh, I can hardly bear to speak of it, ducky," Torchy said, pretending to be faint. "It was *too* awful. I was just going to take him back to see these new cars that were hooked on to the train? They belonged to some friends of mine who run a circus. *Well,* halfway through the next car back of ours who should I see but the coppers waiting to arrest us? So naturally, I pushed Willie ahead of me into the next car. It was dark and while we were feeling around, trying to find a way into the next car where I was sure my friends would be waiting, I'm afraid he sort of accidentally blundered into the lions' cage." She bit at her thumbnail and twined a curl of her red hair around one red-nailed finger, trying to look contrite and embarrassed. "Well, then of course I went for help and who should I meet but the little blond gel, Juli. She was lying low too, you see, having gotten separated from you, dearie," she said to Anna Mae. "So I popped in with her where my friends were and asked them to help me get Willie away from the lions.

"That particular band of Gypsies have always been such charming people, so—colorful, you know. One can't believe all the stories one hears, now *can* one? But there have been some changes in their politics lately and my old chums aren't in charge anymore. Fellow who was running things was an ugly young stud who informed me quite rudely that they were *most* particular what they fed their lions and asked me not to interfere. He sent some fellow to go tend to Willie and the lions and dismissed me rudely, saying *they'd* take care of Juli. Well, naturally I was *quite* suspicious and I came looking for help, which was when I saw darling Brose being abducted by the bobbies."

"Gussie went after Willie," Anna Mae said.

"Oh, yes, I *knew* that," Torchy said smoothly, "and I saw that she had him away from the lions so I thought I should try to help darling Brose by using my *in*fluence and here we are!" She finished brightly, then looked pouty. "I *do* so hope you'll convince Willie and Juli and Gussie that I was only trying to help in my small way."

Privately, she thought, You'd damn well better convince them since I'm going to all the trouble to restrain myself from making this road turn into a tunnel that bores straight into the heart of a sacred fairy knowe and watching your silly faces as the end of the road closes off and the road goes down and down and ever down so that you're lost in the world of *my* ken and kin.

"We know you didn't mean no harm, honey," Brose said, patting her on the shoulder gingerly. He didn't sound awfully convinced; in fact, he sounded quite *wary* of her actually, but it would have to do. Maybe later, when she had the protection of the ashes of the written ballads, she could toy with them all a bit. Nothing as prosaic as another car crash. Some nice terminal sexually transmitted diseases for the younger ones and perhaps Brose the good shepherd could be devoured by a wolf if one was handy. Enough time for that later. She could call out the Hounds of Hell, the Hound of the Baskervilles, or Huckleberry Hound for that matter, whenever she liked, it was all just a matter of the proper timing.

She had found out at devil central that Willie and the others were at Abbotsford so she decided to fool her traveling companions by doing the unexpected and being genuinely helpful, much as it pained her, and so, faithful as a triple-A road map, she gave them the very best directions for the very fastest, straightest roads and short cuts that truly would lead to the estate and not into some bog or hidden tarn on a deserted moor.

"You're pretty helpful all of a sudden," Ellie said suspiciously, "and awfully sure Gussie and Willie really are at Abbotsford."

"Oh, I rang up at the station, after I got out of the loo. I described them to the lady at the manor and she said they were there. So it's all come out all right, you see. Just so there are no hard feelings about the misunderstanding. *I* had rather thought we'd all end up meeting at The Plastic Card because that's where I told the Gypsies to bring Juli—before they became so *rude* I mean."

"Gee, how convenient this all is," Ellie said with an edge in her voice.

"Don't knock it," Faron said. "What I wonder is how they got away from the cops."

"Torchy found out we were cleared," Brose said. "The Irish dude turned his sorry self in."

"God, that *is* convenient," Ellie said.

"Yeah, for somebody," Anna Mae replied sourly.

"I do *try,*" Torchy said modestly. "You're just sour because you've had such a rum go lately, poor dear, but cheer up. Not long now and we'll meet the others at old Wattie Scott's and we shall all be reunited and partying in some pub before you know it."

Her cheery pronouncement served mostly to shut everybody up and they rode for a time in silence.

As they crossed into Scotland they left the broad highway for the scenic side roads leading to Scott's Borders. A dank rain drizzled from a curdling sky onto a road as twisty and slippery as a fresh-caught haddock. If another car should come, either it or the van would have to leap one of the stone fences that veined the fields like the lines of some huge jigsaw puzzle or drive into freshly clawed muddy land waiting to be reforested. The plowed land was invariably flanked by neat little evergreen trees planted in precise rows about two feet apart.

"Sheep raising and Christmas tree farming are big business around here, huh?" Brose asked Torchy.

"Christmas tree farming indeed," she said sadly. "That, my dear man, is what the government is doing to try to replant the great Caledon Forest that once covered all the lowlands and borders of Scotland." She bit off saying any more. She was not at all in accord with the rest of the devils about this particular development. The

Greed and Avarice Devil and horrid old Threedee were
proud of this sort of thing but it didn't appeal to her. Her
job could be done as easily in forest as in pub and she
missed the leafy cover . . . among other things. The
new chemical developments were fun for a while, but
although the drugs caused plenty of misery, their devo-
tees didn't take them seriously enough. Oh, the addicts
were well and truly caught but they were never quite—
awed.

In her younger days, when things were simpler and
she depended on grandiosity for effect and, often, poteen
or whiskey for a mere catalyst, her victims and disciples
alike had feared her, longed for her, and were in awe of
her power and beauty. Aw well, ducks, her Torchy Burns
self told her, we're none of us these days what we once
were. Nowadays, the only entities that received the sort
of admiration she had once attracted were those bogeys
who operated under the auspices of the Superstition
Squad. It was the fault of the damned board. Back when
each devil was either an independent or, at times, an in-
terdependent operator, when life was primitive and the
pickings were easy, people were in awe of all sorts of
things. But then someone got the bright idea for the
board.

The board was very modern. Very keen on statistics.
Statistics could be manipulated even more easily than
people, who could be manipulated by statistics. Anything
to seem *rational.* Rationality, the board claimed, wooed
people into thinking that the forces of the Opposition
were not just ineffective, but nonexistent. The Debauchery Devil didn't think that was much fun. She much preferred her ranting and raving religious television stars,
who were, like musicians, among her best people. Just
one of them, she firmly contended, did more to drive the
general populace away from the Opposition than a whole
academy full of scientists or a whole computer full of
statistics.

She supposed she was rather an old-fashioned girl in
her own way. She much preferred the good old days
when she alone, not some silly movie star, could so en-

chant a mortal that the poor sod would wander around forever pixilated after experiencing, and then being denied, her intoxicating world. After a bit of what she had had to offer, mortals were simply too depressed to face their simple little lives again.

The problem was, her present position didn't allow for such magical opportunities and that got *her* a bit down. It simply wasn't very *personal,* when those you led down the garden path had to be led through the mouth of a bottle or the end of a needle. Not at all like seeing one's own razzle-dazzle reflected in the eyes of one's victims. She missed their society, their attempts to woo her with milk and bread, poetry and yes—music. She missed having people she had never summoned dream of her, long for her, yearn for a glimpse of her, half fearing, but willing to give up lives and sanity not for some silly potion brewed in a sterile laboratory but for the unearthly glitter of her own eyes, to be caught in the web of her hair and enthralled by the cadence of her voice.

But she was lucky, she supposed, (and who better to be lucky? one of her names was Lady Luck—her gamblers called her that) to still have a job of any sort. She who had once been queen of the underworld, spirit of the forest, guardian of the rivers, was now the empress of street corners and casinos. But she still had followers, and it kept a girl going.

The underworld was a total bust now, of course, drilled by mines and such. These spriggy new forests, while rather touching, were hardly tall enough or thick enough to hide even one pair of lovers six miles into the woods without passersby being able to see bare flesh through the trees. And that ambitious upstart of a demon, sponsored by the Expediency Devil, the one called PW (Pollution and Waste, which sounded grandiose to her for such a grubby kid) had hold of her waters.

So here she was, with this crummy assignment, doing in her own disciples. It wasn't even much of a challenge. Music was an addiction all by itself and once she separated the musicians from the music, they'd be easy enough prey.

Even Willie, who seemed as if he should have been quite easy to overcome because of his drinking, still kept from sinking into the pit that was Torchy's particular corner of her particular hell because of the music. Without it, in he'd go so deep he'd never hit bottom.

Torchy had absolutely *no* idea what was keeping Julianne together now that the music had been stripped from her. If only the silly thing could hear herself try to sing now that she could no longer hear, that would probably do her in! Of course, with all of her mystic tendencies, she'd undoubtedly end up on the streets as one more crazy baglady. You couldn't get most people to believe that the supernatural things the girl saw were *real,* even though they were.

Gussie was one of Torchy's very special minions, a bartender, and she was older than dirt and probably wouldn't last long enough to worry about anyway.

Brose might survive the loss of music as long as there were animals and nasty little juvenile delinquents for him to help, but the other devils could no doubt take care of parting him from those outlets as well.

Once Gunn's mind was safely wiped of the music, she could safely be tucked into a prison for her radical organizational tendencies—either that or taxes. You could always count on the Accounting Devil to come up with something in that department.

As for the Randolphs—well, Torchy thought she might do a very special song for Faron—not the kind the other devils were trying to erase, one of her very own, the kind she did when she went for a little swim. It should be irresistible to a serious collector. And his poor wife would be so upset she'd eat herself sick or else she'd try to compete with Torchy's unattainable allure by starving herself thinner and thinner until she died of anorexia.

Torchy yawned. It was all very dreary, actually. Mortals were so—well—mortal. A shame about the music having to go—their love of the music had lifted this lot out of the ordinary, however fleetingly, and she would miss that.

Of course, old as she was, nobody had ever told

Torchy Burns about it not being a good idea to count her chickens before they were hatched.

The van drove up the long gravel and dirt drive leading to the manor house.

"Maybe we're too late," Brose said. "Looks to me like they're about to close."

CHAPTER X

▲▲▲

Meanwhile, inside Sir Walter's mansion, the docent was saying, "I'm verra sorry but we'll be needin' to close up." She glanced disapprovingly at the banjo, which Gussie passed to Willie as if it were a hot potato.

"What a wonderful place," Gussie said, oozing downhome charm. "I do wish we had time to stay longer and see the books more closely but I suppose it really *is* time to go."

Willie and the banjo were already at the door, Julianne trailing behind. him. As Gussie reached the doorway, however, she felt a pressure on her shoulder. "Please," Sir Walter's ghost said. "You mustn't go, just as it's getting dark. Yon instrument has called me from my grave and you canna just go off without explaining this whole thing to me. It's simply not the done thing at all, dear lady."

He was standing in front of Gussie, his hand touching her. The docent called to her to come along and she tried to step forward.

"No, truly, I'm afraid I must insist—" the ghost said. And that time, in the gathering gloom, as headlights cut the fog rising from the Tweed that ran so near the dining-room window, Gussie heard him, and stepped back inside the house.

The docent, oddly, did not seem to notice and somehow forgot to click the key in the lock and the bolt onto the padlock. Juli and Willie, far ahead of her on the path,

Willie pacing with his head in the air and Juli stopping to sniff a rose, failed to notice that Gussie wasn't with them.

The docent strode ahead of them as if in a trance. A car door thunked shut in the parking lot and five pairs of footsteps coming met hers going on the walk. As the docent tripped past the last person, a certain redhead, the docent thrust her bosom forward and caused the plaid of her pleated skirt to swish back and forth as her walk changed to an undulating sway.

Torchy Burns laughed her bawdy laugh. The docent's old man would get a kick out of that little good deed of hers.

"Willie, luv, there you are!" Torchy caroled. "Where did you *go*? I waited and waited for you."

The banjo resumed playing "Whiskey in the Jar."

"For the devil take the women, Lord, you never can believe 'em," Willie said to himself.

But as Willie passed Juli, the banjo played "The Rose of County Down" and Anna Mae said, "I wonder what it wants to tell us by playing 'The Parting Glass.' "

"Isn't that 'Rollin' Down to Old Maui'?" Brose asked. "Maybe it thinks we should all bug out of here and go to Hawaii. I'm for that."

Faron cleared his throat. "We may have a problem here."

"Buddy, we already got one," Willie said. "In case you hadn't noticed. Where the hell have you folks been?"

"We could ask you the same question, MacKai," Anna Mae Gunn said.

"Now that's funny," Willie said, looking slitty-eyed at Torchy, who was beaming back at him just as innocently as she could, which was to say, not very. "I'd think our little native guide could have told you about my close encounter with her pussycat friends and siccin' those ethnic rape-artists on the Widah Martin, which, I want to tell you, I almost got myself knifed tryin' to rescue her."

He might as well take the credit for his good intentions if not his actions. Julianne couldn't hear him to contradict him and Gussie—now just where WAS Gussie?

Torchy rocked her high heel back and forth and looked at the towers and stones of Abbotsford with the mist rising around it like it bored her half to tears. "Well, now that we're all together and you've found each other, can we go somewhere and get warm and have a little drinkee? This place is creepy, don't you think?"

She thought the last was a masterful stroke. Of course, if anybody should know creepy, she should.

"We came here looking for the ballads," Faron said. "Did you get a look at any of Sir Walter's books, Willie? Did you notice a copy of the *Minstrelsy* or maybe Percy's *Reliques of Ancient English Poetry*?"

Willie shook his head. "Naw, that stuff's all under lock and key. There was a copy of *Field and Stream* in the men's room though. No—wait—I think Gussie might have gotten a copy of one of those books in the gift shop. Had something to do with minstrels anyway. She was reading out of it as we looked at the house."

"You won't find out anything very important about your songs here, ducks," Torchy said pettishly. "Everybody knows the old scribbler was a terrible one for changing things around. Why, they claim he made up ever so many of the songs he 'collected' himself."

The imposing front doors of Abbotsford's hall swung open and Gussie stood framed in the doorway, asking in an offended tenor with a broad burr, "Who in the world would so besmirch my honor as to accuse me of such a thing? It was that Ritson, wasn't it? Brilliant man but frightfully literal-minded."

And to their surprise, Gussie strode forward in a lordly manner, knelt gallantly before Torchy Burns, took her hand and kissed it. "Your Majesty. I can't tell you how honored my home is by your visit."

Before the nonplussed Torchy could do more than nod majestically, Gussie had likewise kissed Julianne's hand. "I'm so sorry for your recent tragedy, my dear," Gussie said, still in the tenor that was much lighter and more quavery than her own husky alto.

Julianne stared down at her. "Gussie?" she asked, then stared hard at her friend as Gussie's image blurred and her white hair rearranged itself, her hazel eyes brightened to blue, her sweat suit took on a more formal and tailored cut and her bosom seemed to be merely the ruffling of a shirtfront.

"I'm in here too, Juli," Gussie's voice called, and the image wavered so that they saw Gussie through the blur. "But I'm sort of giving somebody a lift. I know you may find this a little hard to believe, but—"

The banjo keened the chords to "The Unquiet Grave."

"Well, hell, if you can accept that Sam Hawthorne is influencing that banjo, maybe you can accept that Walter Scott wants me to get you to take us to Melrose Abbey to see if we can't have a powwow with another spook who's not only a relative of his but a wizard."

"Oh, well, if that's all he wants, darlin', we should humor him by all *means*," Willie said with a hard glare at Gussie/Scott. "I was just a little concerned there that he was going to make you throw up pea soup or some weird shit like that."

▲▲▲

Willie drove the van this time and Gussie huddled in the passenger seat. Brose, Anna Mae, Julianne, Ellie, and Faron were in the back. "Ah, my worrud, this carriage is a marvel," Sir Walter's ghost said of the van. "And I can only hope, my dear Mrs. Turner," Gussie said to herself in her tenor voice, "that the personal nature of my intrusion isn't causing you discomfort or embarrassment."

"Oh, no, sir," Gussie's alto voice assured him, "no trouble at all. You just come on in and make yourself at home. If you got any questions at all, just ask."

"Most magnanimous of you," the ghost voice said.

"Shucks," Gussie's voice said. "We're in a state of emergency. They used to teach me in Sunday school that the body is the temple of the holy spirit—well—usually my own holy spirit—but since your holy spirit needs a place to light while you try to help us out with this thing, I figure my body just got requisitioned for a while."

"Very sensible. Now then, would you care to explain the nature of your difficulty to me?"

It was a long story to squeeze into a short van ride, but fortunately with the ghost's mind and Gussie's so close, she found she was able to sort of silently fill him in as the others talked.

He heaved a sigh as three of them stopped talking simultaneously and said, "Ah well, then, I see now why the skirlin' of yon instrument called to me. 'Tis a verra dangerous matter when foreign folk seek to destroy a people's spirit by taking their songs—did you know that in Scotland it was once as forbidden to play the pipes as it was to wear the tartan because it spoke of Scottish pride? And in Ireland the English burned not only harps but harpers who were the living memories of Ireland. You folk stand in the stead of those pipers and harpers in your own country and this instrument is a wise and powerful thing indeed to lead you here to win back your songs. But how to do it, eh? It may well be that the trip to Melrose Abbey will avail us nothing, the Wizard Michael being dead more years than I and so, perhaps, deader, ye ken?"

"Oh, uh-huh," Brose said, not having the foggiest idea what he said. "That makes sense."

The banjo had been playing "The Unquiet Grave" over and over for the last thirty minutes. "Sometimes I wish there was a way to turn that thing off," Willie said.

"At least it keeps time with the windshield wipers," Ellie said philosophically.

"Makes it sound like a martial tune, doesn't it?" Faron said. "As if the lover died in battle."

Willie switched on the lights and two moon-pale beams gleamed through the raindrops to illuminate rain-slicked cement. Fog rolled across the road in gauzy swaths. Julianne sneezed and huddled back, smashing into the shattered instrument cases.

"Lovely night, isn't it?" Sir Walter's ghost said conversationally.

"Not very," Ellie said. The banjo played "Cold Haily Windy Night" again.

A patch of fog completely enveloped them and Gussie thought, "Here we go. Back into the Twilight Zone again. As if what's happening now is what you might call normal."

And Sir Walter answered her thought, "Ah, yes. Thrilling, isn't it? Haven't had such fun since I was a bairn. Would you mind terribly sticking your arm out the window so I might feel the rain?"

She was starting to comply when the van plowed through the fog and emerged in front of the spires, arches, towers, and ruined walls of Melrose Abbey silhouetted against the dark and roiling night, ebony against black.

"Do we have to get out of the car?" Julianne asked plaintively. "It's so cold."

The ghost offered to lend her his jacket until Gussie reminded him that he didn't have one anymore and neither did she.

Willie was slamming the door to the van after everyone had emerged before any of them realized Torchy was no longer with them.

"I thought she was right behind me," Ellie said.

"All I need is that redhead mad at me for leavin' her behind," Willie said.

"It's her responsibility to mention it if she needed to go to the bathroom or whatever," Anna Mae said. "We have more important things to do than wait around for her."

Ellie craned her neck looking up. "This place is BIG!"

Faron shrugged. "Mostly it's old. The Oral Roberts Power of Prayer building in Tulsa is bigger. This is more impressive though. This feels *real.*"

"Wh-where do you think this guy is, Gussie—I mean, Sir—?" Ellie asked.

"In his grave as he's been lo these last four—excuse me, madame," the ghost said to Gussie. "Can you inform me of the century?"

"Twentieth," Gussie said. "At least, it was when we left Tacoma."

"Lo these seven centuries," Sir Walter said.

"Then, excuse me," Brose said, "but unless it's the

Scotch version of Memorial Day and you want to put a boo-kay on his grave, what the hell are we doin' here?"

"Easy, Brose," Anna Mae said. "We've had pretty good luck with ghosts so far and maybe this relative of Sir Walter's ghost *can* help."

"Well, so what, we wait another century or two for him to get around to seeing us or do we go hunt him up?"

"The Wizard Michael Scott was a man of muckle importance," Sir Walter said. "He was in high courts and the counselor to kings. I'd rather imagine he stands on the formalities and will rise at midnight in the customary way. At least, that's what the stories all say. I myself have nevair met a speerit before, except for me, that is, and I don't seem to have done the thing conventionally."

"What time is it, Anna Mae?" Willie asked.

"Ten-thirty."

"Let's look around," Faron suggested.

"Do we climb over a gate or something?" Willie asked.

But Julianne, who had wandered ahead of the rest of them, walking in widening circles to keep warm, stood shivering by the abbey door. "It's unlocked," she called in a voice growing ever more toneless and nasal as her deafness alienated her from the sound of her own utterances.

"Aha," Sir Walter's ghost said. "As I supposed, we're expected."

CHAPTER XI
▲▲▲

The cook got to that point in the story just as all of the lights in the restaurant came on again. The dishwasher, waitresses, and two of the regular customers groaned with disappointment. But just then, thunder cracked as if a piece of the skyscraper above them had broken off, the lights died again, and the cook continued her tale.

As if a night like that with the wind and fog and rain in an ancient monastery looking for a long-dead wizard wasn't Halloweenish enough for everybody, Gussie was trying to get used to sharing her body with a ghost. Hell, she hadn't shared it with a man on a regular basis for close to twenty years except for a one-night stand once in a blue moon. And this was a whole lot closer than being in bed together—it was like being pregnant with somebody else's homemade film, full of voices and pictures that weren't hers, even when Sir Walter wasn't talking. It made her giddy. Not that he wasn't as polite as he could be. It simply didn't give a lady much privacy. She had never been quite so close to anyone even before she ran her old man off.

She felt a little like a ghost herself with her cold wet feet and her stringing hair trailing water all down her back and face, her eyes all starey from trying to see in the dark.

As she passed through the gate, reminding Sir Walter that they had to physically open the gate and go between the doors, not through them as he had been used to doing, she saw Julianne wafting ahead of them, like some-thing out of a Wilkie Collins novel.

At Willie MacKai's back, the banjo was still playing that song and now more than ever the words came back —Gussie realized Sir Walter was feeding them to her.

> "Cold blows the wind o'er my true love
> And gently falls the rain
> I never had but one true love
> And in greenwood he lies slain
> I'll do as much for my true love
> As any young girl may
> I'll sit and mourn all on his grave
> For twelvemonth and a day."

But as they crept farther into the abbey, the song changed to a major key and the tune became the one that urged them to "Take it to its root," the song that the banjo had taught Willie and Juli to write during the traf-fic jam from hell on the Oregon Trail. Willie stopped, listened, then continued on, stalking silent and wary, looking all around him like the soldiers on patrol in the war movies did. Anna Mae Gunn walked a little to his left as if she were on tippy-toe and if she were a cat her ears would have been swiveling all different directions. Brose Fairchild pitty-patted beside her with little reluc-tant steps, the irises of his eyes all surrounded by whites and his wiry red-gray hair seeming to stand on end more than ever.

"You seem ill at ease, good woman," Sir Walter's ghost intruded on Gussie's thoughts.

"I am," she muttered—no need to speak loud enough to wake the dead, so to speak, when the dead was right here inside her head, cozy as another pea in a one-pea pod. "I can understand how the atmosphere wouldn't especially impress you but it scares the bejeezus out of me. And I can't help wondering where that red-haired woman got herself to."

"Oh, as to that, who knows about such as she," he said, dotingly, Gussie thought.

"You evidently know her better than we do if you think she's worth bowin' over and so on," Gussie said.

"Aye. I know her," he said. Though he hadn't quite recognized her in the long-distance visions he'd had when he first arose from the grave, the moment he met her he'd known her for what and who she was. He had been a sheriff and a lawman in life and he had seen a lot of deviltry—enough to knock sense into any ordinary man. But he was also the biggest romantic of his age and lived more in his head than he did in the real world most of the time and a little thing like dying hadn't changed that. Gussie did not know what to make of the image he showed her of Torchy Burns with her red hair blazing under a golden crown with stars all over it and wearing a gown of velvet green decorated with silver trim and little silver bells. She just supposed that he liked redheads, which figured, him being Scottish and all, and that he was having the kind of fantasies about her that if he were a modern man, he would have dressed her up in a slinky evening dress and diamonds and maybe a mink coat. (Well, maybe not a mink coat what with the way people were reacting to those things these days. But most men having fantasies about redheaded women didn't worry about animal rights politics or much of anything else at the time.)

"Here it is," Julianne's toneless voice floated back to them, an echo that didn't repeat itself. "I found it," she said. "Michael Scott."

"Is he—uh—up?" Brose asked in such a small voice he had to repeat himself.

Faron and Ellie had been inspecting everything around them with interest but now that Julianne had found the tomb Ellie's eyes were big as saucers and Faron's Adam's apple traveled up and down, up and down. They had already encountered several ghosts in the course of their journeys but the ghost of a wizard was surely something special. Both of them were big fans of fantasy novels and they knew that the quintessential question when it came to wizards was a paraphrase of the one Glenda the Good had asked Dorothy Gale, "Are you a good wizard or a bad wizard?"

Neither of the Randolphs had shown less courage than any of the others when faced with actual ghosts, but then they hadn't had time to be afraid of the ones they'd seen before. The other ghosts may have appeared on atmospheric nights too but they didn't have the fanfare of being announced by a descendant who was possessing a friend of the Randolphs'. The Wizard Michael Scott might have been a great philosopher, scientist, and scholar but he was also, like all competent magicians, enough of a ham to know how to make an entrance.

Ellie scooted closer to Gussie. She was shivering so hard her rain-wet goose bumps stood up like white caps by the light of the drowning moon poking through the roofless portion of the abbey.

"Gussie, ask Sir Walter what this Mike guy is like."

"He doesn't know. He never met him."

"But he's going to wait until midnight, huh?" she asked.

"It's only eleven," Anna Mae said. "God, I'm freezing."

"Me too," Ellie said, jumping up and down vigorously to demonstrate her point.

"Maybe there'd be time to go back to Abbotsford for blankets or something," Gussie said. "I didn't lock up, Walt, did you? You don't mind if I call you Walt, do you? And you call me Gussie. Seeing as how we're getting so close and all."

"Seems imminently practical to me, dear lady. I doot mah dear wife would mind even were she alive, and would join me in begging you to call me what you will. Walter or Wat, as you would have it, so shall I answer to it."

But his pleasant speech broke off abruptly and Gussie felt him stiffen and freeze within her, before with even more alarming abruptness she found herself turning and tearing back for the gate.

"Sir Walt—Wat, simmer down. What is it? Where are we going? You don't have to return to the grave at midnight do you?"

In her mind an anguished howl let rip. "The swine! The dirty swine have returned. They're after my bukes, Goussie. We maun save my bukes."

He headed her straight for the gate. "Whoa, Walt, if you're going that way you have to leave me behind. Even if we don't go through walls I can't run all the way back to your place."

"We must!" he cried. "I canna bide here trapped while they destroy m'life's wark!"

Gussie was too involved with the distraught ghost to notice what the others were up to, but Ellie, who had been close by, grabbed Faron. "Come on, we'll drive you back."

"What about the wizard?"

"There's an hour. The others can stay here. Once we get back to Abbotsford Sir Walter can unpossess you and haunt the vandals into submission if we make it in time. Brose, you got the keys?"

He tossed them and there was a clink as they hit the paving stones, then Ellie, Faron, and Gussie/Sir Walter piled into the van and drove like bats out of hell for Abbotsford.

A diesel eighteen-wheeler with the legend Circus Rom on the side was parked outside Abbotsford and the front door stood wide open.

"Oh, my God, Wat, I'm sorry. I should have locked up," Gussie said. "Might as well have printed an invitation."

But she was only able to aim the thoughts at him as she ran for the house. Sir Walter forgot that she was no longer young and he had been dead more than a hundred and fifty years. He took the walk up to the house like a sprinter and Gussie passed Ellie and Faron, and did not hear the scuffling from behind her when the young couple came abreast of the circus truck. But Sir Walter carried her along so fast she did make it to the door before something came down on her head and she crumpled on the threshold just as a bright orange light blossomed from the open doorway to the library.

CHAPTER XII

▲▲▲

As midnight approached by the luminous phosphorescent-green hands of Anna Mae's watch, the air in the abbey's confines grew even more dank and chill. Anna Mae and Brose draped their arms around Julianne, knotted with cold in her flimsy T-shirt, and Willie paced furiously. The banjo had played only softly for some time but as the second hand swept once, twice, and thrice around into the last second of the last minute of midnight, the instrument struck such a chord as it once did when its dead owner Sam Hawthorne would leap onto stage and, with that chord, announce to the audience that he was about to begin a song and that they were by damn expected to sing along.

"They're not *back* yet," Anna Mae said. "Where can they be?"

"I sure hope we don't need no formal introduction from his Sirship to meet this dead guy," Brose said. " 'Cause it feels to me like we're about to."

Julianne didn't say a thing but all of a sudden she opened her mouth and commenced singing along with the banjo, just like she could hear it, the "Take It to Its Root" song. Willie stopped in midpace, hoisted the banjo up to help it along with his fingers, and sang as if trying to overpower the noisiest bar in West Texas, "And take it to its root," and Anna Mae joined in with her strong alto with the vibrato quavery as a ghost's voice is supposed to be but generally wasn't, "Take it to its root" and Brose

Fairchild joined in with his bluesy, boozy baritone as if he was singing a Gospel harmony, "Take it to its root."

And on the lid of the tomb, a lichen as luminous as the hands on Anna Mae's watch commenced to growing and growing, trailing here and trailing there, clasped to the stone, filling in its runners beside other runners, bulking up on top of itself. Like no lichen ever seen before, it bore tiny leaves that grew larger as the organism grew, leaves that looked now like rose leaves, now like birch leaves, now like the leaves of some brier, all intertwined and growing quick as poison ivy or kudzu or wild blackberry vines. The people watching this growth overtake the stone tomb lid might have thought they were watching a Disney fast-forward nature movie except that the leaves shed actual light, and in time, not to anybody's great surprise, these leaves began taking on the shape of a man wearing a long gown and some kind of a hat or helmet and clutching a big old book to his breast where lilies usually went on the breasts of less learned dead.

Pretty soon, though no one could have said exactly how long it was, everybody being too mesmerized to check their watches, they saw that eyes and a nose and a mouth had dented into this mass of foliage, and that you could tell the head from the helmet and the book from the breast and the hands from the book and each individual foot from the other and if he had been wearing argyle socks under his gown, you could have seen the pattern.

After a while the thing's shoulders began to rise, separating from the lid of the tomb from which they seemed to grow, though some trailers still attached like long streamers behind the leafy form, and the knees bent and the whole thing scooted forward until it was sitting on the edge of the tomb lid, its feet swinging back and forth like tree limbs blowing in the wind. The leaves seemed to melt all together and Willie and his friends could see then that the glow was coming from inside of them and taking them over, the same way Sir Walter's form had sometimes shone through and over Gussie's own self, and the stems of the leaves took on the appearance of veins in the hands, neck, and breast, and some roots seemed to be the Wizard's hair flowing beneath that funny hat he wore, as if someone had stuck an old funnel on top of a topiary rosebush.

The foliage parted of its own accord where the mouth should be and rows of thorns turned into teeth and a pair of roots turned into lips as the creature from the tomb of the Wizard Michael Scott spoke.

"Ah suppose," it said, "ye'll be wonderin' why ah've cawed ye aw here te nicht."

▲▲▲

The wailing of banshees, Gussie knew, omened death— her death? Heavy feet thudded past her and she thought they must be the feet of firemen, but she thought firemen would remove a corpse rather than just walk over it, wouldn't they?

The wailing must be of fire trucks then. Did they have fire trucks out in the country like this? They could get water from the Tweed, no doubt.

She struggled to waken and another shrill scream brought her alert.

Her eyes flew open and the fluttering of her lashes caused her head to roar with pain. Her eyes shut tight again against the blaze of light pouring from the far end of the hallway. She still lay crumpled on the threshold of Abbotsford.

Another shrill scream, followed by an emphatic "Damn!" in a female voice.

My God, Gussie thought, the place is on fire and someone is still in there. She tried to rise, pulling her legs over the threshold and into the hallway where her head and shoulders had lain. As she gathered herself inside, a familiar presence flooded her mind and a gentle burr told her, "Your wound wasna mortal, auld lass."

"Someone's in there, Wat. Gotta—"

"Not unarmed. Nivair unarmed," the ghost said and as they stood together reached her hand up and drew down a long dirk from the weapons displayed in the entry hall along with the armor and carvings.

The scream came again. In the distance, Gussie heard the bells and sirens of fire trucks, but they might be too late to save whoever it was. Pulling up her sweatshirt to cover her mouth, she and her ghostly hitchhiker plunged forward into the billows of smoke and flame, past the library, with the flames licking the books to death on every shelf on both levels, spurting through the windows, devouring the carpet, running along the grooves in the hardwood floor into the study, where the screams were turning to shrieks.

Torchy Burns was sitting on the marble mantelpiece over the fireplace. Her ankles were bound.

"My God, when the fire gets this far that chimney will be like a candlewick," Gussie cried.

"Thanks for the cheery thought, ducks. Get me out of here."

"I can free her," Sir Walter's ghost said. " 'Tis nearly midnight, and we spirits are strongest noo." Sir Walter's ghost didn't really know that for a fact exactly, but romantic that he was he believed that it was true of all haunts worthy of the name, so with spectral dignity his silhouette cut through the flames and bearing aloft the fire-burnished dirk advanced to free the captive lady.

The knife had no sooner sliced through Torchy's bonds than she yelled, "Stand back!" and Gussie retreated into the hall toward the nearest door, where the air was somewhat clearer.

Before it seemed quite possible that Torchy could have won her way clear, the redhead ran past Gussie and out into the courtyard. The ghost reentered Gussie as she sprinted after Torchy.

"What happened?" Gussie asked as the first fire trucks pulled up and started drawing water from the Tweed.

"No time to talk. We have to get out of here," Torchy said.

"Aye," the ghost agreed wearily. "The Wizard Michael will have arisen and I'll not be there to meet him."

The diesel truck was no longer in the parking lot, but the van was, keys still in the ignition. Torchy jumped into the driver's seat and didn't quite wait until Gussie was seated to make a wide U-turn and roar down the driveway, taking little detours into sheep pasture to avoid the three fire trucks coming the other way, the Selkirk one, which boasted only a bell, the Galashiels one, which had a hook, ladder, and a proper siren, and a pickup truck from the town of Melrose equipped with a garden hose and six volunteer fire fighters, most of whom looked to be well over seventy-five, in the rear. There was also a little car with a light on the top, the driver of which seemed to take no notice of them. By the time Torchy had dodged all of these and was back out on the road again, a few bicycles and cars were also headed into the driveway toward Abbotsford. Gussie was sure somebody was taking down their license plate number and that they were already tagged as arsonists.

With every fire truck that they passed she felt a swell of anguish and when she heard the ghost moan she realized it was coming from him rather than from herself. "Oh, God," she said. "Wat, I'm so sorry. Your beautiful house—all your books."

When the ghost sighed in response, the sigh escaped through her lips mournful and puzzled.

"At least you're okay, Torchy." Gussie only said this because she was a southern woman and this was the polite thing to say, even if it was insincere, since she wasn't sure if she had been given the choice whether she would have saved Torchy or Sir Walter's library. Then she remembered. "Oh, Lord, Faron and Ellie! Where are they? Stop, Torchy, turn this thing around. They might still be in there."

"Sorry, ducks," Torchy said and drove on like a bat out of hell.

"Wat, make her stop."

The ghost was within her but was less communicative than before. "Eh? No need. They're not in Abbotsford, your friends."

Torchy screeched to a halt outside the abbey, which appeared as empty as it had when first Gussie had seen it.

Gussie was barely out of the van when Torchy disappeared into the building.

Once more Sir Walter's ghost almost ran Gussie into walls as he tried to go through them in his haste to reach the tomb.

CHAPTER XIII

▲▲▲

Gussie arrived at Melrose to find Willie, Brose, Anna Mae, and Julianne standing in a line like guilty school-children while a greenish glowing figure sitting on a long stone casket glowered at them all.

The banjo for once was silent.

"W-Wat—that green guy. Is that—?"

"Hush," Sir Walter's ghost said to her and to his foliage-fleshed forebear. "Greetings to ye, kinsman."

A breeze seemed to flutter through the leafy apparition as it looked straight across at him and said, "And to you, bairn. I see ye found a steed to bear ye to me."

"Who's he callin' a steed?" Gussie demanded. "I may look like the old gray mare to you, buddy, but it isn't very damn polite to say so."

"The grave is nae a courteous place, kinswoman. Yer forgiveness—" The Wizard's voice was rough and rustly, the wind soughing through him.

"She's nae kin, Michael, but a visitor—"

"She's kin. She bears part of ye in her mak'up, bairn, or ye'd no be able to blend to her sae weel."

"Aye?"

"Yer dead, Walter Scott, and hae been dead lo these mony years, though fewer years than I. Long has yer body rotted in yer grave and long has yer spark been wi' yer Makker. But the wee bits of ye that were yersel'—yer cares and woes, the things that ye looked after—those things hae gone tae other wights. There's a Scott laddie

98

who cares for yer family name as once ye did, there's a policeman in Aberdeen who is evenhanded wi' the law as once ye ware, there's this one and that one who carry on this or that bit of ye. This woman, whose great-grandsire's wife was Laidlaw and a relation, bears yer ane love of story and ballad and yer ane lack o' voice to sing."

"I think the man's sayin' Gussie's your *soul* sister, Brother Walter," Brose said. "Ain't that nice? But the point is, Mike, this banjo here told us we have to learn us some songs and that right here is the root of 'em and we still can't find any. Back home, this banjo was lotsa help because it could give us tunes, but hell, every song you folks got over here has the same tune as six other songs."

"And as Faron said, every one of them can be sung to the tune of *Gilligan's Island,*" Gussie added and then decided maybe she should have kept her mouth shut since the Wizard probably wasn't a big TV fan.

The banjo played a tune that could have been "Lady Margaret," "Little Musgrave," or the American version of "Omie Wise."

The Wizard said, "Aye, aye, ah'm weel aware of the limitations of yer implement. Tha's why it's fetched ye tae the bairn Wat and him tae me. T' Wizard Sam Hawthorne tawd me o' yer woes and o' the great conspiracy tae undo the bindings we set on t' world in sang shortly after he died and ah do understand the argency o' yer difficulty. Tha's why I fetched Wattie doon. It's his province amang ma folk, tae guard the char-ums. Tha's why he 'gan collectin' them when a' was bein' lost before."

"The collection is gone—they're all gone," Sir Walter's ghost said. "With the burning of Abbotsford the last copy of *Minstrelsy,* the last of Percy's *Reliques,* are gone. You feel it, don't you, Michael Scott? The loss of it—and my home, my books, my life's work destroyed."

"For a dead man yer aye too attached tae things of this world, Wat," the Wizard told him. "And 'tis true the collections are gone but 'tis true as well that when these people returned to their ane country, nane o' them but yer lass there"—he indicated Gussie with a pointing finger—"nane o' them would remember a thing. Too late noo for printed collections. The only way for them to learn the char-um songs is to live the char-um songs."

"Just what's that supposed to mean?" Willie asked. "How can you live a song?"

"Not easily," the Wizard said. "For those songs were nae written of easy times but of perilous times and woeful. Ye ken that peaceful, happy times may be easy on a body but they mak' bluidy puir sangs."

"Like the Chinese curse," Anna Mae said. "May you live in interesting times. But there's no way we can do that, is there? Live in those interesting times, I mean."

"If there warn't, d'ye think I'd hae risen frae ma rest and spend frae midnight tae cockcrow in counsel wi' ye?"

"Why until cockcrow, kinsman, when I may roam the day as well as night?" Sir Walter asked.

"Photosynthesis," the revenant Wizard said, raising a leafy arm. "Ah'd sore need prunin' were ah tae stay aboveground the day. Not tae mention alar-umin' the tourists somethin' fierce."

"I did wonder at your shape, kinsman, for according to the ballads are we spirits not supposed to return in our earthly guise?"

"Under normal circumstances, aye," the Wizard said. "But this be a special case and tha'st been dead lo these two centuries and ah lo these seven and there be no remnant of us either one large enough tae mak a rev'nant. Fartunately for me, mah enemies rejoiced and sang o'er mah grave and made these briers and rose leaves grow therein and from these I ha' shaped a boddie. For you, more than for the common man, the things o' the spirit was the sum of ye, and so yer disembodied spirit was able tae return as in the past they nivair war. And when ye had need o' a boddie, why, the crisis itself sent ye the lass in which ye bide."

"Ain't it kind of a large coincidence that out of all the people in the world, one of us should turn out to be related to him—even distantly?" Brose asked.

"We Scotts got aroond. Ye'd be surprised tae find how many distant relations we have throughout t'warld. And as for the speck of Wat the lassie bears, why, bairn, I

dinna think ye've the time nor the backgroond tae understand mah theery o' t'fission o'souls."

"I bet you're right about that," Anna Mae said. "But
you were going to tell us—is there a way to reclaim the
songs without the written collections?"

"Aye, there's a way, but it's a hard one and full of
danger. To win the sangs, the four of ye maun live the
tales behind them and live yet tae sing o' those same
tales."

"Will ye mak us a spell then, kinsman?" Walter Scott
asked.

"If they agree, aye. They've no been given much
choice in this matter and they stand tae forfeit this life
and the next for tales long past and gone. For 'tis in
earlier lives that the char-ums lie and the sang that maun
bear the char-um."

"*There* you are!" trilled a familiar voice from behind.

"Wha's *she* doing here?" the Wizard asked, which was
a relief to Gussie who was beginning to think he knew
everything.

"This here is Miss Torchy Burns," Brose said. "She's
been helping us out."

"Ach, aye?" the Wizard asked.

Gussie was disgusted to find her mind crowded with
reverence and awe for the woman she thought seriously
needed therapy, or at least a little growing up.

"And why, madame, have ye coom?" the Wizard demanded of her. "My business is theirs and none of yer
ane."

"Now, how can you say that, Mick?" Torchy asked.
"When the very stuff that covers you is my business?"
She flipped her long and lovely fingers at his leafy coat-
ing, which didn't make much sense to Gussie, but then
Torchy said, "And so are these coverings. You poor dears
are freezing to death. The grounds keeper here is an old
beau of mine and I 'appen to still have a key. I'm sure he
won't mind loanin' you these and I took the liberty of
making us all a thermos of tea."

"Mighty nice of you, darlin'," Willie said, clutching a
plaid blanket around his head and shoulders like an In-

dian brave in a John Wayne movie. Julianne had two—
Anna Mae wrapped the one Torchy gave her around Julianne as well. Brose tried to give Torchy a hug but she put
him on hold with a flattened palm and began pouring tea
into the cups she'd apparently also brought from the
caretaker's cottage.

"Irrigation, Mick?" she offered. "Wouldn't want you
to wither before you made us privy to this great scheme
of yours."

The Wizard seemed to quail before her, which puzzled
Gussie, who thought he must surely be the most magical
thing in all of Scotland at that point. But Sir Walter's
ghost didn't seem surprised. She wished there wasn't so
much going on so she could ask him. From his mind she
caught nothing but admiration and adoration for the
blasted woman and she supposed she shouldn't find it
strange that even dead men can make fools of themselves
over a certain kind of female. But the caution in the Wizard's response was not admiration, nor was it reverence,
though it was certainly respectful.

"It's nae sae mickle a scheme, lady," the Wizard said.
"We've the implement amang us and awe. The danger is
the being caught in the far realm and—weel, it's what ye
maun call a reverse of my theery of fission of souls . . ."

"Can you explain it without the mumbo jumbo?"
Brose asked.

The Wizard took out his nervousness on Brose. "Ye
black and heathen hoond, do ye doot me?"

"Man, it's not that I doubt you, I just plain have trouble under*standin'* you," Brose replied. "I don't talk Scottish or tree either. How do I know this ain't some special
effect or somethin'? You don't look nothin' like the ghosts
I saw along the Oregon Trail. I think I like American
ghosts better, pardon my ethno-cent-ricness."

The Wizard rolled his leafy eyes and looked around,
as if searching for something. His gaze settled on Juli and
he mumbled a few words and waited impatiently, tapping
his book with a twiggy fingertip.

"Furthermore," Brose was saying, "It's too cold to
stand around here while you jive us."

Julianne gasped and her hands sprang to her ears, feeling them, then cupping them, cleaning them with her fingers, and letting her fingertips linger for a wondering moment on her lobes. "Believe him, Brose," she said in a voice hoarse with emotion. "He's real."

Brose asked, "Yeah, so who is he really? The Jolly Green Giant?" before he realized that Juli had responded to his spoken remarks.

"He did it!" Juli said, pointing at the Wizard, then asked, "You did, didn't you? You did give me back my hearing?"

The Wizard shrugged and rustled as the leaves of his face arranged themselves in a modest guise. "Aye."

"Brose, I can hear. He restored my hearing. Is it permanent? Can I keep it?"

"It depends," the Wizard said.

"For Christ's sake don't toy with her," Anna Mae told him harshly. "The woman's a musician. Will she be able to hear or not?"

"In this life, aye, but to keep the music, she may have to give up many things and who knows but that her hearing may be amang them."

"And I expect the rest of us are gonna have to give up some stuff too, is that right? My daddy always told me you didn't get somethin' for nothin'," Willie grumbled and then said to Torchy, who handed him a silvery metal cup with something hot and smoky-smelling in it, "Thanks, darlin'. Don't suppose you have that flask with you with a drop of somethin' stronger do you?"

"Oh, I think you'll find it strong enough, luv. Try it."

The Wizard's eyes darted to her and he didn't object or interrupt while the rather rude exchange between Willie and Torchy went on, or while Willie gave her a little sideways, negligent hug, which produced a smug look on Torchy's face. At any other time, Juli might have thought of Torchy's expression as bitchy, because Torchy looked right at her, as if expecting Juli to mind what Willie did. Right now, Juli was so glad to have her hearing back that she beamed a beneficent smile at both Torchy and Willie and Willie made a thumbs-up sign at her. Torchy changed tack, and said sweetly, nodding to the silvery cup full of warm liquid she had given Julianne, "Well, I think your recovery calls for a bit of a drink, don't you, Juli dear? Don't be shy-y. Drink up, luvvie. The rest of you too. Do."

The Wizard glanced at her as if for permission to begin. She nodded graciously and again her expression was sly.

"Ahem, my theery of the fission of souls goes as follows," Michael Scott began, laying his book on the knees of his leafy gown and thumbing through the heavy pages, periodically murmuring to himself while Torchy Burns looked on in amusement and all the others shifted from one foot to the other. Gradually the fog began to lift and the darkness to lighten, just a tad, and still the Wizard leafed through his book, murmuring to himself.

CHAPTER XIV

▲▲▲

"And did they ever find out what the theory was?" asked the twelve-year-old at Camp Prairie Grass, where the campers all sat around a pond and listened to their old counselor tell them the ghost story.

"Well, yeah, but it was all in Scottish so Sir Walter had to tell Gussie and she had to explain it in simple English. I think the old wizard was a little apprehensive about talking about it, if you want to know the truth. He was a philosopher, you see, as well as a magician, but he lived during pretty early Christian times in Scotland and they still liked to use barbaric practices like burning folks at the stake and torturing them to death to enforce all the gentle teachings of Christianity. Michael Scott wasn't exactly a pagan, but he would have been considered a heretic if he'd told people what he really thought."

"So what DID he really think?" asked Spotted Owl Sokorski, a girl unfashionably tanned and unfashionably brown-haired and pretty as any ballad's nut-brown maid.

"It was kind of like what he told Sir Walter about Gussie. That when folks die, the material part goes to the grave and the essential inner part of them—what the Egyptians might have called the 'Ka' might go to heaven or hell or wherever—but there are lots of other parts to a person—I suppose intellect might be the best way to put it, or personality. That energy, like the energy created by the decomposing body, gets recycled into new folks."

"Like family members—maybe like genetic material?"

"Yeah, I think that's part of what he meant. Between you and me, I think he thought the Ka sometimes got redistributed too but was too chicken to say that. And Torchy Burns intimidated him."

"Why? Did he know she was a devil?"

"Nope, neither he nor Sir Walter knew her as a devil. But they knew her as something that mattered to them more, since they were of a people who were often Christian mostly on the surface. Sir Walter, church-going man that he was, would rather, like True Thomas, have seen Torchy Burns than Mary, the Queen of Heaven herself."

"Why?" asked Sequoia Thomas, whose parents owned the camp and had hired the counselor specifically to tell this story, which they had heard her tell at a convention.

"Because he knew what she used to be."

▲▲▲

"So that's it—kind of like getting beamed back instead of up, like on *Star Trek*?" Brose asked when the Wizard had explained his theory. "You sort of split us up into component parts and reassemble us when we get where we need to be, that right?

"What the hell," Brose said. "I always wanted to do something like that. Can we call you Scottie, Wiz?"

Michael Scott's root-defined mouth curved in a hoary smile and he nodded once and said with the dignity of a lofty oak, "Gin thar be no furthair objections, I'll tell ye what ye maun do tae reclaim the ballads." He looked meaningfully at Torchy Burns but she merely smiled a sweet, encouraging cheerleader's smile.

"Hand me the instrument, please," the Wizard Michael instructed. " 'Tis in the nature of its spell that ah cannae magick it awa' frae ye."

Willie, feeling a little like Dorothy trying to take off her ruby slippers to save Toto, reluctantly handed it over, then took a long sip of his tea, not because he wanted it but to steady himself. He wished if something was going to happen to him, it would just go ahead and happen. The Wizard moved almost as slowly as a plant grows. Actually, Willie could already hear himself telling the others, "I had the weirdest dream last night and you were all in it. There was this Leaf Man. Who would have thought I could out-hokey Hollywood?"

Gussie meant to drink some of her tea but she didn't like that smoky smell. Since she'd been in the fire, the smell irritated her throat, and before she could bring the cup to her lips she broke into a coughing fit.

Julianne, Anna Mae, and Brose all took the opportunity to wet their whistles too. Willie offered some to Torchy who gazed up at him real sweetlike and said, "Oh, no, I've had more than my share, luv. Drink it *doon*. There's a dear."

She was looking more and more like she was so tickled with herself she could bust. Gussie could not imagine what the woman was so chuffed about.

The Wizard Michael Scott said, "Ah shell instruct the instrument to play a ballad as it was played in mah ane day. Ah weel spare ye m'singin', but ah wot and ye will wot which ballad is bein' played. Ye folk are each of ye a different sort, very like the folk in the ballads. When ah play a tune of a distressed lady of noble blood, ah expect yon lassie"—he nodded to Julianne—"weel respond and when ah play of a roguish laddie, ye"—he nodded to Willie—"maun respond. A doughty warrior perhaps yerself, Moorish man, and ye, dearie, are the woodswoman, the dark sister, the brown gel who is the remnant of the auld folk amang the mortals. Ye, auld woman, are the mothers, the hags, the midwife, the nour-ice, the woman of counsel."

"And me?" asked Sir Walter.

"Ah'm that sorry, laddie, but bein' dead disqualifies ye. Ah wot not but that ye'll return tae yer grave as the spells tak hold."

Torchy cleared her throat. "Wait a mo, mates. This is gettin' a bit oversimplified-like. It isn't going to be all as easy as Mick makes it sound or quite the lark you seem to think it'll be. You see, you've only got seven years to recapture these songs of yours—"

"Seven *years*?" Willie asked. "Who said anything

about seven *years*? Hell, darlin', I don't think they're gonna let us stay that long."

"You disappoint me, Willie luv. You haven't let a little thing like mortal law stand in your way so far. And it doesn't matter, you know. Truly it doesn't. Natural law always has dominion over the laws of mere mortals and —ahem—*super*natural law, of course, takes sovereignty over natural law."

"Do you always have to be the center of attention?" Anna Mae asked her angrily. "Can we get on with it now?"

"Oh, I really don't believe I'd do that without hearing a bit more, dearie."

"But the Wizard said we only had until cockcrow," Julianne said, "and it's getting lighter already. We have to get the songs back. Not that we haven't appreciated all you've done for us, Torchy hon, but you don't understand all of this. It's really a very cosmic situation."

Torchy laughed a loud, long, derisive laugh and her cockney accent broadened and slowed to a West Texas drawl as she said, "No, *hon,* it's y'all who don't understand. I understand more than any of you, even more than Mick here."

Willie's eyes widened as her accent altered. *"Lulu*belle —" he said. "Lulubelle Baker! Why in the hell didn't I recognize you before?"

"Easy, sugar. I didn't want you to. Besides, if you'll pipe down and pay attention, you'll learn that Lulubelle Baker and Torchy Burns are only a couple of the names I'm known by. Mick and Wattie both know me as someone else entirely, don't you, boys?"

Both ghosts—the Wizard in his rustling state and Sir Walter using Gussie's body—bowed in response.

"Now then, shall we get on with this, since you're all so eager?" Torchy asked.

"I hope to tell you we sure as hell better. You're one of those critters been killin' off our friends, siccin' the cops on us, all that stuff. I don't think we have much to say to each other. Wiz, buddy, you can pull your rabbit out of your hat or the brier patch there that you're wearin' or whatever, but lay it on us. I don't want to hear another word out of this lyin', cheatin', low-down excuse for a female."

"Why, Willie, how sweet of you to say so!" Torchy taunted.

"Wait a minute, here," Brose said. "*I* want to hear a little more about this seven-year business."

"It's a good idea to know the rules ahead of time," Anna Mae agreed.

"I'm very relieved to hear the voice of reason enter into all this paranoid hysteria," Torchy said. "Mick, luv, I'll tell you what. You're in a rush and we have loads of time. Why don't you play the tune on that—uh—play the tune that will send our friends where they want to go, but then after I've had a chance to have a wee chat with them over a nice cup of tea and let them know what they're getting into—you naughty wizards always keep the catches to yourself, trying to be so mysterious—why then each of them can make his or her own decision and play the tune for himself or herself when he or she is ready to go bye-bye. Isn't that fair?"

"Yeah, sure, if it'll work," Brose said.

"Oh, it'll work. Won't it, Mick?"

"If ye so will it, lady, wark it will," the Wizard replied.

"I so will," Torchy said in a formal tone that was neither her working-class British accent nor her southern Lulubelle Baker one.

The Wizard's root-veined hands stroked from the banjo no strange and eldritch tune but one they'd all heard a million times, or so it seemed. Each of them recalled its strains coming from fiddles, banjos, guitars, mandolins, dulcimers, concertinas, every sort of instrument at every folk festival, jam session, workshop, and around every campfire they'd ever been to. And each of them recalled a different set of words to it, while realizing that any lyrics they could recall to any of the ballads would have fit the tune.

The Wizard played it one time through and Julianne, Brose, Willie, and Anna Mae nodded that yes, they could play that and Torchy snapped her fingers. "Enough then. Cock's about to crow, Mick luv. Back to the clay with you before someone thinks you're a vegetarian vampire and runs a tomato stake through your heart."

The Wizard finished silently and the banjo reappeared in Willie's hands. Immediately afterward, somewhere on the farms to the west, a cock crowed and the leaves and roots that formed the Wizard began to wither back into the lid of the tomb.

Torchy laughed. "Only ghosties have to go to bed when the boy chicken sings. The Trust people don't get here till ten. We've plenty of time. So, you lot, come along with me. Bring your cups. We'll want several strong cups of tea and a nice long chat before you go making any rash decisions."

CHAPTER XV

▲▲▲

She led them to the caretaker's cottage where the door was open, an electric space heater was humming, and the kettle was already on. She set their silver cups in front of them, one by one, on the pretty primrose-covered tablecloth. She looked very homey and North Country matron in gray-green cord pants, green wool socks, gray running shoes with green stripes, a dark green turtleneck jersey with a heavy heathery gray-green cable-knit sweater that was complimentary to her red hair, demurely tied back in a jade-green Duchess of Windsor bow.

"Now then, my dears," she said in a completely *new* accent—a touch of Yorkshire, perhaps, northern but wavering between upper-class Scottish and country English, "I always find a spot of tea so warming and conducive to sensible discussion, don't you?"

"Who *are* you?" Anna Mae asked. "The Wizard just did what you said as if you made out his paycheck. Is this another setup or what?" She glared at Gussie—or, probably, at Sir Walter, within Gussie.

"Well, dearie, I know you'll find this a bit hard to take —though no harder, perhaps, than Willie found what my Lulubelle Baker persona had to tell him—but you see, oh, my, this is a little awkward to say without sounding arrogant or undemocratic or anything but— it just so happens that another of the little hats that

I wear is, um—no gay jokes now—I'm the Queen of the Fairies."

"No shit?" Brose asked.

"None at all," she said seriously. "I'm very well known in these parts—better than anywhere save Ireland, perhaps. Sir Walter knew me at once, didn't you, Wat?"

Gussie's ghost guest nodded, thrilled to its nonexistent marrow.

"And since most of his magical powers come from me, I suppose your assessment, Anna Mae, that I pay Michael Scott's check is not too far off the mark."

"Well, if you're so damned powerful why didn't you just help us already? Why make us go through all this rigamarole?" Willie asked.

"Because, my sweet, as you've already mentioned, I *am,* nominally, mostly, formally, on the record, anyway, officially working for the opposition. You might recall that song about a protégé of mine, a boy named Tam Lin? Very promising lad, he was, but as roguish as you, Willie. Got some bird in a family way and ran off on me just when I needed him most."

Julianne said, "The ballad says you were about to pay your tithe to hell by using him as a sacrifice."

Torchy/Lulubelle/the Queen of the Fairies nodded agreement. "Oh, yes, handpicked him and groomed him for the position myself, I had. But unfortunately, at tithing time, he was playing hide the sausage with that Janet bird."

"So you couldn't pay the rent!" Gussie said.

And Sir Walter said, "Aye, that's how it was, even as you feared, lady, in the ballad variation that went, as I recall:

> "Up bespak the Queen of Fairies
> And she spak wi a loud yell
> 'Aye at every seven years' end
> We pay the kane to hell
> And the koors they hae gone round about
> And I fear it will be mysel'.' "

The woman in green reached over and patted Gussie/ Walter fondly on the cheek. "There, then. You *do* see how it is, don't you? A girl has her position in this world to maintain and so I embarked on a new career." She sighed a deep, put-upon sigh. "Still, I do try in my own little way to reward those who have pleased me in the past. I'm sure you'll never know how often I've been on the very precipice of a descent into the truly *tacky* parts of hell because I managed to finagle some little advantage here and there that would give you people an 'out,' despite your stubborn refusal to be realistic—I'm not awfully *fond* of realistic, actually, so I can sympathize with you. So from time to time I've been able to stir things up a bit when you get in a jam. If I can't actually help you, I can at least create opportunities, you see?"

"Oh, so you take the credit for every time we've been able to escape from a trap you've gotten us into? Is that it?" Anna Mae asked.

"You *do* see, then, don't you?" Torchy beamed approvingly. "Why, I've been like a fairy godmother to you, a guardian angel, a—"

Gussie's cough erupted and continued for a few seconds as she looked up over her glasses at Torchy.

"Well, I suppose there's no sense in getting sloppy about it. But I've been a peach and I do think you should *trust* me when I tell you that while I can see where you'd want to do this thing auld Mike's set up, I don't think it's a very good idea and I *don't* think you know what you're letting yourselves in for. More tea, Willie, luv?"

"Sure."

"Like I said, you'll only *have* seven years—"

"What's this seven-year jazz?" Brose demanded.

"Why, luv, when you put yourself under an enchantment and oblige yourself, so to speak, to Fairie, it's always seven years, didn't you know that?"

"He's a bluesman really," Julianne apologized for him. "He's not really into the Celtic stuff."

"Oh. I do see. Well, then, I'm very glad I've got a chance to explain a few things to you. Seven years is quite the common contract unless, of course, you do something to make it permanent and you certainly wouldn't want to do that."

"Why not?"

"Well, *dar*ling, think about it! They did not make songs that lasted for hundreds of years out of days of long, dreary peace and quiet or the contented moo of the livestock. Ballads are full of treachery, murder, lost love, rape, war, etcetera, and in order for you to do what Sam Hawthorne and this implement of his want you to do, you'll have your hands full in seven years going into a new persona just long enough to live out the ballad situation, claim it for your own, and emerge into a new one. The whole scenario is perfect hell and there are so few of you to do it."

"There's Faron and Ellie," Gussie reminded her.

She smiled a phony, society-lady smile, lips-up-lips-down. "Sorry, dear. They're out of the picture. My minions took care of them back at Abbotsford. Besides, they didn't hear the tune Michael Scott played, and you'll find you can't really teach it, you know. Spells can be like that."

Sir Walter sighed. "My Lady, Your Majesty, *you* burned my Abbotsford?"

"Don't be such a puppy, Wattie dear. Grow up. You're dead. You don't need a house. If you want to haunt something you can haunt the ruins. Much more appropriate anyway. And I may be a tad more simpatico to this operation than my bosses really like, but I must do my job competently, don't you see? I couldn't allow any of the printed collections to fall into your hands or it would be as much as my job is worth. And I have *no* desire to be busted to pitchfork patrol. Plays perfect *hell* with one's manicure."

"But if you destroyed all the collections and we have to go to the source to reclaim the songs, then we don't have any choice but to do what the Wizard said if we want to get the songs back, do we?" Julianne asked.

"No. You don't. Actually, you haven't got any choice anyway. It's the tea, you see. Water's from the river in Fairie and I'm afraid boiling doesn't do a thing to the enchanted quality. Once you drink it you're into me for the seven years. Sorry. Part of the job. Of course, I could just take you on for seven years and you wouldn't have to do the musical enchantment bit. We'd have lots of fun. Oh, I don't have much in the way of jeweled underground realms anymore and a court and such, but I have plenty of other folks at my command. Probably most of them are motes of my former subjects, Michael Scott would say. People who still want to get away from it all with a little glamorie—these days they find it in a bottle or a syringe or a dab of fairy dust rather than by falling asleep on some knowe or the other—and some of them look for it in sex or try to win it, but they're all my subjects, you see. You, Willie, have always been, though without the special allegiance you'd owe me if you went the route I'm proposing, and you too, Brose, before you broke faith with me. Juli has been looking in all the wrong places though she would have come around sooner or later, I've faith, with a little nudge in the right direction. You, Anna Mae, were going to choose one of the other routes—in the ballad days, they'd send you to Bedlam the way you've been carrying on and you'd have gotten worse by the time we were done with you, especially after your dear friends in the capital had you committed for all of your strange delusions and hallucinations, whether you had them or not—but then, you see, given proper medication and stimulus, you really *would* have had them. I've grown very fond of you all and I wouldn't be too taxing a mistress and you'd get to do things you already like—just no songs and no stories of any sort, I'm afraid, except for certain orchestrated misdirections in a good cause."

"I don't think this seven years at finding ballads sounds all that bad," Brose said.

"It's no longer than it would take you to get a doctorate in folklore if you had to start as a freshman in a BA program," Juli said. "And it is what we started out to do. It's not like it would be *real.*"

"Oh, it's real, okay, ducky." Torchy smiled the lips-up-lips-down unpleasant little smile again. "You'll see if one of you is fool enough to try it—your body is gone and it doesn't come back unless and until you've done all your gathering—and followed all of the rules and regulations, of course. If you slip up, well, then, you stay there and all of your little motes get to come back as somebody else—and I promise you, they'll be so scattered even your best friends would never want to know the people you'll come back in. As for that little spark the Wizard was so fond of, why, if you break the rules that's forfeit to me, of course. And you've all heard the ballads. I needn't tell you what deliciously gruesome things are apt to happen to your bodies."

"The Wizard didn't say anything about any rules," Anna Mae said.

Torchy smiled again. "My dear, that's because we're playing by mine. The tea water, you know."

"And just what might those be?" Gussie asked.

"Oh, they're not complicated. It's just that you will only come to as the ballad character at the moment that the situation is happening—as it truly happened. Oh, and that brings me to the last little rule. It's my favorite and very simple really. You'll find that a lot of these situations boil down to two things—sex and death. If you get laid *or* murdered, you lose, game's mine. You have to get out just before either of those things happens, or come in just after they happen to the character, but not with you—er —*in* character. Clear?"

"Not especially," Anna Mae said antagonistically.

"Good. Then you do see that it's much more sensible to take me up on my proposition. More tea? In for a penny, in for a pound, as they say. Oh, yes, there is one more thing. Riddles. You'll have to answer any riddles put to you correctly or you lose again."

"Is there any way we can *avoid* losing?" Willie asked.

Sir Walter's ghost cleared his throat. "It is customary, Your Ladyship, to give some sort of magical encouragement or enabling device to folk on a difficult quest. You were kind enough, though you forbade True Thomas to eat or drink or speak to any others while in your realm, to provide him with earthly food and drink and to speak to him yourself. You've made it much more difficult for these folk. Have mercy, lady, for you once loved music as well as they."

The woman in green first frowned, then looked thoughtful. "Your appeal strikes, if you will pardon the expression, the right chord with me, Wattie. Very well. Though I know I'll get in hot water for being such a softie. I'll tell you what. For every song each of you survives collecting, I'll throw in seven other associated ballads, free of charge. Now that couldn't be any fairer, could it?"

Sir Walter cleared his throat. "It raises the incentive, lady, but 'tis not the sart of thing tae help them survive the task."

"You *do* drive a hard bargain, but then, I forget, you were a lawyer while alive," Torchy said, smiling a brittle but fond smile. "Okeydoke then. Let me think. An escape clause. Oh, I've got it. Very well. Here it is. You see the extra lengths of string at the tuning pegs, curled into little rings when last Mr. Sam Hawthorne strung those strings that always stay in tune? You will not be able to take the banjo with you to the other side, but if you decide to go, when you have played the first note of the tune, you may clip off one ring each and wear it on your middle finger where it will remain while you are within the ballad. If you find yourself in one of the forbidden situations, you have but to twist the ring three times widdershins around your middle finger and the string will sound the tune that will take you to the next ballad. What could be fairer?" she asked, her smile deepening to a dazzle beamed in Gussie and Sir Walter's direction. "I think that takes care of all the details. The caretaker will be here at ten. That's three hours from now which is more than ample time to make up your minds. I'll be back with the car then to pick up any of you who have been sensible."

CHAPTER XVI

▲▲▲

Gussie and the musicians sat stunned for several moments listening to the stutter of the engine as the woman they knew as Torchy started the van Terry Pruitt had loaned them and drove away in it.

Afterward, the cottage was so quiet Gussie heard the tick of Anna Mae's watch. No one looked at anyone else for a few seconds, each person staring at the pink and white tablecloth and at his or her teacup.

"Well, are we going to sit here for the three hours or use what we know and do what we came here to do?" Anna Mae demanded. By now, Gussie knew her well enough to know that Anna Mae got angry mostly because when she didn't know what else to do, getting angry gave her the energy to move.

"Be my guest, little darlin'," Willie said, handing her the banjo, "I got to give this a little more thought myself before I, personally, go getting myself exploded into motes."

"Thanks, MacKai," Anna Mae replied. "It's good to be able to count on you for such a positive attitude when there's something tough that needs doing."

But Willie's back was turned to her, since he had risen to his feet and started pacing away from the table. So he didn't see that when Anna Mae took the banjo from him, her hands were not quite steady, and she set it on her lap to keep it still and strummed it in a general way once or twice to calm herself. Brose watched stone-faced and Julianne with wide, agonized eyes as Anna Mae took a deep breath, placed her third finger on the third fret of the third string, and picked the string.

"Anna Mae—the string ring," Julianne reminded her.

Brose tightened his lips and Willie, pacing back toward them, looked as if he was trying hard not to bolt.

Gussie plunged into her Mexican basket bag and pulled out a nail clipper, handing it to Anna Mae, who clipped off the first little circle of extra E string at the peg and wound it around the middle finger of her left hand.

She closed her eyes and took another breath so deep her skinny little chest swelled like a frog's and then she picked the tune, what would have been the chorus, what would have been the verse, and when nothing happened, she played the chorus and verse again, and yet again. Brose let all the air out of him as she shrugged with bewilderment and handed the banjo to him. He was still looking at the wire string ring on the left hand in which she'd held the neck as she handed him the banjo when he realized that there was no finger there anymore, and then no ring, and no Anna Mae.

Brose held the banjo and kept looking at where Anna Mae had been, as if he expected her to come back. Tears welled up suddenly in Juli's eyes and rolled down her cheeks and Gussie dug a minipack of Kleenex out of the basket bag and silently handed Juli one, then blew her own nose. "It's okay, Gussie," Juli said sniffing. "It's just —wow—did you feel that shock wave run through the ether when Anna Mae disappeared?"

"Was that what it was?" Gussie asked. "I thought it was seeing her just go 'poof' that gave me cold chills."

"Still, it didn't seem to hurt none," Willie said. "I think we would have heard her scream if it did, don't you?"

"Aw, shut up, MacKai," Brose said.

Willie looked mildly surprised but not offended. "You want to go next, Brose?"

"I gotta think about it, man. I got responsibilities at home. Who's gonna look after my critters? What'll the kids think if I don't come back?"

"I—I could go next," Juli said. "I expected to feel the shock but I think it's just a natural part of using so much power. I mean, I'm not afraid—well, not very much. I heard what Torchy says, and I know maybe you people think I'm nuts when I tell you so, but I *have* talked to George and—I don't care what that woman says, I haven't done anything wrong and I don't think if this kills me I'm going to go to hell or anything so—"

"Hold on there a minute, darlin'," Willie said. "Sam Hawthorne gave this banjo to Mark Mosby who gave it to me. I'll go next. Hand it over, Brose. Been nice knowin' you, buddy."

"Willie—" Gussie said, raising a hand to touch his sleeve. In spite of the way he had hesitated, she had the feeling that now, rather than having really thought things through, he was just closing his eyes, holding his nose, and diving into it. "Willie, you don't have to. What do you know about Scottish ballads anyhow? That redhead likes you. She wouldn't be too hard on you and you got to admit that if she forced you to lead a life of endless debauchery, you probably wouldn't notice much difference from the way you usually carry on."

"Aw, Gus," he said, plunking the first note and clipping off the string ring with the nail clippers Anna Mae had left lying on the tablecloth, "I didn't know you cared. But I'm too old to get broke to harness good now and I don't think I could just walk away from that particular lady when the going got rough, so I might as well do what I hired on for. If I'm not back in seven years, send in the cavalry, will you, babe?"

And he placed the ring on his finger, held the banjo so the head was close to his cheek, and played the tune for all it was worth, three times through, real quick, and handed the banjo to Julianne, who was sitting nearest, as if it were hot.

As soon as she had it in her hands, he was gone, with nothing to show he had been standing there but a little lifting of the edge of the tablecloth as if there were a sudden draft.

Julianne murmured apologetically to Brose, "I'm going to go next, okay?" And he nodded mutely.

It gave her fleeting joy to hear the note her fingers plucked and she clipped the string ring and placed it on her left hand on her middle finger beside the Navajo silver wedding band she still wore. Then she played the rest of the song, three times over, relishing the notes, a little smile on her face and her lips moving as if she was singing to herself. She smiled with her head cocked a little to one side as she handed the banjo back to Brose, whispered, "Here I go," and relinquished it—and was gone.

"It takes 'em suddenlike, don't it?" Brose said to Gussie and she nodded. She wished he'd stay. She didn't want to be the last one. She was feeling more and more scared with every one who left, more and more alone—well, except for Walter Scott, of course, but he was different.

On the other hand, she didn't want to influence him but she said, "Brose, before you—before anything happens, give me a hug, will ya, hon? With people disappearin' right and left like this, I need to feel something solid."

Still holding the banjo, he enveloped her in a great bear hug and gave her a big sloppy kiss to boot. He was still damp from the rain and sweaty and his shirt smelled reassuringly of horse and dog and the dust from feed stores and his arms were strong and real. He held her so tightly she knew he had been feeling the same way she did but hadn't thought to say anything. Finally, when she thought her ribs were going to break if he held her any tighter and she needed to draw a clear breath, she stepped back and he released her. And while she was putting her basket bag firmly on her arm in preparation to volunteer to go next, he struck the first note and was clipping off the string ring and putting it on as she looked up.

The song came out more syncopated than it had with the others, and he played it with the lonely concentration he always gave the blues, then laid the banjo on the table. She tried to stare hard at him the whole time so he couldn't disappear but she had to blink and when she did, he was as gone as if he'd got up from the table on his own two legs and gone outside.

"Oh, my," she said. "Oh, Lord. Walter, what do you make of that?"

"I think," the ghost replied, "upon further reflection that it's an ill curse she's cursed you with indeed to survive in times past using only the words of ballads. For I know better than most that trying to survive with only the help of literature is a chancy venture."

"I guess so. But I'll have to try. Can you find your way back to your grave okay?"

"I s'pose I'm still hoping I might join you."

"Alrighty then, let's give it a try," she said, and she picked the banjo up and set it in her lap as she'd seen the others do, but it felt unnatural and awkward to her. She tried to fit her fingers around the neck at the same frets as she'd seen the others do but her fingers were small and she had to clamp her whole hand over the frets to get her third finger to reach the third fret of the third string. When she plucked the sound came out as a dull thump, but she hadn't heard anybody say she had to play it beautifully, just that it had to get played. She set the banjo down while she took her nail clippers from the table and wriggled the string ring loose and set it on her left middle finger as the others had done, then picked up the banjo again.

And had absolutely no idea what to do from there. She wasn't a musician and she assumed that, like the others, just watching the Wizard play was enough to teach her the song. But it wasn't. She had never played a banjo before in her life and apparently she wasn't going to start now. "Help me out, Wat. How do you play this thing?"

"I don't know, lass. I once played the piano but I nivair laid eyes on sich a thing as that until you brought it here. As you heard Michael Scott say, I'm not verra musical, except in a listening and collecting sort of way."

"Yeah," she said. "Me neither. Well, hell." She set the banjo on the table and stared at it as if it had betrayed her. Finding no comfort there, she rose and began the familiar motions of doing something useful, clearing the table, the sort of thing she had done her whole life. No sense in leaving a mess for the caretaker when he got home. She started to empty the water from her teacup into the sink but remembered it was supposed to be magic water and saved it in another cup instead. Then the dregs of tea wouldn't go. As she started to brush them together with her fingers to throw them into the trash, she noticed what funny-looking tea leaves they were, irregularly shaped and black and gray and one was even white, with what looked like writing on it. She peered at it and saw the words "Tam Lin" and whistled to herself.

"Walter, do you think this is what I think it is?"

"It's my buke," he said. "The cannibalistic witch burned my buke and was sairvin' it up to you as leaves in her cursed tea."

Gussie was scraping together the last of the ashes into a little tea ball the custodian had in the drawer by the sink when she heard a car door thump and, before she could look up, saw Torchy peering over her shoulder.

"Only you left to keep me company? What a shame. But what's your pleasure, ducks?"

"Solitude would be nice," Gussie said. "But failing that, I'd like a little more explanation, which shouldn't be too hard for you, girlie, as much as you like to hear yourself talk. What's with giving us ashes of book for tea?"

"Ah ah ah, you're forgetting your position, dearie. You're mine now."

"Because I drank the water from your polluted fairyland river?" Torchy nodded. "Wrong. Here's the water," she said, holding it up. "And here's what you used for tea leaves." She held up the tea ball. "And I couldn't play the song since I'm not a picker and I didn't have Pete Seeger's *How to Play the 5-String Banjo* book handy. So I guess I'm still a free agent, dearie. So I ask you again, what's the idea of using the ashes of the books in our tea?"

Torchy laughed lightly. "Oh, surely you see!"

"Oh, surely I don't or I wouldn't be standin' here askin' you, would I?"

Torchy's laugh deepened as she sat down, and took on a convulsive up-and-down quality that had the Fairy Queen pounding the table and gasping for air. "But—it's —so—ob—vi"—she hiccuped—"ous."

She let them guess while she recovered from her hilarity, then said with a wide white smile, "Oh, come *on* now. Don't you *get* it? It's just too rich, really, but as I warned you, it won't do to have my colleagues saying I was too easy on you people. I had to make it at least a *little* challenging. So I mixed up the ashes and served them to you so that the affinities would be scrambled, you see. Your friends won't find themselves in the ballads Mick predicted—that would be too easy, not to say too boring, and I'm far too creative for that sort of typecasting. No, this will be ever so much more fun."

"What do you mean?" Gussie asked.

"You'll see. If they're lucky that is. I don't suppose you'd like to just give me the banjo and call the whole thing off?"

"I don't suppose so," Gussie said, before she'd given it much thought. She didn't even want to ask the woman what *she* thought calling it all off meant, and anyway, Gussie didn't figure the banjo was hers to give. It was Sam Hawthorne's in the care of Willie MacKai and in her care till Willie got back. If Willie had wanted to give it to Torchy Burns he'd have done it himself.

She started to say as much to Torchy Burns but before she could open her mouth the woman was gone and the banjo was playing another familiar ballad tune.

PART II

▲▲▲

The Borderlands

CHAPTER XVII

▲▲▲

Willie had hoped that the Debauchery Devil's fondness for him might let him end up in his favorite kind of ballads—that is, the bawdy kind. But as the kitchen at the cottage disappeared, everything was blurry for a while but a song he remembered Buffy St. Marie once singing: "The Lyke-Wake Dirge."

> "If ever thou gavest hosen and shoen
> Every night and a'
> Sit thee down and put them on.
> And Christ receive thy soul."

He remembered those words without really knowing what they meant except what you had done for or to people in life was supposed to be yours in death. For better or for worse. The Golden Rule and all that. God, was this a trick and he was in hell and hell was one long hard-shell Baptist fire and brimstone sermon?

No. A path opened in the haze around him and he saw a field of grass hedged with yellow broom all around and a pretty girl and a handsome devil of a guy pulling up some greenery in a slow and significant way. He followed the path to the couple, took a step, and joined them, blending . . .

▲▲▲

Something clacked close to the bed. Willie shot out a hand to throw back the bed curtains and waddled to the window. Wherever he was, it sure wasn't Texas. Below the window was a lush garden of unfamiliar flowers, with stone walls rising from the garden to the bower and up another two stories where the walls were cornered with towers and toothed with businesslike battlements. The place was a whole lot bigger than even the main house at the L.B.J. ranch.

But he noticed something else as he reached his slender, shapely hand up to wipe his long golden hair out of his eyes and pluck a strand from off his milk-swollen breast. There were a few more profound differences to his situation than mere geography. He was female. Not only female, but pregnant.

Another clack and a clatter as the stone fell short of its mark and a familiar, beloved voice said, "Sarah, cum awa' wi' me." And though the voice had a Scottish burr instead of a Texas drawl Willie would have recognized it anywhere. It was his own voice.

And down below stood a man the spitting image of Willie MacKai from his long elegant legs to his tousled hair with its gold glints in the sun, his gleaming eyes, his proud bearing, and the hint he gave of being barely able to stand still for needing to pace. So if that was Willie MacKai down there, Willie MacKai wondered, why did he seem to be here? Had he sprouted a twin? Then he opened his mouth and a soprano drowned in honey sang out to the handsome devil below, "Ah canna cum noo, love. My father and brothers are back frae the campaign and they ranted sae loudly ah had nae time tae explain tae them aboot our marriage. Be wary o' them—ah had a dream last nicht and ah fear it portends us ill. Ah dreamed we pu'd t'heather and birk up on yon hill. Gae there straightwa' an' ah'll meet ye as soon as ah may."

Disoriented, Willie asked, *"Who am I?"* and was answered, *"Why, Sarah Scott, the sorrowfulest woman in the world and yet—with only a little luck, I could be the happiest. Ah look at him, yon laddie, fast and slippery as a moss ranger stealin' frae my window. Was there ever sic a bonny sight as him in the plaidie I wove for him wi' my ane twa hands?"*

For although Willie still recognized his spirit as himself as well as a part of Sarah, Sarah only knew him as part of *her*self. To her he seemed to be that little voice everybody has that chides and counsels and argues with them—the voice of experience, the voice of conscience, the voice of caution, the voice that balances and weighs our inclinations with our restrictions. Willie, with unsettling direct access to Sarah's thoughts and to her feelings, both emotional and physical, no more wished to upset or thwart her than he would have himself in his own body. If he had become part of her, then part of her had become him as well. He had become her alter ego and she, for the moment, his. She was, most urgently, his business.

His spirit, joined with hers, shared her enthusiasms as he looked through her fond eyes down at her true love. *"No, never. A good man, a good choice,"* he agreed with her. *"Look at his seat on that horse! You've got good taste, Sarah Scott. He's a very bonny lad—"*

"Aye, a flower amang men," Sarah added, sighing so heavily her breasts ached and a loving warmth melted within her loins. Delicately, soothing herself as she would soothe a horse, she smoothed her nightdress over her thighs, then let her hands clasp over the dome of her belly. *"I canna see how Father overlooked him though he's anely a second son instead of a first and his brother inherits. He's a better man than a' my three brothers pu' taegethair, will mak me a better husband and my father a better son. We'd be happy in a bower in the broom if need be, if only my family would not stand between us."*

"A bower in the broom? With no fireplace to cook for him and no loom to make him clothes? No stable for his horse and no cradle for the baby? And don't forget the bed. Without those things how can you be happy? He may be able to live wild, but you'll soon be a mother. It's not like you can get a job or go to college. You're going to want to keep house for your man and your baby. Women are like that. You know it's true. You say you'd be happy with little, but would you truly?" Willie knew all about this kind of

reasoning from the girlfriends he'd had who'd sworn they'd be happy on the road with no money and later, even without babies, proved themselves dissatisfied with the arrangement.

But Sarah twirled herself (and him within her) around as if physically flinging off care and crowed, *"How foolish tae trouble myself with such questions. Aye, oh, aye, I could be happy and my bairn would be happy and so would we all if only we were allowed! It's that dream has me fey! That and my time bein' sae near. What shall I wear? The brown dress or the gay green?"*

"The green goes better with our eyes and brings out the color in our cheeks. Better go for the green at least until we get our figure back." Willie, as a performer, knew the importance of all aspects of image, even though he'd never had to deal with being pregnant before.

Sarah grabbed the green dress and slipped it over her nightie, which Willie realized also served as their mutual slip—er—shift. The effect was charming, though a bath wouldn't have hurt them. There was no time for that, however. Sarah's lover was waiting and Willie, in Sarah's body, felt soft and glowy and full of hope, yearning toward the man who waited for his love up on the hill in the den, for his caresses and his loving words.

And this didn't seem unnatural to him. He was a part of Sarah Scott and instead of finding her feelings and her yearnings strange, in her body they felt natural to him, exotic—impossible to feel so incredibly turned on without an erection, he would have thought, but he felt it. Maybe it was because the true love was so much like himself—maybe it was some kind of an urge for his consciousness to rejoin his real body, to be one with himself again. On the other hand, hadn't true love been described that way? He'd never believed in it himself, especially. Lust, sure. Wanting a woman because she seemed desirable, like a partner who could expand his life a little. That was understandable. But that never worked out. And it never started with this kind of need. Had any of those women ever felt for him what Sarah felt, what he was feeling, for the man who waited on yon hill? Yon—

he was even starting to think with her accent. But it only seemed right. The landscape outside the window looked very much like that that he'd been passing through the last two days. More than that, it felt like home.

"Enough trouble in the world without borrowin' more," Sarah thought. *"Father will surely be reasonable—will understand he maun recognize our marriage now, with the bairn on the way. 'Twas just the shock of it cumin' upon him all at once that upset him."*

"And what about the bruise on your cheek?"

"He didna mean tae strike me sae hard and he wouldna let my brothers abuse me, for he said I was but a stupid girl and easily set on my back and my brothers laughed at that, for often enough they tried to corner me after I grew bubbies and before they went a-campaigning. He's a rash man and he had mickle drink inside him."

"You're soft in the head. Your father's cruel and he'll never relent. Even if he did, how could it work out?"

"I've my tocher lands that are a' my ane and we could live there when the babe is born. Cook says 'tis a boy and she has the Sight. If it is a boy, Father will forgive me sartain, for John's wife and Michael's wife have borne only daughters and Robbie's yet tae wild tae settle doon. Father will forgive us once I gie him a grandson tae dandle on his knee."

And Willie thought, Maybe this is one of the happy ballads after all? Sarah should know her people better than he, and he felt like whistling as Sarah pulled on their kirtle and tied it up with ribbons so it wouldn't drag in the grass. Willie enjoyed the grace of her movements as she made herself ready to meet her lover. She swayed on shapely brown legs from a central pivot of her hips. How strange to carry nothing between the legs and so much to balance above, the breasts, the belly. Her fingers briskly touched her head, loosening pins and sending a cascade of Rapunzel braids to the floor, long, long yellow hair. She picked up an end to untwine it, and picked up a brush with a bone back and boar bristles to tame the unbound locks.

A flurry of hooves thundered in the courtyard.

"Oh, Lord," Willie moaned. Not a bawdy ballad after all then.

"Oh, dear Lord—" Sarah gave voice to his moan, flying to her window. Her three brothers, six of their men, and her father were mounted and riding hell-bent out the front gate.

"They heard us! They saw us!" Sarah gasped.

"Wasn't too bright to arrange a tryst where they could hear us," Willie told her. *"Need to warn the lad. The old man's laid a trap."*

"He has, oh, he has and I must spring it and warn my love else he think I've betrayed him."

"Can we make it in time?"

"Every day this twelvemonth half I've run and never walked tae meet him. Ah, but I'm sae baig wi child noo. Nae time tae fetch a horse, nae time tae ask for help. I'll mak' it because I must."

But even the stairs were treacherous, though she'd climbed down them and up them since she was a toddler. They were narrower now than her shelf of breast and belly and she had to stand sidewise to see where to put her feet. Three times three stairs she climbed down and twice as many took her over the rushes and out into the courtyard and across the footbridge toward the meadows.

"I must reach him first! I must! They'll kill him they'll kill him they'll kill him if only because I love him—"

"You're killing yourself. Slow down. Hear how your heart pumps almost through your breast? Hear your breath roar in your ears? Your lungs will burst if you keep this up. Your legs have failed and your eyes have failed and we're blacking out and we won't reach him in time, poor sorry son of a bitch."

And black out she did, sprawling to the ground in a swoon where she lay senseless to the world around her, though her spirit, and Willie's, wandered in the dream world, where their dreaming eyes opened to behold a horse's hooves. Next they saw the booted feet and bare legs of Sarah's lover, so like Willie's own bodily feet and legs, and higher yet were the lover's strong-veined brown hands clasped on the reins, his slender waist, and his chest in its rough cream shirt with the scarlet scarf at the neck—but above the scarf, which proved to be no scarf, was nothing, nothing at all. The horseman riding toward Sarah was headless and Willie recognized his own body as the one that sat on the horse. Sarah screamed a scream drowned in her swoon, but it roused her so that she opened her eyes, and the headless horseman disappeared.

"Too late, too late—" she breathed as she ran headlong forward, tripping on her skirts, her belly and her breasts bouncing painfully, her insides shooting knives into her groin and heart, her legs burning as if her bones were fiery brands.

"You'll never make it. You're too weak, the baby's coming, you'll burst with the effort, it's too far—"

"There! The hill is there! Only a little ways!"

"What's that clash like pots and pans at suppertime?"

"Gramercy, it's the clash of swords!"

"And that? The horses are screaming . . ."

"Maybe they've just started. If I throw myself between them, they'll have to stop, won't they? For my sake, as they love me, they must—"

"If they don't, it's all the same, isn't it?"

"Aye." And all thought was swallowed by the drumming in her ears and the waves of pain from her belly and loins.

"Listen."

"Silence."

"Why?"

"They've stopped."

"Who's that riding down the hill?"

"I see now—it's Father and my brother John."

"Do you see him?"

"I do not."

Her father's hand lifted in a greeting, half weary, half jaunty, and she could barely lift hers in return, but as he drew nearer she fell against his stirrup crying, "Father, dear, I'm so glad to see you. I had a most doleful dream . . ."

"Ye've done o'er much o' dreamin', lass. 'Tis time noo tae get on wi' real life. We've revenged ye agin yer seducer, though we lost Michael and Robert and six men besides in the deed."

He looked down at her with anger suffusing his blunt features, his thin mouth and his bulbous nose, his flaccid cheeks huffing and puffing still with the aftermath of his effort. His hair was gray, his skin lined and cracked with the weather, but his eyes under brows like thunderclouds were absolutely cold, staring into her and through her as if she were an inconvenience, a wart on his hand, a stain on his sleeve.

"He said to find you," her brother spoke up, mockingly. "He said to tell you he forgave you your betrayal o' him. Ah wish ah found it sae easy."

And brushing her off, her father rode on and her brother beside him.

"They didn't even ask how you were, and you so near your time."

"Gin they cared how I fare, they'd never have let matters come to sic a pass."

"They could have offered you a ride to the house."

"They could have left me and mine alane and I'd never need a ride. I'd walk from here tae the ends of the earth to undo what I fear done."

"Maybe he's just wounded," Willie said, *"I think that might be it. I don't feel anything. I can't believe they've killed him. I can't believe that dream was real."*

"I can believe though I'm loath tae think it."

A hand curled out over the crest of the hill, its fingers spread as if relaxed in sleep. But the nearer she drew and the higher she climbed, the more apparent it was that the hand belonged to the body of a dead man, his chest cleaved open. The grass was slick with blood in a trail leading to another, whose severed arm lay to the left of a tree root, his body with his free hand still clasping the stump, to the right.

And Willie knew from Sarah's memory that this was her brother Michael, who had once slaughtered her pet lamb and laughed at her when she wouldn't eat mutton for her supper. He had died from hemorrhage when his sword arm was severed. Beside him was a hired man, his skull split to the bridge of his nose, his brains and blood leaking from the cleft. Her brother Robert was beside him, but she ignored them all, the servants and her brothers alike, and never drew a breath the entire time she walked across the hill until she saw him.

He lay facedown, as if napping, his clenched hands arrested by death in the act of tearing at the heather between his fingers. His sword had fallen to one side and the blood on it was still red, the smell of hot metal and gore simmering from it in the sunlight. The dream was not accurate, Willie was glad to see, for his head was still on his neck and the killing wound was from the sword that still stuck in his back. Willie could not recall having seen brother John's sword when they met on the trail. John it was then who must have surprised Sarah's lover from behind.

"You took eight of them with you though, buddy," Willie thought fiercely.

"Aye, they bought him dearly but not sae dearly as it's cost me." And Sarah pushed and pulled until she turned him over and Willie looked into his own dead face. The mouth was quirked as his quirked when he cut himself shaving. The eyes were glazed as his were glazed before his first cup of coffee. He might have been looking in the mirror but for the blood.

Sarah, on her hands and knees, stroked the corpse's hair and began to kiss the wounds and Willie did not somehow find it morbid when she licked and sipped the blood, as if by doing so she could take her lover into herself once more.

Two ravens sat in the tree above them, casting speculative beady eyes on the corpse.

"Get lost, you buzzards!" Willie wanted to cry, but found he had no voice without Sarah, who wearily made shooing motions with her hands and tried to tug her love by his arm away from where he lay. "I'll bury ye mysel', love," she said, and stepped backward on her long braids. She fell and her belly exploded with pain again.

She scarcely cried out, but Willie felt the pain that had

only been anesthetized by her deeper pain and he said, *"Take the sword from his back and cut off that hair. What do you care? He'll never stroke it again. Make a harness to lift him with."*

And with the rope of her hair lapped under the arms of the corpse of her lover, she tugged and pulled and dragged her love to the foot of the hill.

Her father and her brother were returning with men and shovels for the burying of the bodies and her father glared down at the top of her shorn head and commanded, "Stop. John, tak' that body frae your sister. She looks aboot to swoon."

"He's a little goddamn late to be worried about your welfare now," Willie growled.

Sarah looked up at her father and said in a voice made flat with pain, " 'Tis like my dream, Father, all full o' woe and weale—"

"Enough!" her father roared. "I won't have ye greetin' thus o'er this sneakin' seducin' dirty dog. It ruins the aftermath of a good battle. I cam' home for comfort and rest and what do I find but rebellion and sorrowful speeches. Nivair ye mind aboot him. I'll find ye a lord tae wed ye to who's twice the man and wi' his ane siller besides."

But Sarah jerked aside when her brother would unwind the hair from the knot across her chest and although he was stronger than she and not above striking her, as he had often done before, he shrank from her now.

Her father dismounted and reached for her gently. "I promise, I'll find ye anaither, worthier lord."

She didn't resist as he folded her in his arms.

"Let go of her, you old hypocrite!" Willie said, and just then the baby inside her burst from the womb and tore it from her as baby, placenta, womb and all plunged from her body in a torrent of blood.

She fought and clawed at her father as he eased her down on top of the body of the slain man, and she screamed, screamed and screamed, wrenching at him, until the ring on the middle finger of her left hand was half ripped from her finger, torn sideways in her struggles.

As her strength failed, a strain of music came to her and to Willie within her from far off, and Willie knew the song that went to the music.

> Last night I dreamed a doleful dream
> I knew it would bring sorrow.
> I dreamed I saw my true love slain
> On the dowie dens o' Yarrow.

And with remembering the song, he remembered that he mustn't die with her here in Yarrow. *"The ring. You must twist the ring twice more, backward—"*

She slumped so that her cheek was against her lover's wound and as the song played Willie saw that her love was waiting for her. *"The ring, Sarah, the ring,"* Willie in her mind said and the slain lover waiting for her echoed, *"My ring, love, my ring—"*

That which was Sarah and that which was Willie tangled together more tightly than ever as she died, drowning in her blood. Willie heard the song clearly, and desperately dived for her spirit that was abandoning his own, trapped in that dying body, *"You can't go yet. Stay and release me. Sarah, this isn't all of you. It isn't all of him. It isn't the end. There's the song, Sarah, the song they made for you and him . . ."*

And through her rang the second verse and with it the realization that this pitiful short life she had lived and was losing, that her lover's life, was not the end, and that they were avenged and remembered at once in all the time thereafter.

"The ring. Twist the ring. Backward—"

Her arms were limp over her love's body and her hands, dragging in the heather, clutched it in her death throes, the heather against her left hand working the ring slowly around, and ever slowly in a full counterclockwise twist . . . .

CHAPTER XVIII

▲▲▲

"Wat, are you still there?" Gussie asked. She felt lonesome, after weeks and months of being surrounded by people, to be driving down an empty road in a borrowed van in a foreign country all by herself.

"Aye," the ghost said as mournfully as ghosts are supposed to sound.

"What do we do now?"

"What ye will," the ghost said indifferently.

"Wat, come on. Give me a break. You've got to help me. This is your country, you're the ballad expert, and all of this supernatural business is a lot more your kind of thing than mine."

With great effort a faint voice inside her replied, "I'm no the man by day I am at night, lass. Leave me be. Return me to my grave for I maun rest me."

"Oh, no, you don't, buddy," Gussie said, gunning the engine and heading for Abbotsford. "You're not going to pull that poor-dead-me cop-out on Augusta Turner. You helped get us into this and you have to help get us out."

Abbotsford did not look very much different than it had when she first saw it, except that the doors were ajar and the windows were broken. The stone roof and the slate tile roof were still intact. The lawn and gardens and the front courtyard/parking lot looked like a giant garage sale. Some of the furnishings hardly appeared to be damaged, but when Sir Walter groaned Gussie saw the remains of the Spanish Armada desk. The docent from the day before and two men were there, ignoring the water-logged upholstered chairs, the charred dining-room table, to paw through a sodden, smoking mass of books and papers. Swirling smoke veiled the house, as the fog had done last night.

Gussie watched from the van. Was it safe to go up to the house or might someone have reported spotting the van driving away from the fire last night? She didn't know. She didn't care. She wished she too had a place to rest—though preferably not a grave. It had been a long night.

Sir Walter spoke softly. "Did you know that the walls of my study were covered with hand-painted silk? Oh, yes, a present from my publisher. Blue, of a Chinese design. Charlotte, my wife, was delighted. She would have liked it for the parlor but I liked to rest my eyes by looking at the pattern. Is the dog anywhere out there? I'd hate to think something happened to it. I have grown fond of it."

"Oh, Wat."

"I think it rather sad that things don't seem to have spirits after all. Some would think that sacrilegious I suppose, but many of the old peoples were animists, you know. They believed that things did have a life. Swords and such."

The banjo, tucked in Gussie's basket bag, had been noodling to itself, and changed tunes suddenly to the line in the hymn that went, "Some glad morning when this life is o'er, I'll fly away."

"Oh, aye. There's you, of course. But some people thought there was no special enchantment needed. That all things had lives of their own. If so, mine have been murdered. Better that they had been divided up among my creditors than this."

"Do you want to go to the house and see what the damage is?" she asked.

"I do not."

"Okay, then I'll take you back to your grave. You—uh—you can get in this time of day, can't you?"

"Aye, that I can."

"Fine." She started the motor again.

"But, on reflection, I'd prefair to bide with you. I've been dead a lang time and it seems obvious there is some reason for me to be active in the affairs of the living noo."

"Blast that Torchy anyway for what she did to your home. Wat, I don't know what fairy stories you've heard, but that is not a nice woman."

"Of course not. She's not supposed to be a nice woman. Even human queens seldom are, as you'll ken frae your history. As for Abbotsford, there's naught to be done aboot it. What else might we do?"

"I think we'd better start by trying to find the Randolphs. We can go to the police if all else fails but if Torchy kidnapped those kids, the police either wouldn't know anything or would deny they knew anything or were, who knows, responsible for it. And we're going to have to do something about latching onto some work visas or else find a way to hide and a way to get by over here for seven years. I haven't been a saint most of my life, but I never figured on becoming an outlaw at my age."

"I was always on the other side of the law myself," Sir Walter said. "But I canna say as much for my ancestors. I'm not acquainted with the laws we'll be breakin', lass, but I do hope we can do it with style."

"I hope we can get away with it, period," Gussie said. "I think now, though, what we have to find is that Circus Rom truck. The circus stopped in Edinburgh. I'm going to head up that way."

▲▲▲

"Whoa-o!" said the man sitting next to the storyteller. He wore an ancient tie-dye tee, baggy jeans, and a beard that hung in two braids to his waist. He was probably about twenty-five, too young for the sixties the first time around, not a "productive citizen." Other nonproductive citizens or at least not-productive-enough citizens were also stretched out over the carpeted floor of the gutted bus known throughout the Sound area as the Silver Snail. Six people at the far end were playing cards, one couple was necking,

and across from the group an artist tried to sketch between jolts. The jolts were to remind the passengers that the cheap transportation and the room to stretch out the Silver Snail provided were accompanied by such no-frills dues as no-shock-absorbers-either.

Most of the twenty-seven other passengers, however, had gradually found themselves drawn into the group surrounding the little curly-headed granny type in the pink jogging suit. She had been saddened to notice that these days no one brought a guitar, a banjo, or even a harmonica with them. Only ten years before, such things would have been an expected part of the trip. She had a hard time understanding why people chose to do without instruments now, and then it occurred to her that maybe it was because so many of the songs were still forgotten. Even people who had once been interested in folk music wouldn't remember anything to play. It wasn't only the old ballads gone now, it seemed, but pop music that had passed into the hands of ordinary people who liked to entertain themselves—that too had somehow vanished. Now these people were content to sit passively and let her entertain them with no participation on their parts except the occasional remark or bit of discussion. Sad. If they took in what she was saying, however, if it made them curious, maybe this state of affairs wouldn't continue much longer.

The man with the braided beard said, "So the dude ended up in some woman's mind, huh? And then she died and meanwhile old Sir Walter is running around in that lady's mind and they're looking for those other folks and all of this is for a few tunes? Why don't they just, you know, turn on the radio?"

"Get real, man! You can't play that stuff on the radio anymore. Any deejay caught spinning some song with stuff about guys wanting to boff their sisters or fathers hitting their daughters or guys killing other guys because of some babe, not to mention the woman miscarrying right there at the end of the song, shit, man, anybody played a song like that or sold it to some kid in a store would do a hell of a lot more time than guys who actually do go around boffing

*and beating their nearest and dearest, not to mention mur-
derers."*

*"I guess that's right. At least then they didn't have all
this censorship stuff."*

*"Unless you count getting beheaded if you made a joke
about royalty or singing a derogatory song about the
Douglases in their castle, forgetting to change the clan to
Ker,"* the storyteller said. *"Censorship in those days was
often fatal."*

*"You sound like you know all about it from personal
experience,"* a young mother nursing her baby said. *"Like
you were alive back then."*

*"In a manner of speaking, I suppose you might say I
was."*

▲▲▲

Faron came awake with a jolt inside a dark room full of
rattling things. The room was freezing cold and seemed
to be moving. When his eyes adjusted to the lack of light
he saw that he was lying with his nose pointing up at the
nose of a wooden horse. He seemed to be lying on a
merry-go-round platform.

Something warm bumped him and he surmised, correctly, that it was his wife.

"Ellie, you okay, babe?"

"Hell of a headache, about to freeze to death, otherwise fine. What hit us?"

"The arsonists, I guess. Gussie? You here?"

After a long moment with no answer Faron shrugged,
then realized Ellie couldn't see the shrug, and said,
"Guess not. There's a merry-go-round here."

"The truck said something about a circus. Must be the
kind right out of a Ray Bradbury story, huh? Like 'Something Wicked This Way Comes.' Wish we could ride this
painted pony out of here. Oh, shit."

"What?"

"We missed the ghost. The Wizard's ghost. I bet it's
already up and everything's all over and we missed it
all."

"Well, not quite everything. If everything was over—

solved, how come we're still here? You wouldn't happen to have a match or a lighter or anything, would you?"

"No, but I've got my combination flashlight and key chain in my pocket," she said, and with a click a thin beam of light pierced the gloom like a laser sword.

"They don't seem to have been all that serious about holding us here," Faron observed. "Didn't even tie us up. Let's see if there's anything we can use to escape. A crowbar would be handy."

"And maybe a motorbike so we could just zoom out of here. Got the time?"

"Yeah—about one A.M. Say, you don't happen to have a compass on that key chain do you?"

"No, that's on my Swiss Army knife. I'll bet we're heading for Edinburgh though, what do you think?"

"How do you figure that?"

"It's the nearest city. Easier to get lost in a big city than out on the roads someplace. Hey, what's this?" Her foot had bumped against a smallish, curved-sided object. She reached down and touched it with her hands, feeling along its sides, which bulged, drew in and bulged again, followed by an elongated piece. The flashlight beam bounced off of something black.

Faron was crawling under a tarp over some other piece of equipment and called back in a muffled voice, "Well, what is it?"

"A fiddle."

"Yeah?" He stumbled back toward the beam of light.

She had already opened the case and held the fiddle in one hand, the bow in the other. "Why don't you play it? Maybe *it's* haunted by the ghost of Stradivari. The way this trip's been going, I wouldn't be surprised at anything."

"I don't think Stradivari's ghost would be much help to us. Probably has the attitude of the symphony musicians: if it ain't classical, it ain't music. Feels nice though." He lifted the fiddle to his chin and the bow to the fiddle and sounded a note, tuned, sounded another note. "Gorgeous tone, huh?"

"So play something."

Faron hemmed and hawed and sawed around for a few minutes, then launched into a Cajun tune he'd gotten off an old Doug Kershaw record, "Diggy Diggy Lo." In between choruses he took proper breaks and sang, Ellie pitching in with harmonies and an occasional "Ahh eee!" for atmosphere.

"That warmed me up. Play something else." He started "Louisianna Man," which he remembered just fine since, to the best of his knowledge, Doug Kershaw was still alive and, the last Faron had heard, was traveling around Australia. One chorus and one verse and one bridge into the song, the truck sighed to a halt and Faron halted too. "Look, they might come back here and try to stop us," he told Ellie. "If they do, I'll try to distract them and you make a break for it. Now's our best time, before they decide to tie us up or take us someplace else."

"Okay," Ellie whispered.

Footsteps crunched across gravel outside while they held their breath. Voices speaking in some foreign language were raised and then one of them said something that had the tone of "Yeah, yeah, sure" and the argument stopped while more crunchy footsteps grew gradually fainter, then died away altogether.

Faron exhaled the breath he had been holding since the truck stopped, and at that moment there was a scrabbling near the rear of the truck and the doors swung open, the night air rushing in upon them.

"Out with you, you two," a voice said. It sounded old, anxious, and with a northern English or Scottish accent overlaid by another, more exotic accent.

"Okay, okay," Faron said, and scrambled for the doorway. "Where to?"

"Hide in the woods. Run! Giorgio, he's gone to piss but he'll be back soon. Go!"

"Okay, thanks."

"Wait."

"What?"

"My violin. My wonderful nephew-in-law no longer

lets me make her sing. He tells me to burn her but I don't do it and now, hearing you play her, he says he'll break her in half. Take her and keep her safe. Now, go!"

They went, hoping that Giorgio had a very full bladder.

CHAPTER XIX

▲▲▲

Anna Mae Gunn knew something had gone wrong when she emerged from the haze that had suddenly swallowed the banjo and the kitchen after she passed the banjo on to Brose. For a moment she found herself staring back at a young man whose rakish grin reminded her of Willie MacKai. He was dressed in fancy old-timey clothing, humming a black humor of a tune, at once both lilting and minor, wind rippling a black tarn. He opened his mouth to let fly with a particularly strenuous note and she found herself on the inside looking out of his eyes, into a mirror where he admired himself very greatly.

"And will you love me and me alone forever and ever, my darling Clark?" asked the nude woman on the bed, and Anna Mae knew at once what the mix-up was, because the woman on the bed looked like her. She should have been in that place, not this one, but here she was.

"You know I will, dear, in my fashion," Anna Mae's host replied with a laugh.

"You've given up those little trips you take to the shore then to visit our local banshee?"

"Now how would you know about something like that? I won't have you distressing yourself with idle gossip, my poppet."

The woman, his wife, the mayor's daughter, threw her pillow at him. "Everyone knows about you and her, Clark, and I swear, if you go near her again, I'll be so shamed I won't dare hold my head up anymore. She isn't human and everybody knows it."

No, she certainly wasn't and Margaret the mayor's daughter most certainly was human. You could see her skeleton right through her skin and feel it too. She was bony, not bonny, this woman.

"Why the hell'd you marry her then, sport?" Anna Mae asked.

"How many times will I have to ask myself that and will I ever be content with the answers?" her host responded, as he thought, to himself. For he, like Sarah, thought of the new voice within him as simply another of his own inner voices. He had from time to time harbored many voices as critical as Anna Mae's but usually managed to silence them at least long enough to embark on some new venture that would rouse them again. Now he sought to appease these new doubts with a barrage of justifications. *"Here I am the best catch in the country, good-looking, fair-spoken, well off, thanks to the woman my wife says is not human, and God and my mother know, I am a solicitous son and so can be expected to be a dutiful husband. So dutiful that I put aside my own preferences to do the right thing. And now I wonder if it's the right thing at all."*

"Doesn't sound to me like you were doing her any favors."

"Oh, but of course I was. I saw her father's note didn't I? She had gotten herself so worked up she threatened to die on the spot if I didn't marry her. That moved my mother's heart to pity—that and her well-endowed dower. 'How will you provide for me when I'm old, Clark? Me and your sisters and you with no daddy. You can't just lark about the country doing nothing in particular all your life. You need a wife and family and a position,' she said. And I asked, 'Mother, have I not always provided for you since Father died? Have you ever wanted for anything?' That was a big mistake. She had a list. But she's my only mother and it's little enough I can do that makes her happy. So I saw no reason not to accommodate this rich girl about to die for love of me. I can look away from her

sharp chin and the little mustache and if her hipbones are enough to disembowel me, I can always pad her with pillows."

"Or maybe get a fat mistress," Anna Mae said sarcastically.

But the man, who was as much her new self as Sarah had been Willie's, was immune to sarcasm.

"There's a thought. But I have to explain to the current one about the wife first. I dread this. She is a sweet, dear girl and I owe her so much. She's always looked after everything for me. In fact, the things I've been able to get for my family already are gifts from her. I just sing this little song and she comes running with whatever I need. I'm tempted to call her in now and let her have it out with dear little Margaret."

"Don't you dare!"

"No, I don't dare, it's true. At least not here. But who knows, maybe Lillian will take a shine to Margaret and provide for us all."

"How do you expect her to do that?"

"If she can find sunken treasure to supply me and my mother and sisters with goods, surely she can find enough extra to support my wife as well. If I explain it to her that I won't get the time to come and see her as usual, or a moment's peace to myself if I allow my wife to control all of the family's fortunes, surely she'd rather keep helping out than lose me altogether, hmmm?"

"We are a little mercenary about this whole thing, hmmm?"

"That's not being entirely fair to myself. What am I good at, really? I am pleasing to a lady's eye, can bespeak her as she desires, and also have a facility for horizontal refreshment due to my natural endowments. I'm an artist, in my own way, and were I talented with paintbrush or lute, and born to a miller's family, though I might concede to my family's wish that I go into the miller's trade that ill suits me, still I might wish to privately pursue my own art form on the side, might I not? I don't see a particle of difference between the cases."

"Hmph," Anna Mae replied. Damn Torchy Burns and

her infernal spells! The bitch *would* have had to make Anna Mae play conscience to some insufferable antique cock-of-the-walk. Which ballad was this anyway? It had to be one in which he murdered some poor girl and threw her in a convenient body of water for bearing him some tangible fruit of his "artistic" labors. *"So you really don't give a damn for either of the women, do you? It's all a game to you."*

"Well, not too much of a damn," he replied. *"Though if it were left to me alone, I prefer my mistress, for she is sweet to me as she uses me and I believe she loves me. But how much of a damn do either of them really care for me? My wife needed to marry me, if not some other, so that she could say to her gossips 'my husband this and my husband that' and complain of me or brag on me, never for my own sake but for hers. I give her the position of a married and respectable woman, not one who has been left by the wayside. I will naturally supply her amply with children. As she has a rough tongue and is not the fairest lady in the district, my services are not those she could acquire for the fee of her considerable but not inexhaustible dower, and well she knows it. In having me as well as her own wealth, she will be the envy of her friends. And if I amuse myself elsewhere with gaming and dalliance, who can blame me? A man must have some diversions from toil."*

"And your mistress?"

"Her exploitation of me is one for which I have more sympathy. She has more than the normal female liking for screwing. Moreover, she is outcast because she has no family and, as far as the world can see, no fortune, and she is uncommonly fair, which, coupled with her love of displaying and using her pretty self, makes her an enemy to all other women. Were it not for me, no wife in town would be safe of her husband and they'd try to burn Lillian for a witch, I vow. Fortunately, I have too much need of her to leave her time to make a whore of herself with others. I fancy once the honeymoon is over, that one in my bed will be withholding her favors in order to win her will of me in less amiable pursuits. We shall see who has whose will of whom! But for now . . ."

Aloud he said, "Come and walk with me, my love, and wear the wedding present that I gave you so I may show off to all of your other admirers the magnificence of their loss."

"Oh, Clark, you say the sweetest things—"

She pulled a long scarlet gown over her head and clasped her waist with a magnificent jeweled belt. "I do love this," she said, Anna Mae thought quite sincerely. Her eyes beamed with what she certainly thought was love.

"Faith, but she should," Anna Mae's host thought, *"it cost me fifteen crowns."* To his wife he said, "It pales by comparison with your beauty, my own."

The garden at the fine house where Clark and his lady lived was in full bloom, rich emerald green with manicured trees and bushes and rows of flowers in shades of rose, pink, yellow, and violet. Lilacs and roses, daffodils and violets, the ground studded here and there with little white gillie flowers among the paving stones that glittered with shards of wild gemstone crystal.

The bride sighed. "Do you mean it, Clark? Do you really think I'm beautiful?"

"The most beautiful woman in the world," he assured her, mentally amending it to "the most beautiful one I see in front of me, anyway."

"Fairer than the fair maid who lives by the stream?" she asked, looking down and biting her lip as if afraid.

He didn't answer, hoping his silence would restrain her, but she looked up at him with searching, tearing eyes. *"She does love you,"* Anna Mae said.

"Perhaps she does," the host replied with surprise that was immediately smothered by bitterness denying that she might love him, wanted to love him, *could* love him for himself alone. *"But if she does,"* he continued, *"it's only while she thinks she does not have all of me. Once she has me in her power, she'll despise me. Women are that way, as I well know. Why else did my mother send my father away?"*

"There could have been a lot of reasons. She said he left."

"He would only have left if she made him leave. Once he got her with me, she had no more use for him. She had her dower money and she says he was a wastrel. But he would never have left me behind, would he? No, she forced him away once she had what she wanted of him. I'm not about to make the same mistake."

And Anna Mae thought, *Poor silly boy. Just a grown-up kid who resents his mother for running off his father. How fucking Freudian.* But a pang pierced her wondering how her parents had come to leave her, to put themselves into such danger that they died and couldn't raise her. They'd left her with adoptive parents who were well off and who cared for her, but she'd never fit in really. And much as she might sniff at this man's rationalizations of his filthy behavior toward the women in his life, his art-ist/miller analogy made a certain amount of sense to her. Her adoptive parents expected her to earn her living in the white man's world. They said they wanted more for her, and she knew that meant more than she would have had on the reservation, more than many women of her people had, more than dancing for tourists, playing her guitar for tips in smoky honky-tonks, probably between taking guys to some back room, or wearing out her eyes and fingers with beadwork while raising her own tribe of brats by some itinerant rodeo bull-riding alcoholic. They encouraged her to develop other skills—clerical and po-litical—and she was thus set up to be the lackey of a white man who wanted her, not even for her beauty or sex appeal or amiability but so that she would betray her own people. She was as cynical about men as Clark here was cynical about women and she supposed both of them had pretty good cause. She didn't really want another man particularly, or another kind of man. But yeah, she would like to just be left alone to devote herself to music, to what she was good at and what she understood, she'd like to be able to make a living and be happy doing that.

In Clark's time, it wasn't that cool for a man to be an artist of some kind. Even minstrels were often out of fashion and ended up trying to play in taverns for bread. They slept in stables or in the rain instead of in kings' halls. Painters could only make it in major cities, where wealthy patrons vied with one another for fashionable portraits. This guy might well have some other artistic talent than "horizontal refreshment." The sensitivity to his partner's need for romantic fiction might well have developed into something less whorish if he were encouraged to pursue it, but she could see that there didn't seem to be that opportunity. She just wished that he could see that the woman in front of him, whose manners might not be as pleasing as he thought, was not anxious to be the domineering bitch he thought she was.

"You should listen to her," Anna Mae argued. *"Whatever her reasons may have been for getting you to marry her, she loves you now. Look into her eyes."*

" 'Now' is the key word. I have to make sure she continues to love me."

The bride put her hand on his sleeve and he recoiled as if they had not touched other body parts so intimately throughout the night, as if she had no right. "Clark, that woman is evil," she said. "Please. You married me. You agreed to do this. Don't go to her. I fear—"

"You see? It's starting already. She wants to control me," he thought but said with a throaty laugh as he tickled his wife's sharp chin, "Don't you worry your pretty head about me, my love. Here you are trying to take care of me already, but I'm a grown man and I can take care of me and you as well. Haven't I told you enough times that there's no one as fair as you? Now you'd better go send your thank-you tokens to our friends. I have business across town."

The bride swallowed and nodded and went meekly indoors again.

"Whew," Anna Mae's host said to himself. *"She's mild enough now but I expect that as time goes by, I'll have to be firmer and firmer to get her to let go. Faith, I feel smothered already."*

He saddled his horse himself, for their budget did not allow for a stable boy, and besides, he needed some excuse to get out of the house now and again.

The horse was brown as acorns, brown as bark and

sleek and fleet. His love had given him this horse, though as he told the story around town, he had won his mare while gaming in the village two valleys away. As he rode, he whistled the tune he'd been humming when he arose from bed.

"You could be a musician," Anna Mae told him. *"You could learn to play that song on an instrument, set words to it—it would give you an excuse to get out of the house too."*

"I might at that. I'll ask Lillian when I see her. She mumbles the words to herself but I've never heard her sing them out. Perhaps I could learn music, now that I'm a respectable married man."

He rode on until he came to the far edge of the town, where he came to the banks of a river, and followed it upstream and into the hills and the woods.

At length they came upon a woman washing something in the water. Her long fair hair fell over her shoulders as she scrubbed and her high round bosom bobbed sensuously to the rhythm of her hands. Her legs, long and shapely as birch saplings, curved under the crescents of her hips and she sang to herself in a soprano clear and high as wild bird song. Only when he dismounted did she turn to him, brushing a sheaf of fair hair away from wide grass-green eyes that reflected the play of light on the river.

He sang out to the pretty woman as he bent to cuddle her from behind, cupping her breasts, squeezing gently as she worked, "Wash on, wash on, my bonny maid/That wash sae clean your sark of silk."

She laughed and sang back a response, rubbing backward against him so that he rose to the occasion, "And weel fare you, fair gentleman/Your body whiter than the milk."

The disembodied Anna Mae felt as if she'd been plunged into a bath of lava with the sensations she received from this male body. She didn't like it. It went against everything she thought should happen. *"You're nothing but a two-timing son of a bitch!"* she screamed with all the venom she'd built up from the betrayals she'd experienced.

But she was trapped inside him and there was no place else for her rage to go. It reverberated through his head and beat against the inside of his skull until he stopped fondling his mistress and fell back, clutching his head. His very hair throbbed with the blinding pain.

"My head, my head!" he groaned, scrubbing at his face and scalp with his hands as if to scrub the pain away.

"What's the matter, love?" the woman asked.

"It hurts me sore, Lillian," he sobbed. "I can't bear it."

"Can't you then? My poor dear."

"Can't you see she's mocking you, shithead?" Anna Mae screamed. *"You think she didn't hear about your wedding? Where do you think this is, London, that you can screw everything that moves and have it not get back and hurt somebody? You ignorant bastard, this woman has given you everything she has and you married another one and still expect her to play second fiddle. Dumb shit!"*

"See here, my darling, here's a little bane-knife. Cut a bit off my sark here and we'll bind it around your brow. That'll make it feel better."

But she kept chirping her little song as she tied the piece of silk around his head and as she sang, Anna Mae felt her rage growing and growing, and although she realized she was under the woman's spell, she could do nothing to restrain the tidal wave of anger and contempt that, to her host, felt like self-contempt and self-hatred.

The scrap of silk only served to bind the anger in and bind Anna Mae to anger and she called Clark Colville sixteen different kinds of a fool and told him what ought to be done to a man who acted the way he was acting. "My head is worse than ever!" Clark groaned. "Sorer and sorer it aches."

And Lillian shrugged and returned to her washing. "I know," and sang her little tune with the words "And sorer sorer ever will, till you be dead . . ."

Rage to answer her own rose up from the man within Anna Mae's host and he drew his knife. He couldn't kill

Anna Mae without killing himself but he lashed out for the betraying female—even though he'd set her up to betray him—who mocked his pain. She laughed, evaded the blade easily, and to the wonder of the host's pain-dazzled eyes did a backward flip, her gown glittering suddenly like sequins and ending, not in ankles and feet, as Anna Mae had been sure there were when the girl sat on the bank, but in a long scaled tail. By the time Lillian hit the water she was half fish and swam away laughing.

Clark barely managed to keep his seat as he rode home. His mother, sister, and younger brother stood talking in the garden with his wife as the steed carried him, half-dead with the pain of Anna Mae's roaring, the roaring of his own self-loathing that Lillian had magically amplified with a silent spell and with the binding of her sark had bound the rage inside him to continue until it should hound him to death.

"Mother, Mother, take off this sark and braid my hair. My lady, make my bed. Brother, you take my sword and spear—"

"Faith, Clark, what's wrong! A little headache? God's blood but you've always gone to pieces over such trifles."

"No, Davey, listen to me. I have seen the false mermaid. Lillian. It's true what they say about her. Go ahead—take my weapons. Unbend my bow until you're big enough to pull it. 'Twill never be bent by me again."

His wife rushed up to make the bed and his sister and mother guided him up the stairs. His mother braided his hair until he fell asleep. "A sudden fever, I suppose." Anna Mae was quiet now, for the headache hurt her of course too, and in her last roar she felt something break within the man's head. A stroke perhaps? Too many sweets, that was for sure.

As her host fell asleep, she was dimly aware of the family murmuring outside the door. "A sudden fever. It takes them like that sometimes," his sister said.

"Please let me go in to him," the bride said. "I could put cool rags on his head. I could hold his hand and comfort him. I could—"

"Now, dear, I've lived with Clark all his life, and I

know best," his mother said. "When he's sick he wants no one but me to tend him and he wants little tending at that."

And Anna Mae heard and Clark heard his wife's heartsick weeping.

"She does love me, doesn't she?" Clark asked himself, and the fresh, now-undeniable realization cut through his pain for a moment like a ray of sunshine piercing a storm cloud. *"She'll miss me and be true to me although we've been man and wife but one night. And Lillian will go find some other fool."*

"Lillian should have cut your nuts off," Anna Mae snapped.

As if mentioning her invoked her, the mermaid appeared suddenly at the foot of the bed, singing her little song. "Will ye lie there and die, Clark Colville, will ye lie there and die?" she asked, her white teeth glittering in the glow of the single candle his mother had left burning at his bedside. "Or will gang to Clyde's Water to fish in flood wi' me? I'm ruined around here because of your accusations, but if you'll be true next time, you may live and bide with me, though you'll have to behave yourself this time and agree to my terms."

"I will lie here and die," he said angrily.

"Had it all wrong, did you, sport?" Anna Mae asked. *"Your lover is the one in control, your mother is the one who will continue to benefit by you even after your death, and your wife is the one who truly loves you."*

"Aye," he agreed. *"And I've learned one thing. I know now that my time is near and that my chiefest enemy is within me. Living with Lillian or living with Margaret, it's all the same. It's living with myself that causes me such pain."* Aloud he said, "I will lie here and die. To spite you and all the devils in hell, I'll just lie here and die."

Lillian disappeared with a look that, to Anna Mae, said, "So long, sucker."

Before Clark died, Margaret escaped his mother long enough to be at his side and hold his hand, which he held on to most gratefully. His speech centers were affected by now and one side of his body paralyzed, as vessel after vessel broke behind his handsome face. His eyes flickered to his wedding ring, which he wore oddly on the middle finger of his left hand, having averred that it was too large for his ring finger. With his good hand, he tried to twist it backward, but could not.

"Does it bother you, love?" Margaret asked. "Do you want me to take it from you that you not lose it?"

It cost him great effort to shake his flaming head from one side to the other. His fingers feebly twisted the ring again and through a haze of pain he beseeched Margaret with his eyes.

"I don't understand, love," she said, taking that hand in hers and twisting the ring backward as she had seen him do. But when she looked to his eyes for further instructions, they were staring beyond her into nothingness.

CHAPTER XX

▲▲▲

Gussie and Sir Walter picked up Faron and Ellie shortly after they left Abbotsford.

"We walked through the woods, kept behind fences, anything to get away from where the guy let us go so that if his buddy found out we were gone he couldn't come back to the same place and get us."

Ellie yawned. "Can't we find someplace to sleep? I'm whipped."

"That's unanimous," Gussie said.

Walter Scott assented silently within her, by which she knew that he was really out of steam, mist, ectoplasm, or whatever made ghosts run.

At the Galashiels tourist office, set in a mobile home in a vacant lot next to a fire station, they found a brochure of places to stay in the Borders and found what was called a self-catering flat big enough to accommodate them, a stone cottage that had once belonged to the gamekeeper on a much larger estate. The estate was given over to black-faced sheep and "belties," the lowland belted cattle. Faron phoned ahead to the owners, who lived in "the big house," the former mansion of some squire or other, and when they drove up the maze of winding graveled roads that led to the place described by the owner, they found the cottage as advertised, smack in the middle of a pasture surrounded by cows and sheep. A little red car was parked on the gravel patch in front of the stone cottage and the door of the cottage stood open.

A woman wearing a bandanna on her head, corduroy pants tucked into black rubber wellies, and a patched blue windbreaker was inside, making beds. She extended her hand in a businesslike but friendly fashion. "Hello, I'm Janet Carr. You must be Mr. Randolph, who rang up?"

"Yes, ma'am," Faron said. "This is my wife Ellie and this is my wife's aunt Gussie."

"Nice to meet you. How long will you be staying?"

They hadn't discussed it.

"I only ask because we can just take you as we usually have tenants from the States who stay all summer, but the lady's had a bit of heart trouble this year and can't travel yet."

"How much is it?" Gussie asked.

"A thousand pounds for the three months is our usual rate, or eighty pounds a week."

"May we pay you for today and tonight and let you know tomorrow?"

"That will be fine. I simply need to know if I can accept other reservations."

The house actually had more than enough room. Four bedrooms, two adjoining the living room on one side, two adjoining the entrance hall on the other side of the living room. Each bedroom was furnished with a wardrobe, a bed, a bookcase stacked with old paperback mysteries, and a bedside stand and lamp. A coal stove dominated the living room, augmented by an ancient electric heater. In back of the living room was a narrow kitchen, fully equipped with pots, pans, a few assorted dishes and pieces of cutlery, and an electric teakettle that heated water almost as fast as one of those boiling water faucets Gussie had seen in the States. The entrance hall led from the front door to a back door that let out onto a narrow cement sidewalk around the house, kept from the hill behind by a low cement wall. The bathroom adjoined the kitchen.

Gussie made use of one of the beds, and by the time she woke, Faron was already up, the electric kettle busily boiling. Ellie actually slept *more* soundly than the dead since as evening drew closer, Sir Walter's ghost grew increasingly alert.

"So, what now?" Faron asked.

"So now we try to figure out how to stick around for seven years without getting thrown out," she said, and told him as much as she could about the happenings of the previous night that she hadn't had time to relate after she had found him and Ellie and driven them to Galashiels.

Faron shook his head. "We'll never manage to stay here seven years," he said. "Too many legal complications."

"Maybe so," Gussie said. "But I think we need to use what time we have to try to recover anything we can find about the ballads. They weren't all at Abbotsford, after all. There are supposed to be some in the Edinburgh library, and other more isolated places."

"It's too late to go there now," Faron said. "Damn, you know, Gussie, I can't help but wish if you were going to get haunted by somebody it could have been Professor Child instead of Sir Walter. He's not generally considered a very reliable authority."

"He's been a lot of help," Gussie said loyally. "Anybody could have gotten taken in by that Torchy or whatever she calls herself, and he got us the Wizard's spell to help the others and all that. He's just a little weary now —losin' his library like that was a big shock."

"I didn't know ghosts *could* be shocked," Faron said. "Besides, I don't mean that he's not a nice enough guy as ghosts go, just that his collection was limited."

"I beg your pardon, young man, but I'm forced to take exception to that," the ghost said for the first time that evening. "Why do you find my credentials lacking?"

"Sir, you just never collected as many ballads as Professor Child or researched them the way he did and you, uh, you changed them, sir. You messed around with the text."

"But don't you see? The story was incomplete and I *knew* how it should go. Fragments were lost. I wanted people to listen to those stories and to hear them as I did.

Besides, the originals were in the manuscript folios. I'd like to ask your Mr. Child how many of his ballads he found in the folios and books I collected at Abbotsford. I knew all of the collectors of the day, corresponded with them and collected their works. I read Percy as a boy and besides had Ritson's works, Buchan's, and Motherwell's, amang others. I'm a lover of good stories, and the ballads are amang the best. I could not in a' conscience present them dismembered and incomplete. I assure you, lad, my alterations were altogether in the original spirit of the ballads."

"I'm sorry, sir, but it wasn't good scholarship," Faron said with his square chin jutting across the table at Gussie, quite forgetting her in his argument with her bodily guest. "You didn't say where you'd added things and—"

"Aha! You see! If you canna say where I've made my little contributions, you canna tell my work from the auld songs. That shows you how true to the spirit they were—"

"Nevertheless, it alters the meanings, alters the language, alters the *text* dammit."

"Will you boys pipe down?" Gussie asked. "You're making me dizzy. Faron Randolph, I'm surprised at you. Who makes up new lyrics at the drop of a hat for any song that's ever been sung? You do, that's who. Why, from what I understand of the folk process, any song going is fair game for anybody who wants to sing it and it doesn't seem to me that it's any worse to write down your own version than to sing out loud or record it. What's Wat if he isn't folks anyway?"

"But we need to know the original old versions from long ago, Gussie, so that we can learn things about the people."

"Well, hell, he's old and from long ago and all of us will be to somebody someday. I think this is just plain foolishness."

"Knowing the authentic versions is what makes folk songs different, why they can't all be copyrighted by record magnates and made the property of SWALLOW," Faron said stubbornly, referring to the Songwriters and

Arrangers Legal Licensing Organization Worldwide, which now claimed a broad hegemony over music all over the world, although it had gained the strongest hold thus far in the United States and was just starting to make real inroads in enforcing its "rights" in Europe.

"And a lot of damn good authenticity's done us lately then, ain't it?" Gussie asked, and to her bodily guest she said, "You gotta forgive Faron, Wat. His uncle Vance was a famous ballad collector in America and so he's upholdin' the family opinion or something."

"Gussie, it isn't just Uncle Vance's opinion. He cross-referenced a lot of the versions he collected with stuff in the *Minstrelsy*—"

"I rest my case," said the ghost.

"The sad thing," Gussie said, taking back control of her own mouth, "is that all those songs are no use to us. Wat, you have to help us think of some places we might find those ballads that the devils wouldn't think to look. You mentioned correspondence—can you help us maybe track down some of the letters or books that might have ballads?"

"Oh, aye," he said. "Her Highness is a very fine lady and all that but she never had that much to do with humankind that she knows all our tricks. *And* I vow that if you took all of the ballads out of the libraries and literature of Scotland, not to mention England, Ireland, Wales, and Cornwall, you'd have precious little left—our stories are part and parcel of our lands and people."

All of a sudden the banjo in the corner began frailing a tune and Faron began singing "On the Dowie Dens of Yarrow—"

Ellie emerged sleepily from the bedroom.

"My kingdom for a tape recorder," Faron said during a pause in the timing.

Ellie bumbled back into the bedroom and reemerged with a sketch pad. "Shorthand," she said. "I can always fall back on it."

She wrote down the words Faron sang—fortunately, he had only sung the first verse before she got the pad and it was repeated later in the song. After he sang that version, Sir Walter triumphantly recited six others from memory. To her amazement, Gussie remembered three more—one from a Steeleye Span album, one as Ewan MacColl had used to do it, and an Appalachian version she had on an old Jean Ritchie tape.

When all of them seemed to have exhausted their supply of versions they knew, Sir Walter said, "Someone survived through that one, eh?"

Ellie shuddered. "I don't see how. Everybody died."

"Nevertheless, if one of our people hadn't survived it, I don't think we'd have gotten the song back."

Just as they were getting cocky about remembering that one ballad, the banjo began another one.

"I don't even know that tune," Gussie said.

"I do," Faron said. "It's Clerk Colin or Clark—Colville." And he sang that one and three other different versions.

"A've aneothair vairsion," Scott said and recited it laboriously to the banjo.

▲▲▲

"You're supposed to shut these people down, DD, not make deals with them," the Chairdevil said, visiting the woman known as Torchy at the Gypsy camp, where Giorgio was busy carrying a brick toward the restrained form of his uncle Theo, who had driven the truck and given his forsaken violin to Faron before setting the Randolphs free. Three other men held the old man down, with his hands bound and flattened on another broad stone. Giorgio was going to crush the old violinist's hands as an object lesson, and Torchy was providing the cheering section.

"Come off it, Chair, I'm on very firm ground in that department. Making deals with mortals is a totally conventional, traditional kind of thing to do," she said, smiling at the old man's grunts of pain and the tears rolling down his cheeks. "Give him a little anesthetic out of the last haul, Giorgi-porgy," she said. "Can't have traitors now can we?"

"Tradition of that sort is exactly the kind of thing we're trying to do away with here," the Chairdevil said.

"Look, I've had all the ballad books burned and served them up as tea. What do you want from me?"

"I want that banjo in pieces and those people neutralized . . . or better yet converted. I do *not* want these damned jingles suddenly blasting across the ether in forty-six versions and more spin-offs than a Norman Lear sitcom."

"Hey, I made it as impossible as I could. It's only one little song."

A spasm writhed across Chair's face and Giorgio backed away from the old man, who cursed him. Giorgio's wife crept up behind him with her dagger drawn.

"Oh, say," Torchy said, as the strains of "Clerk or Clark Colville" disrupted the afternoon air. "That's a nice grim one."

"You've got the wrong attitude, DD," the Chairdevil told her. "You're supposed to be keeping track of those specimens of anachronistic noise purveyors, not playing with your little friends."

Giorgio's wife stabbed him in the hip and he dropped the brick on his foot.

"But, boss, these are my minions. They need me here to supervise them. And I can only just keep so good a track of those other people magically—I'm using a lot of juice keeping my own little hell in motion for the four that are back in la-la-la land, so I can hardly be peeking psychically over the shoulder of the leftovers. I think I've pretty well pulled their clawhammers. Get it? It's a banjo technique—?"

The Chairdevil yelled, "Enough! If you can't do long-distance surveillance you'll have to do it in person."

"Boss, they're onto me. Besides, these people here need some encouragement. A little inspiration. You saw what happened with that old reactionary." She tossed her head in the direction of Giorgio's uncle, who now, with Giorgio's wife, held the other men at bay negotiating for less maiming and more of a strong warning.

The Chairdevil waved her protest aside. "I'll send Expediency to whip them into line. I don't care how you do it, but infiltrate the enemy and stop them. You left them too big an out and they seem to be recovering seven songs for every one you make them live through."

"That *is* my fault," she said. "I was the one who encouraged the composers originally to keep stealing verses and lines and melodies from each other. Now all the songs that have any of those all come back at once."

"I like chain reactions better when applied to nuclear technology," the Chairdevil said primly.

"Oh, hell," she mumbled when he had disappeared in the pillar of flame and sulfur that was, though he wouldn't admit it, every bit as traditional as making deals with mortals. "The way he's acting, you'd think I intended to honor that silly deal and give them all up after seven years. Nobody ever trusts me."

If anyone had asked her she would have admitted that her problem with paying attention to her mission was that Willie MacKai was out of commission, on the present plane anyway. She had taken a mighty shine to Willie and considered the three remaining adversaries much less intriguing. Still, she thought she might go peek in on them and then maybe she could take a trip down memory lane to where Willie and Brose, Juli and Anna Mae, were, just to see if she couldn't louse things up for them even more. It was the least she could do.

▲▲▲

"What next in this infernal game of Name That Tune?" Gussie wondered.

While they sat trying to clear their heads, a slender orange-striped cat with a spade-shaped face and a roman nose strolled in and demanded to be fed, rubbing Faron's shins and purring madly, blinking her large green eyes at him.

"I'd like to call home and talk to Daddy and Mama about what's going on," Ellie said. "I also want to warn them about the charge from Norway on the American Express card."

"There's a phone in the bedroom."

"It seems to be sort of an extension of the Carrs' phone. I tried calling out and Mr. Carr answered."

"Well, let's call them and see what the drill is," Faron said. "Unless you'd like to walk up there?"

"I wouldn't mind. Cold as it was last night, it was good to be out of the van. And see how pretty it is this morning."

CHAPTER XXI

▲▲▲

She blew in on a gusty wind, keeping pace with the rider until he reined in long enough to direct his arrow at the dun deer flitting with elfin grace among the fluttering green boughs. As his arrow flew from his bow, she was deposited by the wind and joined with him, a large, sun-bronzed, red-haired man from whose bark-brown eyes she was suddenly looking at the forest around her, the wind she had ridden on biting through the cloak that covered her in his body.

The arrow sought the fleeing deer and found its mark with a soft thud and a squeal, and within her host, triumph and the anticipation of hot venison mingled with regret for the beautiful beast. The hounds at his horse's hooves bayed victoriously, streaking into the brush like jet streams, and the steed, the color of the last leaves before winter, bolted after them, so that the rider had to hang on to the reins with one hand, clamp his knees tight to his mount's sides, and fend off smacking tree branches with the hand that still held his bow.

The deer died cleanly, though, and had not run far. It leaped only a single leap before falling, a heap of slender limbs and bloodied hair, the tongue sticking out of the muzzle a little. Overhead the goss hawk cried and landed on the man's shoulder, its talons biting into the leather pads but never into flesh.

The dogs wagged themselves into a frenzy as the man, with a stroke that would have made Julianne close her eyes had they been her own eyes and not this stranger's, bled the deer and gutted it, dressing it out on the spot.

The clop of other hoofbeats came from the glade beyond and the hounds increased their racket.

"Tha's a beaut, Highness," said a voice behind him, but the red-haired man didn't seem to hear him at first, for the hunter was silently addressing his kill, "I thank thee for thy life that we may eat and live."

Then Juli's host answered his companion, "Aye. Wi' the other one, it's a feast worthy of the hunt."

She didn't intrude on his thoughts at this point but watched with his eyes and listened with his ears, lifted with his muscles and let his feelings flow through her.

"The toun is but seven miles, Highness, are ye sure ye want to bide at yon haunted lodge?" asked a small wiry man as they loaded the deer onto the back of the horses. The dogs coursed 'round them, barking excitedly.

"Quiet, you dogs!" Juli's host ordered, reaching down with bloody hands to scratch ears and to have his fingers licked clean of the deer's blood.

"You're too good to them, Henrie," said the small man. *(Jamie Lochlan, sister's husband,* Henrie's mind supplied the name and position.)

"Ah, but they're good dogs."

"But aboot yon lodge. 'Tis haunted, ye know. Your faither nivair used it because of that."

"Then I vow we'll exorcise it with the incense of roasted meat and that holy water you brought with you from the brewer's," Henrie said.

"A party?" Juli asked, and knew at once the nature of her relationship with her host when he answered her as though she and he were the same, as they were then.

"By God, a party. And long overdue it is," the host said. *"Glad I am to have had the thought."*

They rode through overgrown and overhung trails a mile or so farther. The stones of the lodge were almost obscured by the moss clinging to it and the vines dangling from its eaves. The trees and underbrush crowded close about it, rattling in a rising wind that whipped the riders into the musty, dank building. The lodge stank of old fires and body odor.

"So much for the life of royalty," Juli mused. *"Henrie, baby, you need a gardener and a housekeeper in the worst way."*

"Yes, indeed," her host replied. *"If we're to keep coming here, we will need to make it more hospitable. On the other hand, I wanted a wild place where my friends and I could feel ourselves wild men, at ease with our hounds and horses and hawks and content to eat our catch and speak loudly and indiscriminately and stay up until all hours gorging ourselves and passing gas and giving no offense to the ladies of the house or setting bad examples for the youngsters."*

"You're concerned about the opinions of women and children in your house when you're the King?"

"It's a bit of a bother, to be sure, but I am King of all of my subjects and therefore their servant. Women and children must be considered as well as men for where do men come from but women? All children are future men and the mothers of men and are therefore worthy of my utmost concern and care. Aye, I could almost wish there were a woman here now to minister to the cooking of the meat. My men are rough cooks indeed."

But no sooner had he given form to that thought than the wind blew up so loud and moaning that it gushed through the drafts in the hall, tossing the rushes about, whisking away the dense cobwebs, and rattling the shields hanging up from the walls. So lowly it moaned, so shrilly it whined, so loudly it roared that Julianne, who wanted to ask her host if they had weather like that real often in those parts, literally couldn't hear herself think.

Then suddenly, as if the wind had blown the pilings out from under the house, the whole earth shifted, knocking the King and all his men back a notch. Henrie's dogs yelped and came yowling to huddle by his feet.

That was when the wind burst the fastened door and smashed it open to reveal a visitor.

Julianne screamed a little scream inside the King's head and he almost gave it voice, but instead caught himself, saying, *"I maun stop that. Scares the dogs when I do that, but I vow by the blood, that is the ugliest creature I've ever seen."*

Julianne was staring through the King's eyes at the visitor towering above him. It seemed to be female from her lopsided, low-hung dugs and her filthy, lice-infested skirts. She stood as tall as the roof tree in the middle of the room and she was so big around she had to come in the door sideways. Her teeth were as long and twice as brown as the stakes Henrie and the other men had tethered their horses to and her nose looked like a mace, bulbous and bristling with warts and hairs.

"A fiend from hell!" cried Jamie Lochlan, and that worthy led the exodus of the other huntsmen out the back window of the hall, leaving the King and his terrified animals alone to face the apparition.

"A fiend from hell indeed," Henrie thought despairingly.

Julianne's deafness, fresher in her mind than its cure, had taught her something of what it was like to be an outcast and she was not so ready as she might have been at one time to be repulsed. *"She certainly could use a makeover,"* she said, half whimpering, to her kingly self, *"but maybe she's just a poor sad street person—uh, trail person—looking for shelter from that awful wind. You're not just the King of the pretty people, you know, Henrie. And look how fast they deserted you. Invite the poor thing in. Offer her a place to sit and something to eat."*

Henrie didn't get the time. The creature lumbered up to him like an elephant (though Henrie had never seen an elephant, Julianne supplied the image) and intoned in a rasping and nasal voice flatter than a Bronx cheer, "Some meat, some meat, ye King Henrie, some meat ye gie to me!"

And Henrie, who had had no supper himself, lifted the spit with the by now rather charred deer on it and was preparing to lay it on the table to slice her off a piece when the deer, spit and all, was snatched from his hands and the creature gobbled it down faster than Julianne could have eaten a corn dog.

King Henrie's mind was full of images of his arms and legs sticking out of that ugly mouth as those great teeth broke his backbone. His head was light and his knees felt like noodles. *"Offer her the other deer,"* Julianne prompted, more hesitantly this time. *"She's obviously famished."* The deer wasn't enough, however, for Henrie had no more than started toward it when a great hand with every finger as big as Henrie's forearm reached down and scooped up the deer and devoured it with horrible gnashings and mucousy snufflings, the blood dripping down the monster's chin the whole while.

When she had eaten the second deer, the woman eyed Henrie indignantly again, as if he had only given her two watercress sandwiches with the crusts cut off after she'd been working on a chain gang for a week. "I've given you our catch for the day," Henrie said. "What other meat's in this house, lady, that ye're na welcome tee?"

"Kill your steed and serve him up to me," the creature roared down at him, pointing to the door.

Henrie's horse neighed and leaped, pawing the air, his eyes wild with fright, sides heaving, and came down again with a crack of bone against wood as his leg hit the tree and he screamed again, falling to his knees. "My poor Berry," Henrie cried and rushed to the horse's side. The horse looked up at him with a pitiful rolling eye.

Juli told him, *"I know the giant doesn't look it, but she is a human being and your subject, Henrie. She is so huge, it must take an enormous quantity of food to fill her. And the horse has broken his leg. You don't have any way to fix it, do you?"*

"And besides she'll eat me alive if I don't," Henrie said and with tears, half of fear and half of remorse, raised his sword to do the deed, lowered it, and raised it again.

"Come on, Henrie, I'll bet you've hesitated less when you've had to kill a man," Julianne said. She was originally a farm girl and tended to be practical about animals. Henrie's arm fell and the light died in Berry's eyes.

Henrie dragged the carcass to the door and tried not to watch as the giantess plunged into the horse's belly, eating everything but the skin and bones with choking gulps until, within a matter of minutes, she was sitting back wiping gobbets of raw horse flesh from her mouth with the back of her massive hand.

She opened her mouth and a blast of charnel-house breath hit him like a blow. *"Maybe she's going to say thanks and goodbye,"* Julianne suggested.

But she said, "Mair meat, mair meat, ye King Henrie! Mair meat ye gie to me."

"But she's eaten *it all,"* Henrie groaned, to himself as he thought, and Juli said, *"Then remind her of it, but be polite. She's probably had to face a lot of rejection in her life."*

So he said again, since he was too frightened to think of new and original repartee, "And what meat's i' this house, lady, that ye're na welcome tee?"

And she looked down at the two hounds that slunk shivering and slavering on his heels so close they were like to trip him and his heart sank as she said, "O ye do slay your gude gray houndes and bring them a' to me."

"They've been with me since they were puppies," Henrie said and Juli felt the love and fear pound him like the tide. The dogs whined and cried piteously.

"If you don't kill them, she may eat them alive, Henrie. I know it's not kind and the dogs have been your friends for so many years and they love and trust you and it's a betrayal but see how scared they are? You can't fight her— you shouldn't fight her. Do you think her life has been as easy even as the lives of your dogs? I'll bet big as she is she's like Frankenstein and can't show her face for people trying to kill her. Dogs probably bite her and chase her everywhere. Henrie, how can you, with all your privilege, know what it's like for her?"

He didn't think anything else but he looked away as he plunged his knife into the neck of one dog and then the other so quickly that they died without another whine. Bitterly, he bowed and let the monster woman scoop up first one and then the other of his faithful hunting dogs and with much slurping and smacking of lips over bloodied fangs destroy their bodies.

Julianne knew she was onto something when she compared the woman to Frankenstein, even if Henrie didn't understand the allusion since Mary Shelley wouldn't invent the monster for another several centuries. She had some idea of how the monster woman must feel, ugly, stupid because no one was brave enough or kind enough to teach her anything and instead abandoned her totally to survive by her own devices. How could such a woman be expected to know how Henrie felt about his horse and dogs when she had probably never had a friend in her life?

"Mair meat," the monster intoned. "Mair meat, ye King Henrie, mair meat ye gie to me."

"No friends, eh?" Henrie addressed the tail end of the thoughts of Juli's that filtered to him. *"Then she may as well be mine since I've lost or been forced to betray all of my others."* But aloud he asked with some sarcasm but mostly sadness, "And what's the meat in this house, lady, that I hae left to gie?"

"O ye do fell your gay goss hawks and bring them a' to me."

There was only the one, up on the rafters, but as Henrie called it, the monster snatched it out of the air, breaking its neck and eating it, its tiny bones crunching like popcorn and the bloody feathers floating gently down from her mouth.

"Now," Henrie thought when she opened her mouth again and he saw with horror the feathers sticking to her tether-stake teeth, *"I must slay her or be eaten myself for there's no thing of flesh left in this house but me."*

"You mustn't jump to conclusions. Don't you want to hear what she has to say?"

"In a word, no, but I have no choice."

"Some drink, some drink, ye King Henrie! Some drink ye gie to me!"

"That's not so hard," Juli said.

"I suppose it isn't really, but I sair wanted to get drunk, should I survive this experience," the King said, *"or else have something to marinate myself in should she decide on me for the next course."* Aloud he said, "And what drink's i' this house, lady, that ye're na welcome tee?"

"O ye sew up your horse's hide and bring a drink to me," the woman commanded.

"Sew!" Henrie exclaimed. *"Sew! Who does she think she is? Why can't she just drink it out of a barrel like any ordinary giant? I can't sew!"*

"Yes, you can," said Juli, who did know how. *"Use a piece of the bird bone and some of the sinews left on the bone. All primitive people know about stuff like that."* But the job was slippery, sticky, and gruesome and King Henrie's hands were cold and blue where they were not red by the time he had the sack sewed up of bloody hide and passed a pipe from the wine barrel into the skin for the misshapen woman to drink from.

All of his pains were as unnoticed by her as those he'd suffered from the loss of his horse, hounds, and hawk. She gulped the wine down in one long chugalug, draining the skin, and belched, wiping her great yawning gob, then said, "A bed, a bed, ye King Henrie! A bed ye make to me!"

"There's not a bed in this hall," Henrie thought. *"We were going to sleep on the rushes but they're all covered with blood and manure and entrails now."*

Aloud he said, "And what's the bed i' this house, lady, that ye're na welcome tee?"

Though her eyes were crooked and red and set in holes as black as mine pits, they evidently saw very well that there was no regular bed to be had for she replied, "O ye maun pu' the green heather, and make a bed to me."

"She may be friendless as I seem to think but she's used to servants," Henrie thought grimly, but he braved the wind and pulled the heather, great double armfuls of it and lugged it back indoors and laid it in the least nasty corner by the fire, kicking aside the fouled rushes and laying down half the ground cover from the forest until he judged that it was enough for her.

"It's going to just smoosh out as soon as she lies down," Julianne told him. *"Don't you have any kind of a coverlet or something to lay down for her? It's cold in here too."*

"Freezing to death seems an easier way than what I've feared all night and if I don't volunteer, the demon will

demand it anyway," Henrie said, and spread his cloak over the rushes and invited the beastly woman to lie down.

She had no intention of letting him off so easily however. He was not going to freeze after all. "Now swear, now swear, ye King Henrie, to take me for your bride," she said.

"Oh, God Forbid!" King Henrie said aloud and Juli hissed silently, *"Henrie, for pity's sake, get a grip on yourself,"* and he cried, but silently as well, *"No, this is absolutely out of the question! God forbid that e'er the like betide that that fiend from hell should lay down beside me."*

"She might stink and you may catch a few bugs but she'd be pretty warm," Juli pointed out. *"Take the outside. If you absolutely can't stand it or if you hear your friends coming, you can always get up again."*

"If I'm alive," he replied, but he lay down beside the monster, who smiled cavernously, grunted, and, making the floor tremble again, began to snore.

Henrie was so exhausted from all the killing, hauling, sewing, fear, and just plain being depressed about having to butcher his favorite animals that he didn't have any more energy and fell into a deep sleep.

In his sleep he felt the sunlight streaking through the open front door warm the side of his face, but the silence was what finally woke him. No more wind howled through the night, no more snores rumbled the earth. Instead, warm sunlight and soft zephyr breezes tickled his whiskers and blew away all of the stench of the night's activities, replacing it with the fragrance of the fresh heather and wildflowers.

Moreover, the great weight beside him had lifted. He turned, reluctantly, to see where the giantess was and what she was up to. In her place, between himself and the wall, lay the most beautiful woman he had ever seen.

"I've outlasted the nightmare and come into a dream," Henrie said and Julianne said, *"Hmph! You wouldn't have bitched and moaned so much about killing your horse and dogs for her!"*

"Aye, she's worth any amount of trouble," Henrie said, and aloud he said, clearing his throat, "Oh, weel is me. How lang will this last wi' me?"

And the beauty at his side rolled over and said in the monster's flat Bronx cheer voice, "E'en till the day ye die. For I was witched to a ghastly shape all by my stepdame's skill till I should meet with a courteous knight wad gie me a' my will."

"Of course you were," Henrie said, twirling a lock of her golden hair around his finger, and though he thought she was very beautiful Julianne realized the girl just looked like her embodied self on one of her better days.

Julianne wondered if it was time to twist the ring yet but Henrie, remembering the monster shape, didn't make any moves on the beautiful lady until his false friends returned later in the day with reinforcements, to retrieve what was left of his body as they thought.

Henrie and the girl told them what had happened and he was promised the pick of the litter from Jamie Lochlan's pregnant bitch and the best foal in Lord Buchan's stable, and everyone remarked about how all a man really needed to survive sometimes was enough gold to have the right things and enough charity to give them away. And they leered at the girl standing by Henrie's side. And she smiled back, linking her arm with that of her true love, and delicately spat out the feather that still lodged on the tip of her pointed rosy tongue.

CHAPTER XXII

▲▲▲

The Snail broke down a few miles into Glacier Lake National Park, around midnight.

"No big deal," the driver said. "Just a little overheated, I think. Thermostat blew and the fan belt gave out and I thought maybe one of you guys could hike with me down the road to the waterfall to get some water for the radiator. I sent a relay message to headquarters on the CB and the owner's mom should be driving down from Eugene in her station wagon to bring a new fan belt and thermostat. Oh, yeah, and a jack. I forgot ours this time. So maybe you guys will want to set out signal flares. I don't think you can build campfires around here but you've all got your sleeping bags so you should be okay. You can stay on the bus till Mrs. Tortuga arrives but then you gotta pile out so we can work on this heap. Oh, yeah, one more thing. Anybody got a flashlight?

The storyteller produced one from an extremely battered Mexican basket bag. She hoped when she got to the border she'd be able to replace the bag.

"Thanks, that's great. Anybody got some cookies? We had emergency rations stowed under my seat but I got the munchies."

Mrs. Tortuga arrived two hours later. In the meantime, there were no lights for fear of running down the battery. The only lights to be seen were the stars and moon, high above the fog that boiled over from the river basins and streambeds between the mountains. The passengers who had been reading had to stop reading and the passengers who had been playing cards could hardly do it by braille.

"Now you see here, this is just what I mean," the story-teller said to the group around her. She said it in a kind of declaiming voice, though, so that everybody could hear. "In times past, when something like this happened, people would all sing and everybody would know the songs. Any-body here know any songs?"

Only the peepers and a few night birds answered her. All of the people shook their heads in the darkness, which produced a lot of rustling but nothing in the way of socia-bility.

"In olden times, people thought songs would ward off evil, but of course, we don't believe in that kinda stuff now, do we?" the storyteller asked.

"I, uh—I know the tune to Duck Soul's new hit," some-body said from a dim corner of the bus. "Only I can't quite understand the words. But the tune goes like bop-bop-bop-bop-bop-bop-bop BA!"

"Jimmy, honey," a deep female voice drawled, "from what I can make out, the words are about a mass mur-derer hacking a town to death at night while they sleep— nice beat but if you did try to sing it I'd freak out. Besides, you can't carry a tune either." To the storyteller she said, "So, what's all this stuff you're telling those people? I keep catching something about time travelers and fairies and shit but is it all made up or is there some stuff happening in, like, you know, the real world?"

"Well, yes, yes, there was. After the Queen of Fairies, who was also the Debauchery Devil, Torchy Burns, turned herself into an orange kitty cat to spy on the Randolphs and Gussie, who was possessed by the ghost of Sir Walter Scott, in case you didn't catch that, that devil-woman real-ized she had made herself some serious miscalculations. Her boss, the Chairdevil, had plenty of reason to be peeved with her. Now, Torchy was not especially a worryin' kind of entity, but as the months rolled on, she saw that her soft heart (she liked to think of herself as the original prototype for the whore with a heart of gold) had led her astray again. She honestly had thought the singers were going to *have a much tougher time getting from one song to the next.*

"The reason she miscalculated, I reckon, is because of what your psychiatrists and psychologists and folks in the counseling-type professions call 'projection.' Any of you here not been in therapy?"

"Can't afford it, lady. I do sweat lodges, but I never heard of projection except when you're maybe acting or something."

"It's a little bit like that, I guess. What it means is that you think whatever you would do is what somebody else would do—you sort of lay your own way of behaving on them. Like with some people, if they got a rovin' eye and are playin' around on their lover, they get powerfully jealous over nothin' because they figure if they're playin' around, then naturally their lover is doing the same thing, and they spend all their time tryin' to catch 'em at it."

"Oh, yeah. I heard about that."

"Anyway, when Torchy Burns changed the spell around to suit herself and gave them the out with the ring, she figured they'd never think to use it. Her idea of what would happen was that they would do like her and when they found themselves in somebody else's body, they'd be rude guests and just push that other person entirely out of the way. But she also guessed that that wouldn't be a good thing for them to do because while they were in that other person's body during the other person's lifetime, the visiting spirits would get completely lost and forget all about what they were there for. They'd be out of place in the old times too, since they wouldn't know what ballad they were in or be the same sex or anything, and would act so crazy the other people in the ballad might even think they were bewitched or something. She figured they'd never even get to use the ring. But of course, it didn't work out like that. Bein' a devil, she probably never had to say, 'I'm of two minds about this situation,' and wouldn't realize that sometimes people really are. Any one person has room to be lots of different things and lots of different people within them, though most of us don't get to try more than a tiny part of who we can be.*

"The musicians, who were real used to being guests in other people's houses, blended right in and fitted their spirits to the needs of their host spirits without even knowing how they did it. They took their cues from their hosts and fitted themselves to the character and the situation so well that the hosts in most of the ballads never even realized there was somebody there who wasn't originally part of them.

"Of course, in the case of Brose Fairchild, it was a little different, since his hostess was what we would call psychic and what people back then called a witch."

▲▲▲

Torchy Burns's little joke with the ballad ashes provided the biggest shock of all for Brose Fairchild. *"Hey, man,"* he thought when he arrived in his appointed body. *"I'm not only a chick, I'm white."*

"Not white enough," answered the grim womanly voice that shared his current vocal cords.

"Hey, babe, this is a whole lot whiter than my usual," Brose answered.

The other parts of the woman's mind probed at the part that was Brose and she asked, *"Be you an elf or a demon sent to succor me?"*

"Not exactly. I be Brose Fairchild from Austin, Texas, and since I seem to be inside o' you I don't think I could succor you if I wanted to without it bein' pretty awkward, but if somethin's buggin' you, you could talk to me. Lots of kids talk to me. You knocked up?"

"Knocked up?"

"In a family way? Preggers? Havin' mah bay-bee?" It was a logical guess, being the main kind of peculiarly female trouble with which he was acquainted. In these olden days, as he could guess was where he found himself judging from the dump she lived in, folks didn't have stuff like the pill or even Trojans.

"No, praise be to my granddam who taught me herb lore for such ailments. But I am forsaken. You were not here, I suppose, a moment ago, when this came?"

She picked up a letter from off of her bed. Brose saw

that the little sack of brush she used for a pillow was all
wet. Her eyes felt scratchy dry now, however.

"Dearest Barbara," the letter said, "I'm not good
enough for you. I am in awe of the wisdom of you dark
woods folk and we had wonderful, wild times together.
Your house and lands are tempting too, but I find that I
cannot sleep for thinking of Ellen, who is fair, like me,
and therefore a much more suitable match, you see?
She'd fit in with the family portraits so much better. I
know this is a caddish thing to do after all we've shared
(heh heh) but I just thought I'd let you know. Please
don't wax wrothy or do anything rash. Love, Your Own
(Formerly) Sweet William."

"*Asshole,*" Brose said. "*Reminds me of some pickers I
used to know. Hell,*" he said after thinking it over a little
more, "*Reminds me of me.*"

"*So you see, demon, you've caught me at a bad moment. It seems I will be going through my days with no
true love, and I rather thought every maiden was entitled
to one.*"

"*Your name's Barbara?*"

"*Aye.*"

"*Look, Babs, I got a hot tip for you. Guys like that are
a dime a dozen. You seem like a pretty classy lady. This
house yours?*"

"*It is mine, from my mother's mother.*"

"*And you got a little piece of land too?*"

"*I do.*"

"*Then the hell with him.*"

"*Oh, demon, would you do that for me, really?*"

"*Nah, I mean, forget him. Get along without him.
Sounds like a jerk anyway.*"

"*But how can I?*"

"*Lots of ladies where I'm from do just fine on their
own. What'd you just tell me? You got property. Look in
your mirror.*"

She bent over a tub of clear water she'd drawn for
drinking purposes. "*Hey, you are one fine-lookin' woman.
Black eyes, nice tan, good body, and a way about you.
Girl, what are you moanin' for over one measly little pale-*

*faced no-account no-class ball-less wonder who hasn't even
got the nerve to come tell you in person when he wants to
drop you? Baby, you are just too much woman for a man
like that anyway."*

"You're right," she said, staring not so much at her
reflection as into it for a few moments while her thoughts
spun. *"How can he reject me so? Why does he not love me
enough to keep his promise? Am I too brisk? Why does it
matter that I am brown? Once he thought me fair enough
for him."* Then she sat down and picked up the letter
again, staring at it hard so that Brose felt tears trickling
in the edge of her eyes. *"What shall I write?"* she asked.

"How about 'fuck off and die,' " he suggested.

"How do you spell that?" she asked, and scrawled the
message on the back. When she was done she rolled the
letter and walked out into the field, where some of her
neighbors were sharecropping her land. Brose, whose
body was often overweight and stocky, was delighted at
how gracefully she moved, like the deer that came to ruin
his garden regularly every spring, but with a ferocity
about her determination not to show her weakness that
was more like a mountain lion's. A man looked up from
his work, glowering into the sun a little, suspicious even
as he tugged his forelock to her. His woman ignored her
and kept chopping weeds while other children peeked
and giggled and whispered to each other. To the youngest
child, a boy of about seven, Barbara said, "Take this to
William Graham in the toun." She handed him a coin to
seal the deal. The child took off at a run.

All that afternoon Barbara worked in her own garden,
planting, hoeing, weeding, gathering the herbs and flowers for hanging to dry from her rafters. Just before dark
the boy returned with the letter still in his hand. He pretended to have run all the way but Brose noted the sack
tied to his waist, the purchase he'd made with Barbara's
coin, no doubt.

"The gentleman says you're to come to him, miss.
He's taken terrible sick and says you're a' can cure him.
He says you'll know what he means."

Barbara smiled. "Does he noo?"

Brose said, *"See there, Babs baby. The dude can't live without you."*

"You don't understand, demon. He wants me to come and give back his faith."

"His what? I'd think if anybody's lost faith in anybody else it'd be you losing it in him."

"We plighted our troth," she told him wearily. *"He begged me for months. I knew somehow all along that it would not work, you know. Not, as he says, because he is fair and I am brown, but because my living is earned not just from things of the soil but from things of the spirit, because I read and spin and keep myself to myself but say what I think when I am amang others and he cares only for hunting and hawking and being with his fellows and says that I am rude to speak out so, though he also says he admires it in me. I think he is not yet weaned, sometimes. I think that he wishes me to mother him but also that he wishes to unsettle me as a rebellious child unsettles its mother. He could not stand it that I could pass his letter of un-love off so lightly and now he seeks to make me face him."*

"So he can break you down and see you cry, right? Yeah, that's probably it okay. I used to play that little game myself, just to see how tough a lady really was. That's why I like bein' around critters better. You kick them, they bite you. Fair enough. You gonna bite this dude?"

She shook her head once and he felt the heart within her sink with sorrow. *"I knew he wasn't suitable. I didn't want to become involved with him. But he followed me and flattered me and did all he could to please me until it seemed foolish to give in to my reservations. If I tried to mention them, even gently, he seemed wounded and offended, until I thought, I have never been happy in love so perhaps I need instruction. So I gave in, and giving in, I began to love him. It will be hard to see him without touching him, to speak to him without calling him by the endearments I've come to use, to have him speak my name and not the endearments I'm accustomed to from him."*

"You got the blues bad, Babs," he said and hummed an eight-bar melody line.

"That's strange music. Is it demonic?"

"Nah, it just feels that way. Guess you might say it's what folks use where I'm from to get rid of their demons, or at least make 'em feel at home. Goes with situations like yours."

"Are there words?"

"Lots of words, but you can make up words to fit the situation and you can play to fit the situation. You don't own a guitar do you?"

"What might that be?"

"A musical instrument. Came over from Spain I think. Maybe you folks would have lutes or something."

"Harps, perhaps?"

"Yeah, there's blues harps but you play 'em with your mouth."

"Can you show me?"

He put her hands to her mouth and made sounds like a blues harmonica with her lips. It wasn't as good as when he did it at home and he said, *"Loosen up, baby. You gonna lose this man for your skin, you might's well get some of the spiritchal benefits thereof, know what I mean? Now lissen here and we'll sing you one."* And he sang her one of his favorites, "The Hootchy Kootchy Man."

"Is that your true name, demon? Hootchy Kootchy Man?"

Brose laughed. *"Might say it's one of 'em, yeah. Let's get our beauty sleep now, sugar. We want to look cool tomorrow when we see that man, just so he'll see what he's missin' out on."*

She undressed and washed in a tub of clear water and Brose surveyed their mutual charms before she slid back into her night shift and into bed. *"Umm, um!"* he said. *"That man is a pure fool. No doubt about it."*

The next day after a leisurely bath and washing her waist-length black hair with herb-scented soap she'd made earlier that spring, and dressing in her long green dress with the red and yellow embroidery on the bodice, she set off on the road to town.

Brose sang her other blues songs he remembered, using her husky alto voice. *"You're a natural, babe,"* he said. *"Now it's your turn to make you up one."*

There was no one to hear but the ewes and the lambs so she tried one.

> "I am a brown brown girl
> My eyes are black as sloes
> I'm as brisk as a nighttime nightingale
> As wild as a forest doe."

"Real nice," Brose said. *"Now the chorus."*

> "And I am. And everybody *knows* I am
> I'm a bonny brown girl don't give a *damn*
> For no false-hearted man."

"You're cookin'," he said. *"Keep it rollin'."*

> "My love has sent me a letter
> He sent it from yonder town
> He says he cannot fancy me
> Just because I am so brown."

And together they sang the chorus again.

> "And I am. And everybody *knows* I am
> I'm a bonny brown girl don't give a *damn*
> For no false-hearted man."

They kept making up verses as they drew near the town but they stopped to dance (Brose showed her some rock and roll moves that totally amazed the cows) and picked flowers that she wove into garlands as she sang:

> "Y'know I sent that man back his letter again
> For his love I valu'd not
> Whether that he could fancy me
> Or whether he would not

'Cause I am. Wheeooo—oo-ooo! And everybody *knows* I
  am
I'm a bonny brown girl don't give a *damn*
For no false-hearted man."

On the outskirts of town, people started staring, and
Brose said, *"Better cool it,"* but held her head high and
proud and she walked as if she didn't have a care in the
world, Brose's sly smile twitching the edges of her
mouth. *"Okay,"* he said. *"Where does this mental giant
live anyway?"*

The house was one of the largest in town and had a big
iron door knocker that Barbara brought up and let fall. A
slender elderly woman with fine features and watering
blue eyes answered the door. Her mouth slitted when she
saw Barbara and she turned her eyes away, but opened
the door wide. With much swishing of silken skirts she
climbed the stairs, showed Barbara to a certain door,
then left. Barbara pushed open the door and stepped inside. A man lay in the bed, his hair almost as white as the
linen pillowcase beneath his head.

Three other men were in the room but two of them
were talking in low voices by the window while the other
watched from an upholstered chair to one side of the bed
head.

"His friends," Barbara thought to Brose. *"They hate
me. They told him I was a witch."*

"Hmph," Brose said. *"Probably just want in your pant-
ies themselves. Ignore 'em."*

She walked past them as if they weren't there to the
head of the bed and looked down into the man's face. He
opened his eyes as if he had only just realized she was
there. "Hello, William," she said.

"Barbara, at last you've come. I thought you would
come last night or this morning. It isn't such a long way
it should take you until—" He had risen on one elbow as
his voice rose into a whine but now he sank back onto his
pillow, flopping elegant fingers toward the man at the
bedside and asking, "When *is* it, Humphrey? I've been so
terribly ill. I swear I am dying."

"You do look awful," she said, not answering his implied questions. "Your face is rather swollen, William. You look like a squirrel with its cheeks full of nuts."

"I'll be damned," Brose told her. *"Man's got the mumps."*

"What's that?"

"The mumps. It's a disease kids get. Affects the glands. Just makes kids sick for a little while but on a grown man like this it gets him where he lives." When he explained it, Barbara got an evil grin on her face and then started laughing.

"Beg pardon," she said, hiccuping to the man in the chair, and lowered herself onto the chair arm doubled up with laughing.

"What's so funny?" William demanded.

"You are. You seduced me, flouted and scorned me and, from what I hear, half the women in the town before me, and now you're after another and want me to bless you on your way. But there is justice in the world and you lie before me receiving your reward."

"Barbara, I *loved* you," he said, his voice high and squeaky in his sore throat.

"Stop laughin', baby, you s'posed to act impressed now," Brose said.

"So you said," she answered William. "In that case, I'll give you back your token and two of my own for good measure." She pulled three gold rings from her fingers, and one by one dropped them on his bed. She got so into pulling rings she reached for the twisted wire one on her middle finger and Brose stopped her with a *"Not that one, babe. It's magic."* She was fortunately the kind of girl he didn't have to offer any other explanation to. To William she said of the rings on the bed, "Here. Maybe these will help pay for the funeral."

"Barbara!"

"You'll be wanting your faith and your troth back, I suppose, to make peace before you die."

"I—if that is the way you're going to behave, I should say so."

"Of course, you'll be needing them if you wish to

make an honest woman out of the blonde lady you mentioned in your letter so that she can be your widow."

William set his mouth in much the way that his mother's had been set and closed his eyes as if her attitude pained him too much to bear.

"Very well, then." She took a long piece of bone from her pocket.

"What's with the chopstick?" Brose asked.

"It's my wand," she said.

"Like the fairy fucking godmother?" he asked. *"What're them little squiggles carved on it?"*

"Runes," she told him and, bending over William, touched him with the wand. He flinched, but all she did was stroke him with the wand and said, "My faith and troth I give back to thee so thy soul may have rest."

"Do you have to put it like that?" he asked. "I said I felt badly enough to die—and I must say I feel even worse the way you've been carrying on, but I didn't say I was actually going to die. Your problem, Barbara, is that you've always taken everything so seriously. Can't you forget and forgive? Give a man a little space to breathe? No wonder a man gets sick with you taking his natural urges in such a deadly way."

"I wouldn't wonder but she's put a curse on you, Will," said one of the men at the window.

"Then she's cursed Elinor Elgin's wee brother and sister the same," the other man said. "They look just like him, though not so deathly ill. It's a wonder she hasn't cursed Elinor as well."

"Oh, I'm not likely to forget your betrayal, William, nor to forgive you," she said. "I wouldn't want to be wooed with soft words again. I need no vengeance, however, since the ailment you've caught will be sufficient to make you rue the very day that you were born. I will promise you this however. I do think that though you've broken faith with me so that I may never trust another man, I'll do as much for you as any maiden might her somewhat-truer love. I faithfully promise that I'll dance upon your grave for twelvemonth and a day thereby lining your coffin with rose leaves and heralding your arrival into the hereafter. How will that be?"

He groaned and turned his face to the wall.

Since Barbara seemed neither inclined to die nor to get laid any time in the near future, Brose's spirit stayed with her and learned from her the song of an ancestress who had been similarly betrayed by a winsome youth who had a taste for blondes.

"But this grandma of yours went off the deep end and stabbed the girl and then the guy beheaded her? You people make Frankie and Johnny look like lightweights." He learned the song from her, wondering if somewhere in the Wizard Michael Scott's fission of souls theory, his Barbara wasn't a chip off the old brown block. She had more class than her grandma, though. Brose helped her with her stock and showed her a few veterinary tricks he had picked up on the ranch. She showed him uses for herbs and mushrooms, lichen and fungi her grandmother had taught her. He liked her a lot. She was tough and smart and, left alone, could even be funny and playful. He wondered what it would have been like if they'd each had a body and then decided it probably wouldn't have worked because he never would have gotten to know her so well. She reminded him a little of Anna Mae, but he couldn't say how much exactly, because he only felt her expressions from the inside, never saw them from without. But he loved brushing her long black mane and bathing her sleek brown body with its crosshatch of scars from briers and thistles and its hands rough and dirty from work around her place.

The longer he stayed, the more peaceful she grew too, the less mad at everything. The people who worked for her started to look up and almost smile when she came out to the field to bring them water or a loaf of bread to split for lunch, and accepted her when she worked alongside them.

The townfolk were something else again. Though William did not die, and lived to marry his Elinor (Barbara had sent them a garland of garlic for a wedding present, to prevent further illness, as her note said), neither he nor his friends forgave her and spread rumors about how she was cruel and a witch and had cursed William first to die and then to the more lingering death of an unhappy marriage. After his illness, he could no longer comfortably sit a horse for prolonged periods and his fellows missed his company.

He did not linger at home, however. Within six months Elinor grew as tight-lipped as his mother so that when his bride spoke to him it was as if she were pulling stitches one by one from a winter garment. By the time two years had passed, it appeared she would remain barren. But at the end of three years, with no kinder attitude toward her husband, she bore a son that was the spitting image of the dark-haired and florid-faced man who had once sat in the chair at William's bed head.

A few months after, William began suffering mysterious stomach pains and this time he did die, according to rumor, still calling for Barbara's forgiveness and for his friends to be kind to her.

She walked to the town church for his funeral, but in spite of her threat, she didn't feel like dancing or singing. She took another braid of garlic for the grave but the expressions of the widow and her mother-in-law and all the other townsfolk kept her from stepping forward.

"You've a lot of nerve coming here, you hard-hearted witch," snarled a fair-haired, cherubic-faced boy who was Elinor's younger brother.

Another boy picked up a stone and threw it at her and the florid-faced man who stood beside the grieving widow said, "That's enough, boys. Not at a funeral. She'll get her punishment in hell."

"Goddamn, babe, what do they want from you?" Brose asked when they had finally arrived back home, bruised from the stones and tired from walking briskly, if not running. *"You gave him what he wanted, you let him marry who he wanted, you were a class act through the whole damn business."*

"They want me dead," she said. *"And they want me to bear the blame. And whether I will it or no, I suspect that I shall."*

And that day they said no more, but the older children of her tenant family did not accompany their parents to work. "Mr. Nixon has given them work, ma'am, and is paying good wages," said the woman. "We're only staying the fortnight." The two youngest ones were singing a new song when she went to take them water, which they refused, though they stopped singing.

"A pretty tune," Barbara wheedled. "Come, sing it for me."

"You'll like it not, ma'am," the girl said.

"But I like it already."

"You promise no matter what not to beat us?" the boy asked.

Brose thought, *"Look out, baby, here it comes."*

But Barbara, the smile still on her face, said, *"Better to know than not."*

The children sang, hesitantly at first.

> "It fell about the Martinmass times
> When green leaves all were fallin'
> Sweet William on his deathbed lay
> For the love of Bawbee Allen."

"That ain't fair," Brose said when all the verses were sung. *"It even says he was after your money."*

"That's not unusual," she said with wry amusement.

Brose wasn't amused. *"I remember that song and that ain't all of it."* She had to ask him the rest of it three times before he would tell her and then she smiled. *"My world must be crueler than hell from the way you act, demon. Come, I'll show you now how a deathbed's to be made. I suspect I may have need of it soon."*

They had no need of her preparations that night or the next or for yet another night, but in the meantime, her sheep died mysteriously in her field, her tenants left, and on the last night she drank water from her well and immediately a cramp seized her belly and sweat broke out on her forehead.

Brose had time to help her lay herself on the bed as she'd showed him and to twist the ring thrice around.

When he found himself back all by his lonesome in the fluid haze of the in-between world, he looked for her, hoping she was a ghost too and would stay with him. But when he called for her, the only response he felt was from the churchyard. Someone had made the song come true by planting a rosebush on William's grave and its little red flowers crept toward the place outside the churchyard where the bastards had buried his Barbara. She was still fighting back though, tough little bitch that she was. A blackberry bramble held the roses at bay and within the year, Brose knew, would take them over.

CHAPTER XXIII

▲▲▲

Mrs. Tortuga had come, bearing cookies and lite beer for
the passengers, as well as the required maintenance parts
for the bus. Meanwhile, the passengers took their sleeping
bags and retreated, shivering, to the edge of a "scenic look-
out" point, where they huddled close together, munching
cookies and sharing coffee from the thermoses of those who
had had the foresight to fill up at the last truck stop.

"So, while all this wild stuff is going on in olden times,
seven years is passing on the home front, right? How did
they handle getting to stay in the country? How did they
make a living?"

"I hate to admit this in open company, but they sort of
broke the law a little. After all, what had it done for them
except to support the bad guys against them? The work
permit thing was helped somewhat by the laws changing in
Europe that made almost indefinite stays possible. Faron
would busk part of the day, playing Lazarus the banjo or
the Gypsy's fiddle on the streets in Edinburgh to earn a
little money while Ellie researched. Her folks back home
sold Faron's car and rented out their house for more than
the mortgage payment, which made for a little income too.
They stayed at the Carrs' lodgings, which didn't normally
bring in money during the winter months, when the Carrs
often visited friends in the West Indies. So Mrs. Carr arranged with Gussie to trade caretaking and housekeeping
for rent, which was a major expense.

"Everything seemed to settle down for a little while.

Each month brought more songs, trickling in sometimes note by note, sometimes two or three whole songs in an hour or so. 'King Henrie' came in November, and later that month they got a bonus of first another transformation song, 'Alison Gross,' and then 'The Marriage of Sir Gawain,' which is about a knight of King Arthur's who voluntarily marries an ugly monster of a woman, and then all of the King Arthur songs one after another like a string of popbeads fitting into one another, and then 'The Laily Worm and the Mackrell of the Sea,' until just about all the transformation songs known in the British Isles had turned up. That kept Faron in plenty of material for the Christmas season, even though the first notes of 'The Brown Girl' had not yet come because that song took a long time to end and to hook up with the other songs that were related.

"The research was goin' real well too. The librarians got to know Faron and had heard of his uncle and for a while, even let him bring back to the Carrs' some of the common, popular books about Scottish history and so on, until the orange cat peed on the book one day when she got locked in accidentally, as they thought.

"That cat was one frustrated critter. It had come to the farmhouse to spy on them, but they were all so pooped by the end of the day trying to find songs that they didn't talk about plans much or reveal anything important. Finally, Torchy ended up having to turn herself into a German library-sciences exchange student named Miss Fahrenheit to keep any track of Faron at all, and then she ended up getting herself stuck back in the stacks of the accounting books for the Kingdom of Scotland from decades past. Once she tried to disguise herself as a tourist who wanted to get her palm read, so she could check up on her Gypsies, but the Expediency Devil, who was teaching the Gypsies time management and more efficient ways to process and smuggle their drugs, spied her almost at once. The fact was, her magic was pretty well occupied with maintaining the interference she had cast into Wizard Michael's spell.

"Meanwhile, every day he was at the library, Faron Randolph uncovered some new piece of information that *led the banjo to remember yet another song—the Robin Hood ballads poured in around New Years, and all through the month of February, when he found a book of poetry the Gypsies had overlooked when they looted the Edinburgh library. Later on, Ellie took a graduate course in Shakespearean theatre and a whole bunch of songs based on Shakespeare resurfaced. The banjo kept all of them up every night that week transcribing.*

"The devil board of directors by this time was having to rely on the mischief they had already made, for the music continued on its merry course. The dirty tricks the devils played unraveled the songs in the States and in the British Isles faster than the ragged-ass group of musicians could possibly bring the songs back. When Ellie called her daddy at home, he told her each time of another big collection being destroyed, more musicians being killed in supposed accidents or dying before their time of drug- and sex-related illnesses, of old-timers getting Alzheimer's or throat cancer or something else that effectively put them out of commission, of the media and the schools ignoring anything connected with any kind of man-made music in favor of more and better computer simulations and high-powered games and such.

"But the devils were having a hell of a time too. They'd only concentrated their efforts against the music in English-speaking countries, and had let a few other things slide while indulging that little whim of the Chairdevil's. One day he called them all back in, including the Debauchery Devil aka Torchy Burns, Lulubelle Baker, the Queen of Fairies, DD, and Miss Fahrenheit, and said:

"It's almost as if the Opposition has been playing us along, plotting this diversionary tactic. While we've been messing around with these music mongers, distracting ourselves with their wretched noise, the worst possible scenario has occurred; peace has broken out in several parts of the world and unless we act fast, it may spread like a virus until it consumes the earth. The leaders of the Soviet Union and the United States are seeing eye to eye and some millionaire has actually been using good money that could be used for wild living to get the world powers talking peaceably among themselves and other kinds of bleeding-heart liberal bullshit. The Berlin Wall, one of our greatest monuments, has been torn down. Our minions in charge of oppressing the citizens of several Eastern European countries have been brutally slaughtered. If we are to salvage anything, any massive breakdowns in the economy, any impatience on the part of people who are just about to be liberated to make it happen so fast they undo the whole thing, any further rebellions just for the hell of it, we have got to get cracking."

"You've just about tied my hands," the Debauchery Devil complained, not that she didn't enjoy that sort of thing under the right circumstances, but it wasn't often she got a chance to display righteous indignation, since she disdained righteousness as a rule. "You've appropriated and mismanaged my minions and left all my magicks tied up with your little scheme while I have to prowl around on four paws or hide behind thick glasses and stacks of musty old books. I'm glad we're abandoning this in favor of schemes more worthy of my talents."

"You misunderstand me, DD," the Chairdevil said. "I'm simply pointing out that we need to pull Expediency back where he belongs and you need to behave yourself with more dedication and dispatch. Take back your minions. They're human. You have the chief offenders tied up in your realm for the time being and the cursed instrument is guarded only by two bookworms and an old woman. Have your minions recapture it. I don't care how. Then even if our adversaries do relearn some of the charms against us, they'll have no way of sending them back into this world and we can keep them where they are."

"But that will keep draining me indefinitely, boss," she complained.

"Only for seven years, dear, at which time you fork them over to us—"

"Fork 'em over?" the Stupidity and Ignorance Devil chuckled. "That was a good one, boss. Yeah, fork 'em over right in the—"

"I got it, dammit!" DD snapped.

"I think you've been a little too indiscreet lately, DD, pushing your minions and victims until they expose themselves to the world. I think it's about time we kept our minions staunch and righteous and free of drink and drugs and sexual exploits—it always makes them deadlier anyway when they can feel pure about doing as we like. Then you can come back in, after the seven years, when people are no longer so cynical about looking for the connection between our works and your substances. You're getting a little trite. So I want you to handle this. Have your minions destroy that twanging talisman of theirs and then we'll see how badly you're needed."

▲▲▲

Gussie drove toward Drumlanrig Castle, clan seat of the Scotts and home of the Duke of Buccleuch. Walter Scott was telling her about the Duchess who was once accused of witchcraft, when all of a sudden Gussie felt something ringing under her bottom.

What with everything that had been happening, including living the last few months possessed by the ghost of Scotland's most famous novelist, she didn't wonder for a moment if she was imagining things. First she said, "Did you do that?" to Scott and when he disclaimed any knowledge of it, she pulled over into the broom by the side of the road. By then the ringing had occurred twice more, again coming from beneath the driver's seat. She stuck her hand under the seat and fished around until she touched smooth plastic. "Gotcha," she said to the cellular phone, answering it by the fourth ring. "Hello?"

"Hi, there. Who's this?" asked the voice on the other end.

"Gussie Turner. I think you have the wrong number. Who were you calling?"

"Aren't you the lady that came with the Randolphs?" the pleasant male voice asked. "Remember me? Dan? It's Terry's and my van you're answering."

"Oh! Oh, Dan. Where are you?"

"In Polar Circalen. Above the Arctic Circle. We're on

our way to the airport and were hoping you would bring the van and pick us up. We've got some people we'd like you to meet."

"How was the African festival?"

"Fantastic. We met the coolest guy from Kenya who's into Icelandic music and we thought maybe he could help you guys with your problem."

Gussie had a vision of Terry and Dan standing astride a band of ice, accompanied by an African in yellow Kente cloth tribal dress and carrying an accordion, or whatever it was Norwegians played. Walter Scott, however, was excited. "Many of the magical ballads had roots in Norway and Iceland," Wat told Gussie. "Ask them if they found any Norwegian variants of our ballads while they were there—there's also a German named Grundtvig who found German songs that were at least parallel to the ones we sing here in Scotland."

Gussie relayed the message and Dan said, "Yeah, yeah, Gachero knows all that stuff and besides, we've got some pals from Iceland with us who know *all* the old stories and songs. You have just got to see the way they usually perform them. I wish we could have gotten the whole crowd together, but there's only three who can come, plus Gachero and a couple of other Scottish guys from the band Terry used to be in. How's Ellie and Faron?"

"They're up in Edinburgh researching. Wat—my friend—was showing me some of the historical sites of border ballads and so on. He's an expert on the reivers and such. But Ellie will want to know, were you able to replace your instruments?"

"Sort of. I convinced Terry that instead of a new guitar and fiddle we needed a bunch of African and Norwegian instruments for the same price. Like you said, the clerks never checked the signature and saw we weren't named Curtis. I'm sure Terry can repair her guitar and fiddle when she gets home. One of the guys coming with us is a luthier and he could probably do it for parts."

Dan seemed to be in no hurry to get off the extremely long-distance call and wanted to chat awhile. Frankly,

Gussie was glad of the company. "It's good to hear from you," she said. "The others have—uh—gone off researching too so there's nobody here most of the time but Wat and me."

"So who's this Wat guy, Gussie?" Dan asked jovially. "New boyfriend?"

"You might call him a 'soul mate,' " she said.

"Uh-huh. Well, we're going to be flying back in the morning. So, what do you think, can you pick us up? If not, maybe we can rent a car and meet you. Where you staying?"

She gave him the address and he said, "If we do have to rent a car, is it okay with Ellie's dad if we use the card again?"

"I'll ask her. Can you call back?"

"Sure. When do you expect the Randolphs and those other folks back?"

"I'm supposed to pick up the Randolphs tonight but it will be—a while—before the others return. I'll tell you about it when you get here," she said.

"Cool," he said, and gave her the airline information, then rang off.

"Engaging young man," Sir Walter said. "In bygone days, minstrels were not so ready to share their songs or their territory for fear of losing their livelihood."

"Were minstrels still around when you were alive?"

"Not your traditional sort of minstrels. But we had many of their descendants here on the Borders, beneficiaries, I'm sure my ancestor the Wizard would say, of the fission of souls."

"Is that so?"

"Indeed. Some of the ballads—'Kinmont Willie' and 'Jock o' the Side'—were written aboot business associates of my ane ancestors, the Bold Buccleuch and Auld Wat, for whom I'm named."

"Is that so?"

"Aye, they were bonny men. Bold and daring, brave as bears and honorable—did you know they scorned to kill anyone unnecessarily?"

"No, really?"

"Aye, it was part of the Borders code," he said, and she felt his pride swelling her own breast.

"Sounds like the Code of the West," she said.

"Oh, aye?"

"Yeah. You never got a chance to see the American West, did you, Wat? You'd have liked it. Or at least, you would have liked the movies and books about it. Knowing you now, I wonder if maybe Zane Grey and Louie L'Amour might not have gotten a bit of you when your soul fizzed, if the Wizard's theory is right. You bein' a sheriff and all, I think you would have found it real interesting."

"No doot. But we've a wee drive still if you're tae see Drumlanrig and return in time to collect the Randolphs."

"Y'all drive as much around here as we do in Texas, 'cept the roads aren't as good."

"They were worse in my day," he reminded her.

Drumlanrig was a very long way, southwest of Galashiels, and the phone call had come shortly after Gussie left the Carr estate.

"Yarrow," she said, "is that the same as the Dowie Dens?"

"None other," he responded. "These hills are full of ballads, full of murder holes and the lairs of the reivers where they'd hide during the day on their way back from a raid, avoiding the hot trod."

"I thought you didn't have cars in those days," she said.

"Of course we do, woman. We've been staying in the home of Carrs, who were, by the way, off and on ancestral enemies of the Scotts."

"Now you tell me," she said. "Anyway, Janet doesn't seem to hold any ancestral grudges. She's been very neighborly and helpful."

"Aye," he said. "Would you like to see some of the places I'm talking aboot then?"

The banjo began playing a song, "The Rolling Hills of the Border."

"What's that tower over there?"

" 'Tis a Peel tower, fortification for the Border barons against the English and sometimes against each other."

He told her how the towers could be seized by burning the doors or taking the roof but that otherwise they were impervious to assault, which was why there were still so many standing.

They reached Drumlanrig by midafternoon. Gussie admired the great circular staircase out front and the great circular staircase indoors with the old masters lining the stairwell and the silver chandelier with nineteen stone of silver dolphins hanging from the ceiling. She splurged on a scarf in the Scott tartan, which pleased Sir Walter, who was much better than any tour guide whispering stories and song lyrics to her all through the day.

He was telling her the story of "Armstrong's Farewell," which she knew as "The Parting Glass," when they reached the intersection at Elvanfoot. She thought the sign said to go south for a while to reach the turn back north toward Edinburgh, but the farther she drove, the darker it grew and still no turn until they found themselves at Moffat again.

"Damn," she said. "Faron and Ellie are going to think something's happened. Let's call the library before it closes and have them meet us somewhere that will be open." She stopped the car and got out and fished for the phone again, since she had dutifully hidden it to prevent theft when she stopped at the castle.

The librarians were not all that happy to receive phone calls for patrons, but they relayed the message to meet at the pub near Sir Walter's memorial, the tallest structure in Edinburgh. It looked a little like a Siamese shrine, Gussie thought.

She was insisting to the librarian that there *was* such a shrine when the sort of vehicle that's called a Winnebago in the U.S. regardless of make and a caravan in Britain drove past the parked van, put on its brakes, and stopped. Gussie looked up in time to see rough, swarthy-looking men piling out while the banjo twanged loudly.

"Hold!" Wat said. "What's this the banjo's playing?"

"I don't know, Wat, but I don't think those are Pakistani tourists coming to ask directions. Let's blow this joint." She jumped back into the van, flipped the key in the ignition, and gunned the motor. That was fine in a James Bond movie but the van didn't take it very well and by the time it coughed and sputtered its way into motion, the Gypsies had piled back into their own vehicle and caught up with Gussie. As she passed the Ettrick Forest, the Gypsy vehicle hogged the little road beside the van, trying to run it off the road.

Unfortunately, at that moment an oil tanker bore down upon both of them from the opposite direction. This was not a four-lane highway the three vehicles fought over; this was a one-and-a-half-lane cowpath. Gussie kept driving off the road and down an embankment into the forest, where the van stopped a hairbreadth from the tree fixed in its headlamps like a moth.

Brakes squealed and tires screeched from the road. No explosion. The tanker hadn't hit then. Gussie rammed the van into reverse and hit something with a crunch of metal and plastic.

Through the trees, headlights jiggled crazily.

"The hell with this," she said, grabbing her basket bag with the banjo inside and the keys to the van and taking off through the trees. "You said there were all kinds of hiding places around here, Wat. Do you know where they are?"

"Well—er—no. I know they're here because they were once used, you see, but when I needed sich a place for my stories I moved it aboot to wherever I needed it."

"Well, move one this way," she said, running deeper into the forest, which was better than the Christmas tree farms they'd seen in other places, though not by much.

"You're spry for an auld lass," Wat observed. "Wait! Hark!"

"What?" She paused, holding her breath to hear beyond the trees bobbing in the wind and the tall grass swishing back and forth. From the direction of the road, a set of headlights beamed down to the right of her present position. She zigzagged farther away from them, trip-

ping over a stone and falling headlong against one of the
tree trunks.

"That. Listen."

Somewhere in the distance she heard a call, like an
Indian war whoop, "A', a', a', a'."

And at that sound, though she didn't remember bending her knees or rising to her feet, she was suddenly up
and moving fast, closer and closer to the sound, which
she heard repeated again, this time with words before it.
As she cleared several trees she saw something cheering
—a fire—campers! Maybe even folk song–singing campers, because as she ran closer, she made out more of the
words.

The refrain was a cross between a banshee's lament
and a battle cry: "Fy, lads! Shout a'a'a'a'/My gear's a'
gane!"

A dog howled, and another, anxious baying sounds.
City dogs from London maybe, not used to the country.

She sprinted toward the sound, almost effortlessly.
"This is on me, lass," Wat said. "Now it's nicht and I'm
stronger. Gin that sound is what I think it is, this could
be a wondrous night for the baith of us."

As they sped through the trees, Gussie focused on the
campfire and soon saw that it was too small for a campfire and too high. It flared from a little ridge in the forest,
and burned against the sky, torchlike.

"Aha," Wat said. "I thought as much." Drawing
closer, they saw that the flame indeed emanated from the
torch and holding the torch was a woman on horseback
followed by a small band of men, perhaps ten or twelve.
She seemed to be starting her chant over again. It didn't
scan, it didn't rhyme, but it rose and fell on the night
wind with a wild and angry eeriness that at once made
Gussie's neck hairs rise and broke her heart.

"Weel may ye ken
Last night I was right scarce o' men
But Toppet Hob o' the Mains had guesten'd in my
        house by chance
I set him to wear the fore-door wi' the speir, while I

kept the back door wi' the lance.
But they hae run hium through the thick o' the thie,
    and broke his knee-pan
He's lame while he lives, and where'er he may gang
Fy, lads! Shout a' a' a' a'
My gear's a' gang!"

Gussie's breath rose and fell with the chant and the wind. The woman looked down at her with pale eyes full of fury, determination, and exhaustion. "You there!" she cried down at Gussie. "I claim your aid by law of the trod. Two nights ago my stock was stolen, my goods despoiled, my guest maimed, and my person violated, and I seek my lawful revenge. Have you seen reivers riding near?"

Sir Walter answered as if he and not Gussie had been addressed. Gussie felt her body's blood pulsing with his excitement. "Madame, all my skill is at your service to redress the injustices perpetrated upon you by sich ruffians. My companion and I are fleeing ruffians ourselves."

"Driving a late-model Winnebago," Gussie volunteered and the woman seemed to peer through Sir Walter, who, to Gussie's eyes, was suddenly standing independent of her, rather like a Siamese twin joined back to front.

"What?" the woman asked. "Have you your wife with you? She's standing behind you so that I cannot see her."

"The lady is a close companion. She haunts my every movement."

"Who haunts *who*?" Gussie demanded.

But then she realized that the figures on the hill seemed a little see-throughish and to them, no doubt, Sir Walter looked real and she seemed ghostified. Certainly the longer they stood there, the more solid they and Wat looked and the wispier she felt.

"I regret we have no horse with which to assist you," Sir Walter said. "Our transportation has just—er—died."

"I regret I have no horse either," the woman bit back sourly. "My horses and cattle have been lately driven off by your countrymen and this mare I ride is the charity of my neighbor. You are the first soul my trod has come near on this side of the border and are obliged to help me, horses or none. I know my rights. Neighbor Cuddy, will ye tak' this man up behind you?"

"Aye, Mistress Hetherton, I will."

And Gussie found herself, her haunt, and her basket bag, banjo and all, lifted up beside an apparition who gained more reality as she sat on the equally apparitious horse. Both man and horse even sweated smelly spectral sweat.

"What's she carrying that torch through the woods for?" Gussie asked. "She's going to start a forest fire that way."

"That fire's as dead as I am," Sir Walter said. "Besides, it's the symbol of the hot trod. She must carry the torch to notify all that she takes to the trail in her own righteous cause. Poor lady." He scratched. "Her neighbors are poor too, I wot. Neighbor Cuddy is louse-ridden."

"Don't scratch so hard. Those are ghost lice and they aren't bothering me a bit."

The riding didn't bother Gussie much either. She used to ride with friends all the time back in Texas. But she did wonder about these people. The woman was no beauty, with lank greasy brown hair and a nose like a tulip bulb. Livid bruises showed around her eyes and on her jaw, neck, and naked forearms. She wore a slip that might have been white once but now was dirty, spotted gray, and another garment, loose and ugly and just as disreputable over it. She looked about the age of Gussie's daughter Lettie, in fact, if Lettie had been a hard-liver, heavy drinker and smoker, had ten babies in a row and had let herself get knocked around a lot, she might have resembled this woman. Gussie knew the woman was a ghost but she could also see the ghostly gooseflesh rising on the woman's thin bruised arms. She dug into the basket bag and pulled out the afghan she'd been crocheting for Lettie and Mic. She only had a strip of twenty granny squares by ten hooked together but the woman was small and the piece would make a good-sized wrap for her.

"Can she use this?" she asked Wat, but Neighbor Cuddy took it from her hand and passed it to the woman. Gussie guessed it figured that if she herself could ride a ghostly horse, the ghost woman could warm herself with a piece of a corporeal afghan.

"Your lady is kind," Mistress Hetherton said, dropping back to speak to Wat again and fingering the bright-colored acrylic yarns draped over her skinny shoulders. Her voice wavered between softness as she ducked her head to rub her cheek against the yarns and ferocity as she added, "If I had had such a pretty piece as this to lose when they came to my stead, I'd have strangled them each with my bare hands before I let them take it. My husband left me little enough to live on, but my herds had increased until I had twenty-four good oxen and cows. Now they're gone, all gone, with my pots and pans and all my food, my dishes, every stitch I owned including what I was wearing, the sheets from my bed, my candlestick, and the coats I was making for my grand-children. I would be going after them naked but for the guilt of my neighbors, who never rose nor lifted a hand to help me and my poor guest Toppet when the reivers came. It's a comfort indeed, sir, to have such fine Scotch folk as yourselves enlist in my cause. Besides," she added on a more practical note, "if we find the rascals, and they're too many for us, likely they'll occupy themselves with the likes o' you while we escape." There was no special rancor toward them in her tone.

Sir Walter didn't even seem to notice, but said, "We've been in far lands for many years now, madame. Who now sits the throne of England?"

"Why, Good Queen Bess. How far have you gone not to have heard and how came ye home not knowing? Oh, but I forget. You're Scotch and things be wild here-abouts."

"True. Well, then, I think I know where there will be stronger help than mine for your cause. I have powerful kinsmen whose hold is but a league or so distant from here, on the edge of the forest. I wonder that you did not pass them as you rode."

To Gussie he said, "What an adventure we have before us, auld lass! All my life I've heard of my ancestor, the Bold Buccleuch. The stronghold of Buccleuch is close by. He'll see to it that this poor woman's given justice. I hope he's at home instead of off to Liddesdale, where he was sometimes Warden, a position much like the one I held during my life."

CHAPTER XXIV

▲▲▲

The fog was so thick by now that the people who sat directly opposite her could see neither the storyteller nor the people who sat next to her. As she talked, the driver tinkered and swore beneath the bus, aided by Mrs. Tortuga, who held the lantern. The beam of the lantern glimmered like a rheumy eye from behind cataracts of fog, but except for it, the passengers might have been alone in those mountains and the bus, the driver, and Mrs. Tortuga might have been alone as well.

"So," a disembodied voice said, "I guess that robbery victim lady and her buddy on the horse got them out of that jam, huh?"

"Out of the frying pan into the fire," the storyteller replied. "See, once Gussie and the banjo went with the ghosts, it was sort of like they disappeared too. Now, I know it never worked out like that on Topper but the fact is, Sir Walter possessing Gussie made the difference in whether she was real in this world and hazy in the next, or straddled both planes. He pulled her with him over to the ghost side—not out of malice, mind you, but from the affinity he had with the other ghosts."

"One of those affinities the Wizard was talking about?"

"Similar. Anyway, once she took off with the hot trod, the Gypsies couldn't find her, but then, neither could anybody else. Furthermore, the banjo was in the ghost world too, and that made all kinds of difference, upset the magical equilibrium as it were."

▲▲▲

Willie MacKai was so relieved to hear the banjo he could have bawled—in fact, he reckoned he probably would, next song around. He was as purely tired of being a beautiful young female as a man could be of anything. First, of course, he'd gotten his lover killed off by his family, losing a bunch of them in the process, then as "Tifty's Annie" he'd been part of a girl who'd been beaten to death by her family for falling for the wrong guy.

He had joined May Margaret right after some swarthy galoot named Prince Heathen had raped her, drowned her brothers, stabbed her parents to death, burnt her house, and carried her off to live in a cave where he didn't feed her or give her anything to drink until she'd had a son for him and then he'd half killed her dragging her through the brambles while she was in labor as his men laughed at her. Willie wished to God that Torchy Burns had added to her instructions not to get killed or laid that they couldn't have babies or get beaten to a nonfatal pulp either because that was the god-awfulest thing he had ever been through, bar none. May Margaret was tougher than most of the girls Willie had inhabited though. Once she had her kid and started bawling because she thought her self-appointed boyfriend was going to kill the kid too, Prince Heathen got all solicitous and started behaving himself. He said he didn't mean to hurt her. He was only testing her. Yeah, sure. Well, he'd messed up Margaret's looks real bad and he had to sleep with the results.

Willie wished he could go back and tell Margaret what his next hostess, a middle-aged woman known for some strange reason as Fair Annie, had done. Her old man had kidnapped her when she was a little girl and Annie had had seven kids by him, boys, who he had raised up to be as rotten as he was. Then he decided Annie was looking a little long in the tooth and he began regretting that he'd never gotten a dime's worth of dowry for her, so he started courting another girl and ordered Annie to act like his housekeeper. Fortunately, the other girl had been

brought up on tales of how her older sister was kidnapped to such and such a land by a man who seemed
mysteriously like her fiancé and she thought to ask Annie
who her parents had been. The girls were sisters, and
conspired between them to have the younger girl's body-
guard hang the husband, then both girls went back to
their native country.

Along with his hostesses, Willie had also been knifed
by jealous women, and drowned by his brother, who
didn't want the folks to know he was about to give birth
to his own niece or nephew. *NICE PEOPLE* these ballad
folks. Reminded him of the real tiny little hollers in the
South where sex was so often a family affair. He especially liked the ballad where the brother accidentally
killed two of his sisters trying to get one of the three girls
to marry him, till the third woman laid a little family
history on him. That had been Willie's idea. He had finally started to figure out how to help these gals once in a
while.

He hadn't done so well as Mary Hamilton, who'd gone
to Russia and had been fool enough to abort the King's
bastard and been hung for her trouble. (Willie had bailed
out of that one as soon as he recognized the ballad and
realized that poor girl just had a talent for putting her
foot in her mouth and plain hadn't learned in time to
"just say no.")

But that last little old gal had been a smart one. When
her boyfriend talked her into taking her daddy's horse
and her mama's jewels and running away with him, then
wanted her to strip off her designer clothes before he
pitched her in the river, Willie, as the voice of her common sense, had told her to pretend maidenly modesty.
When the bastard's back was turned, she shoved the jerk
over the cliff and into the ocean. Worked slicker than
deer guts on a doorknob.

Willie wished he could have done more to help these
women but of course if he had, their songs would have
changed. Still, it made him feel a little like a network
news cameraman filming away while people were being
murdered all around him. He wondered if the songs

about the women he had been would make a bit of difference in anyone else's life, but somehow he figured if he ever got to be a guy again, they would make some difference in his own.

The banjo song he heard now sounded like a reprieve to him and he moved toward it, and found himself in a big house by a river, looking through the blue eyes of yet another golden-haired girl in love with a handsome stranger.

▲▲▲

Anna Mae Gunn was glad to hear the banjo too. She had turned her ring just after little Musgrave struck at Lord Barnard while the naked Lady Barnard (who got Musgrave into the whole mess anyway) looked on. The third twist had come just as Lord Barnard's sword touched Little Musgrave's chest, preparatory to skewering him.

Prior to that, she and Annachie Gordon had lost their one true love because Annachie didn't know if he wanted to be tied down until his love was forced to marry a richer man and poisoned herself on her wedding night.

As one guy named Geordie, she had turned her ring just in time to avoid being hanged in a golden chain. As another Geordie, she had turned her ring just before making love to the wife who had the foresight to bring the (heavily armed) clan along before she attempted to ransom his life. It was nice to win one occasionally and most of her hosts didn't get a second chance.

As a blacksmith, she had left her native home and a girl she felt only half hearted about and found a new love, while the girl back home cursed her love's falseness. On the other hand, as John Riley she had tested the Maid of Islington's continuing interest in her love by telling the girl that John Riley had died. The ring was once more turned on a happy note. But as often as her tale ended happily, oftener it had ended sadly, if not fatally.

All of the girls seemed to think that if only they hooked up with Anna Mae's host they would be saved from lives of drudgery, pettiness, shame, maybe starvation. Anna Mae's hosts often felt that they too were trapped and their only salvation was to not get entangled in any one pair of arms that would bring on crushing responsibilities. Most of the men sought to seek their fortunes in the wider world while fending off girls who sought their fortunes in the arms of the men. Anna Mae was just plain embarrassed on behalf of womankind, even knowing as she did that at that time in history, women had few choices and had to depend on love or luck.

So she hoped, when she heard the banjo, that being able to hear it meant the ordeal was over and she could return to being herself. But when the haze parted, she found herself once more within someone else. This time there were *two* wealthy girls to keep her hopping.

▲▲▲

Julianne Martin was having so many thrilling adventures and close escapes and near-death experiences (saved from being death experiences only by the string ring) that when she started the new identity the banjo's tune had led her to and found herself in another heroic-looking male body, she turned aside from the look of yearning in a dark-haired woman's eyes and began to throw up in the rushes. Juli was shell-shocked, she had what you'd call battle fatigue.

She was tired of being valiant through shipwrecks as Sir Patrick Spens and the brave cabin boy of the *Golden Vanity*. Every time Robin Hood made another daring escape or rescue from the Sheriff of Nottingham, she thought she'd have a heart attack right along with Robin, who couldn't seem to stop himself from such heroics. She was tired of being expected to lead and wished with all her heart that people would just run their own lives and stop expecting so much of her and her hosts. She was tired of being noble when one more of her hosts began to die some horrible death, when what she wanted to do was to scream and scream and knew he did too and couldn't because he had, in some part of himself, been dead a long time and knew it. She was tired of the rough hardy life and wanted terribly to be a wimp again, to sleep in a flannel nightie and sip herb tea and pet cats and play gentle songs about nature and love and peace.

She didn't want to always have to earn a reputation or awards, she just wanted to be provided with a nice, comfortable life—but not at the expense of some hapless hero. God, no. If she met another one she'd give him a brotherly kiss on the cheek and offer him a cushion and his choice of videos and if someone broke into the house, she'd brandish her claymore and scare them away herself.

So she was pleased when she parted the mist and found herself in the body of a wandering man whose burden this time was not a sword or a bow but an ancient, decrepit, out-of-tune harp. At least, at last, she was allowed to be a musician again.

▲▲▲

And Brose Fairchild was sick and tired of always having his smart, sexy, strong ladies get rejected, reviled, and picked on by men too dumb or greedy to appreciate them in favor of women with twice their looks and half their brains.

After Barbara, Brose had been a Turkish lady who saved her knight from prison and traveled across the sea to claim his promise (which for once he kept. Brose had had a hard time turning the ring just when he was getting to the happy ending). Of course, the damn fool knight should have sent her airfare, as far as Brose was concerned, but at least he didn't fink out on her.

Brose had also had a hell of a time as a witch trying to escape a wizard with a serious case of horny but after a number of amusing transformations that had ended happily too—to the witch's secret satisfaction, the wizard had proved her match and himself worthy of her and she had let him catch her and "gain her maidenhead," which was supposed to "pu' down her pride." Fortunately for the witch, the wizard, being a guy, didn't realize that to witches maidenheads were a renewable resource. Once more, Brose had had to exit before the grand finale.

So maybe he was feeling extra horny, in a female kind of way, when he heard the banjo song and followed it into the body of yet another dark, intense woman. He knew right away, however, that there was something seriously wrong with this one.

CHAPTER XXV

▲▲▲

Faron and Ellie had to wait two days for the bus back to Galashiels, all the while wondering why Gussie had not picked them up, why she hadn't answered the phone at the Carrs'. Ellie called her parents collect, thinking they might have heard from Gussie, but they only had more bad news about recent musical catastrophes—bluegrass musicians were dying off now and other countries were refusing to admit any American musicians period onto their soil in retaliation for the U.S. policy against foreign musicians. SWALLOW, the Songwriters and Arrangers Legal Licensing Organization Worldwide, had managed to close down all music on all radio stations, all juke-boxes, and any music played on network or public television stations, besides live performances. The exception was one licensed bombshell-rock station that owned a nationwide monopoly. Nobody seemed to notice monopolies were allegedly illegal.

After a daylong milk run of a bus trip, the Randolphs walked home from the Galashiels Road just as twilight faded. A white plastic feed sack billowed from the fork of a tree while the naked branches clawed the sky. No lights shone from any of the houses on the property. Lights also did not show from the front end of the Winnebago parked behind their cottage, so they didn't see the reception committee until the cows suddenly set up an alarm at their presence and they found themselves looking down the business end of a revolver held by Giorgio.

Behind him was Torchy Burns, dressed like a punk fortune-teller.

"We want that banjo, gadjo," the Gypsy said.

"Sure, yeah," Faron said, "but did you realize what you just said had all the elements of a poem—banjo? Gadjo?"

"Giorgio!" Torchy cried delightedly. "I love it. We'll write it together, Faron, dearest, as soon as you've given Giorgio what he wants. Giorgio is terribly musical, you know."

"Is that why he wants to break the old man's fiddle?" Faron asked. "Look, we don't have the banjo with us. Gussie kept it."

"We know she kept it, but she's gone and we can't find her or it. By the time Giorgio found the van, it was empty. So the question is, where did she go and where did that banjo go?"

"You know more about it than we do," Ellie said. "We were in Edinburgh waiting for a bus."

▲▲▲

The hot trod arrived at Buccleuch, stronghold of Sir Walter's ancestors, in time for brunch.

Sir Walter knocked boldly at the gate, and when a suspicious eye peeked out the hole he said, "Please to admit us at once, kinsman."

"And who might you be?"

"Sir Walter Scott, joined on a trod on behalf of this lady and her neighbors. I'm here to claim the aid of my chief and Keeper of Liddesdale, the Bold Buccleuch."

"Ye be Sir Walter Scott?" the man asked and Gussie thought from the way Wat puffed up he expected to be asked for an autograph. "God's balls, they're everywhere," the man grumbled but swung open the gate, admitting horses and riders.

They were admitted to the hall, a dark and dismal place full of stenches and animal noises that Gussie soon perceived were made by Wat's kinsmen slurping away at their breakfast porridge and big haunches of beef. Wat strode before Mistress Hetherton and her group in his eagerness for a glimpse of his romantic forebears.

"I'm come to claim aid of my kinsman, Bold Buccleuch," Walter said in what Gussie assumed was the prescribed manner.

"Good God, man, could ye no' wait until a decent hoor?" demanded a red-bearded man with white flecks of porridge dribbling into his whiskers. The other men looked up. Not a man in the lot would have looked out of place in leathers and spikes, covered with tattoos and riding a Harley Davidson hog. "Had a hell of a nicht. Who might you be, noo? One of my wife's relations, no doot, cum to ask boons at such an unco hoor?"

"No wife's relation but your own great-grandson, Sir Walter Scott, and I've come to you for justice on behalf of this poor woman on a hot trod after vile raiders despoiled her of all she owned."

A shriek rent the morning air and caused the Bold Buccleuch to grab his head with both ham-hands.

"Bessie!" the Widow Hetherton shrieked from outside the door. "That's my Bessie they're milkin'! And those are my oxen!"

The Bold Buccleuch gave Sir Walter a withering look, as if he'd done something incredibly gauche, then, when the Widow Hetherton strode in, Buccleuch's whiskers parted in a broad predatory grin.

The banjo in Gussie's bag broke into the mournful melody of "The Twa Sisters." Sir Walter, impatient at the interruption in an embarrassing and potentially dangerous bursting of one of his romantic illusions, complained to Gussie, "I thought you told me it usually played something to indicate the current situation. That seems to me totally irrelevant."

"Well," she said. "It *is* about how you can't always trust relatives."

▲▲▲

Willie and the Fair Isabelle were thinking that very thing as they hit the water under the impetus of their dark sister Jane's hands. "I told you we shouldn't flirt with

Jane's boyfriend," Willie said to Isabelle as she went under. "Sister Jane takes romance real seriously."

The Fair Isabelle held her breath and flailed her arms but, alas, she had never cared for swimming as the sun darkened her alabaster complexion and threatened to turn it as swarthy as Jane's.

As Isabelle's hands flailed the water's surface, Willie turned the ring once around. On the bank, Sister Jane, seeing the gesture, cried out, once, "Juli!"

Fair Isabelle said, "She is confused. Poor thing, she doesn't realize what she did," and Isabelle tried to dog paddle toward shore. The embankment was very steep and she said, "Sister, just lend me your hand. I'm sorry I teased you and called you dark as walnuts. You can have all my inheritance."

"You'll be even fairer by the time the water has bleached you out for a couple of days," Jane replied, shoving back down the voice inside her that said, *"She's your sister. You were babies together. Whoever the dude is, he ain't worth it."*

"You don't care anything about that guy," Willie told Isabelle. *"Offer to give him up."*

"I'll scorn Sir William," Isabelle gulped, coming up for the second time and the second twist of the ring. "He'll be only yours."

"With you out of the way, he'll be mine anyway, as will your dower lands," Jane said.

Brose, within her, saw Isabelle twist her ring around again and said, *"You see there what she's doin', Janie? You gonna be doin' that when they hang your ass. Now bail her out, dammit."*

"No, she's tormented me long enough. I'm tired of second best. This is the last time she gets all the attention while I go neglected." And with that Jane turned her back and walked away.

As Isabelle twisted her ring for the third time, Willie swam free and left her to her much-sung fate.

▲▲▲

"Tha's aye a fine sang that unco harp ye have there plays, Great-Grandson. It plays a' by its lane?" Bold Buccleuch asked, momentarily distracted from robbing and slaughtering them all by the banjo twanging away in Gussie's basket bag.

Gussie answered, "That it does, sir. It's magic and it knows all of the songs about love and war and right and wrong and justice and injustice that ever were sung. Wonder what songs it's going to play about you?"

"Eh?" He lifted a red eyebrow as thick as the tail of the orange cat at Carrs' and just as mobile. "That sang's very familiar but I canna' recall it."

"Ahem, allow me, laird," said a tall, skinny man, balding and with a trimmed beard. He looked less ruffianlike than the others. "The song is called 'The Two Sisters' or 'The Cruel Sister' or sometimes by the burden it often bears 'Binnorie.' "

"Ah, our renegade Irish harper. How cum ye to know a Scottish tune?"

"Many songs have crossed from one shore to the other until who can say where they began, laird," the man said, but sang the lyrics as the banjo played through them again.

> "Sometimes she sunk, and sometimes she swam,
>   Binnorie, O Binnorie;
> Until she cam' to the miller's dam,
> By the bonny milldams of Binnorie.
> 'Oh, Father, Father, draw your dam!'
>   Binnorie, O Binnorie;
> There's either a mermaid or a milk-white swan,
> By the bonny, bonny banks of Binnorie."

▲▲▲

Giorgio had opened the door and forced the Randolphs inside, before beginning to search the rooms. Before he could get started however, Terry Pruitt's white van, its front grill dented but otherwise unhurt, careened up the driveway and skidded to a stop. Giorgio's wife flung open the driver's door and jumped to the ground as a van-load of Gypsy women, children, and some of the older men swarmed from the vehicle. Even inside the house, Faron could hear the persistent ring of a phone.

Giorgio's wife dove head first back into the van and finally groped under the driver's seat until she triumphantly held aloft the cellular telephone, which kept ringing until she pushed the switch to answer it. "'Allo!" she said.

"This is Sam Hawthorne speaking. I can't come to the phone right now but at the tone I'm leaving you the following message."

Torchy Burns stood in the doorway with her hands on her hips. "Oh, hell! I should have known when I mixed up those affinities that all the dead people would get into the act. That Hawthorne is well named okay—he's always been a thorn in my side and a pain in my ass. I offered him plenty of opportunity but no, he had to be Mr. Clean and now the son of a bitch has the temerity to haunt *me*!"

The tone sounded and was followed by the mournful wail of a banjo playing a tune that Torchy recognized at once. She grabbed Giorgio, saying, "Come on, you fuck-up, I need you to occupy a body." Giorgio's uncle, who was also the maternal uncle of Giorgio's wife, slipped past where Torchy had been standing and saw his beloved violin lying on the table. He didn't even need to tune it since Faron had been playing it the night before, and now he joined in with the banjo, which seemed louder than it could have possibly been over the telephone.

Everyone ignored him except Faron and Ellie and Giorgio's wife. There was a sort of an instrumental bridge, and then Faron began remembering the next part and sang it.

▲▲▲

"You're a miller now, Giorgio. It's your chance to go straight. Whatever you do, don't let that body fall into the wrong hands. You must strip it so it can't be identified. Got it?"

The miller of Binnorie nodded and went to draw his dam while Torchy Burns vanished once more to intercept the boyish-looking man who was the district harper.

▲▲▲

In Buccleuch stronghold, Harper Hawthorne sang the same verse Faron Randolph sang at the Carr estate in Galashiels, both of them singing for audiences of rogues and thieves:

> "The miller hasted and drew his dam,
>   Binnorie, O Binnorie
> And there he found a drowned woman,
> By the bonny milldams of Binnorie.
>
> "You could not see her yellow hair,
>   Binnorie, O Binnorie;
> For gold and pearls that were sae rare,
> By the bonny milldams of Binnorie.
>
> "You could na see her middle sma'
>   Binnorie, O Binnorie;
> Her golden girdle was sae bra'
> By the bonny milldams of Binnorie."

As Juli's harper host rounded the hill, he saw a red-haired dandy, very fine, leering at him. Julianne would recognize that leer anywhere. Her host hesitated. He was a well-known harper, but was little more than a boy and a smallish one at that. His voice had not yet changed, but was still a sweet countertenor, and his hands, more delicate than Juli's had ever been save for the hard calluses on the fingertips, were deft at the making of instruments.

The dandy, who was none other than Torchy Burns in another guise, said, "And where are you going?"

The boy harper, on his way to sing at a school for gentlemen's sons, replied, "I'm going to the school."

"Wait," Julianne said to him. *"This sounds familiar. Remember all the riddles in the King Arthur stories? This*

is the devil and he's trying to trick us. Be careful of your answers."

"I wish you were on yon tree!" proclaimed Torchy, thinking that the Juli harper would have to go there because she, Torchy, declared it.

Juli, who had picked plenty of apples in her time, supplied the harper with the answer, "With a ladder under me!"

"And the ladder for to break," the Torchy/man said between clenched teeth.

"And you for to fa' down," the boy harper replied, getting into the spirit of the thing with a typical bit of preadolescent "Oh, yeah" comeback.

"I wish you were in yonder sea," the red-haired man rejoined.

"With a good boat under me," Juli, the voice of the harper's memory and all of the riddle songs he knew, replied. Fortunately, Juli had lived through plenty of riddle songs already, and Torchy had nothing on the Lady Ragnell and her brother whom Julianne had encountered with Sir Gawain.

"And the bottom for to break," Torchy said, which Juli thought was pretty weak.

"And ye to be drowned," said the boy harper. The fuming dandy vanished in a spurt of flame and Juli's young host ran down the road past the singed spot in the dirt.

CHAPTER XXVI

▲▲▲

In the time of Bold Buccleuch, the renegade harper sang along with the banjo that Gussie and Sir Walter's ghost carried in the basket bag. In Gussie's own time, Faron sang the next verse along with the Gypsy's violin and the banjo, which Sam Hawthorne had patched through from the Other World on the cellular phone. And in a time somehow the same as theirs while at once being a long time before, the boy harper hosting Juli lived out the same song with the sad, bedraggled corpse of a poor young girl crying for revenge upon a cruel sister.

> "A famous harper passing by,
>   Binnorie, O Binnorie
> The sweet pale face he chanced to spy
> By the bonny milldams of Binnorie."

Giorgio, as the miller, had stripped the body of its fine jewelry and clothing before shoving it back into the millstream. Then he took Isabelle's rings to sell for drink to comfort him for his sorry lot in life to be abused by first his wife and then by Torchy Burns.

The Fair Isabelle washed up, considerably the worse for wear, some days later at the feet of the boy harper. The fishes and rocks had worked upon the body until it was unidentifiable but the boy, whose sensitive heart broke with pity, was also moved by a preadolescent attraction for the gruesome, plus, unbeknownst to him, an inbred instinct for the magical he had from being a seventh son. So he fished the battered body out and made of the once-beautiful flesh another beautiful thing.

Some people claim that it wasn't the body itself that was made into a harp, but that the body decayed and fertilized a linden tree, and it was that tree that was used for the harp, but when Gussie Turner looked close at the banjo sitting there in her basket bag as Buccleuch's Irish harper sang the next verses, she noticed some things about that banjo she had never noticed before.

> "He made a harp of her breast bone,
>   Binnorie, O Binnorie;
> Whose sounds would melt a heart of stone
> By the bonny milldams of Binnorie.

> "The strings he framed of her yellow hair,
>   Binnorie, O Binnorie;
> Whose notes made sad the listening ear
> By the bonnie milldams of Binnorie.

> "And what did he do with her fingers so sma'?
>   Binnorie, O Binnorie
> He made them pegs to tune his vial
> By the bonny milldams of Binnorie."

Gussie had been traveling with that banjo all over the United States of America, across the Atlantic Ocean, and across England and Scotland, and never before had she seen that what she had taken for plastic in the tuning pegs did indeed seem to be bone, now that she looked at it, and so did the inlay on the neck. The strings had a funny appearance too. They weren't gut and they weren't metal and they always stayed in tune. They looked like brass and since she didn't play, she'd never really paid any attention but at one time, maybe, they could have been tight-wound and woven hair, transformed, she supposed, by all the magic that was going around. She didn't even want to think about the hide stretched across as the banjo head but now she had some idea of what had hap-

pened to that magic harp from long ago. She thought that
would explain why this banjo, made by that Appalachian
witchman luthier from, perhaps, an older instrument,
had served Sam Hawthorne so well over the years against
so many enemies.

The song continued:

> "He laid the harp upon a stone
> And straight it began to play alone
> O yonder sits my father, the king
> And yonder sits my mother, the queen
> And yonder stands my brother Hugh
> And by him my sweet William, true.
> But the last tune that the harp play'd then
> Was—'Woe to my sister, false Jane!' "

▲▲▲

The storyteller's words pierced through the fog and every-
body listening felt lost and lonesome, up there in the
mountains stranded by that broken-down bus. A little
patch of fog floated away on a breeze and the storyteller
saw, off to one side of her, on a rocky outcropping, three
elk grazing under the trees.

Then there was a rumble and a shriek and in a few
more minutes, a train rushed past them, rattling and roll-
ing and streaking on by, car after car with ghosty people
staring out the lounge windows into the dark, and in the
passenger cars nothing showing but just the blank lids of
lowered shades over the windows.

When the train had passed, the storyteller took a deep
breath and said, "It was Willie MacKai, of course, who
came back into that harp after it was made into a living
thing again from that poor girl's dead flesh. He was the
one who told on that mean sister. And Brose Fairchild
turned her ring widdershins three times on her finger and
then he left her to her hanging, but this time he left, not
out into some haze, but through that harp too. So did
Julianne Martin, abandoning that boy harper as she real-
ized that her role had ended with him. Likewise Anna Mae
left Sir William just before he killed himself in remorse for

his fickleness bringing on the death of his true love and the craziness of her poor jealous sister. Those four souls left through the harp music and stayed with it until it took them where they were next to go. Now, at that point, they felt real close to being themselves again, and within the Wizard's own spell, they would have been free, but Torchy Burns had sentenced them to serving seven years under her and they were stuck in her spell without some stronger magic to free them.

"As for Torchy, she was having the devil's own time figuring out what to do after she'd failed to stop Julianne. I wonder, you know, if she was trying all that hard at that. She didn't like what the other devils had said to her about making everything and everybody pure for a while. She didn't like being counted out of the action. So maybe she just screwed up for spite. Or maybe she was drunk or high at the time. But she left Giorgio to his fate, condemned to be in the miller's dam for finishing off poor Isabelle, and he, if you'll remember rightly, didn't have a string ring to pull himself out again before he died.

"But now that the banjo was in the ghost realm, it was callin' its own to join it."

▲▲▲

"So, ye claim to be my great-grandson," Bold Buccleuch said to Wat when the banjo had finished its song. "I've a good mind to have ye prove yoursel' at arms but I ken yer a lammiter."

"A what?" Gussie asked Wat.

"My limp," he said. "I had a lame leg from boyhood. Now that my presence is stronger than yours, I suppose you seem to have it too. Just as well. I'd never best the Bold Buccleuch in battle," he said fondly. "A proper terror he was."

"I'm touched," the Widow Hetherton said to his lordship. "Ye'll no pick on a lammiter man though ye'll mak' one of my poor guest Toppet, and despoil a helpless widow woman. Fie!"

"Woman, ye'll no rebuke me under my ain roof!"

Footsteps stumped into the hall then, and a man in

somewhat tattered battle dress clomped to the fireplace and speared a piece of meat from the spit.

"God's blood, 'tis Christie's Jock! Laddie, I thought we'd left ye for dead in Northumberland gin I received yer ransom letter."

"And dead I'd be in Northumberland i' truth gin I'd waited for you to ransom me, Buccleuch. I maun use my natural gifts instead. The provost had a bonny daughter, The Flower of Northumberland they ca'ed her. I offered t' marry her and mak' her my lady."

"Ah, and what would your Mary have to say aboot that?"

"I shudder to think on't. But this lassie served to gie me a horse and siller tae cross the border with and then I tuke the siller and hired her a horse and sent her home again greetin'."

"Ah, Jock, ye should nae brak her tender hairt sae sare, mon. If ye'd fetched her here, I'd hae comforted her soon enough."

"That I know, Buccleuch, but I've mony years tae go before I'm sae hard as ye that I would turn o'er tae yer tender maircies a lassie who stole from her parents for love of me. She's nae yet sixteen."

Buccleuch smacked his lips but then frowned. "See that that too tender hairt o' yers gets nae in the way o' business, Jock."

The Widow Hetherton burst into tears. "Undone! I'm a' undone by such ruffians as these!"

"My laird, can't you relent and let this woman have back her goods?" Sir Walter asked. "You're a man of business, I know, but also a great-hearted man, humorous and wise, and you only steal from necessity—"

"Says who?" Buccleuch demanded.

"Well—er—I did. In my bukes. I'd heard about you as a lad, you see, and read the ballads of your exploits and so I wrote bukes about you and these others."

"*Did* ye noo? And did anybody read these bukes?"

Now Sir Walter was on territory where he was sure of himself. "Probably most of the literate world, I'd say, if sales figures are any indication. In my day you becam' a

great hero in Scotland, even in England and America, not
to mention Germany, Italy, France, Spain, and the other
countries where my bukes were translated." He hesitated
a moment, then said in a dramatic voice, "Ye ken, Great-
Grandsire, that we cam' frae a time two hundred years
frae noo, when ye've lang been deid."

"Weel, ah *kenned* tha' mooch. I'm nae sae auld as tae
barely ha' grown sons, nae mair grandsons, nae mair
great-grandsons nae mair great wights o' yer advanced
years, though the resemblance is undeniable—yer the image o' my ane lost Wat. And then, wha' wi' yer unco
garmints and yer misshapen harp, and tha' shadowish
lass a'ways joost behind ye, 'tis clear yer nae mortal
wight. But if I've nae fear of the ghosts of my slain enemies, and I have nane, then why maun I fear the speerit
of my descendant? Now, tell me mair aboot mesel' in
these bukes o' yers . . ."

"The King himself has read them," Sir Walter said.

The Widow Hetherton crept forward a pace and Gussie saw a blade in her left hand, held low in the fold of her
skirt. The hand also wore a wire metal ring on its middle
finger, and the fabric of the skirt caught on it as she
brought the blade up. Gussie, with a dancer's balance
strengthened by a few years of aikido when she was tending bar, reached out with a foot and knocked the Widow
sideways so that she dropped the blade in the nasty
rushes littering the floor. It vanished without a clatter or
a shimmer of light on the blade and the Widow
Hetherton spat at her.

A girl Gussie hadn't noticed before stepped forward
and helped the woman to her feet.

"Now, Jeannie Gordon, ye shouldnae be soilin' yerself
with the likes o' her, henny," Buccleuch called.

"My Jeannie's but thinkin' o' yer reputation, Buccleuch," a young man who Gussie noticed was hand-
somer and not so rough-looking as the rest offered.

"Glenlogie, yer besotted with women noo that ye've
the flo-oor o' the Gordons tae wife. Tell me more about
what ye wrote of me, Great-Grandson."

Gussie noticed as Jeannie moved away from the

Widow Hetherton that Jeannie too wore the ring and a new intelligence peered from the Widow Hetherton's eyes as she too noticed Jeannie's ring. So, at least two of Gussie's friends were here, in the personas of the Widow, living out her ballad, and Jeannie, apparently somewhat after she had almost died for the love of Glenlogie.

And though Wat may have written about Buccleuch and his men in books, there was no ballad in which Buccleuch himself was the principal hero and for very good reason, as she now saw. But Jock was self-admittedly the betrayer of the Fair Flower of Northumberland. She'd have to see his hand. He and Glenlogie were having a chat aside that made her think that she might be right, especially when the banjo broke into first "The Fair Flower of Northumberland" and then "Glenlogie" as if providing theme music for the men. The renegade harper began to sing, with Glenlogie and Jeannie providing harmony, and Jock adding a baritone.

Wat continued to regale Buccleuch with all of the latter's noble (and totally literary) deeds, and Buccleuch was growing more and more thoughtful until he said to the Widow, "Madame, 'tis in my rough-humored though good-natured and totally noble way that I've been havin' sport wi' ye. The truth is that I caught the villains who robbed ye before e'er ye cam' here tae me, and my great-grandson here was right tae bring ye. Let it never be said that a widow lady applies to the Keeper of Liddesdale for justice and goes hame disappointed."

"Then you'll give her back her stock?" Gussie blurted from within the apparition of Sir Walter.

"Aye, providin' my great-grandsire here agrees tae pay me fee for every buke he sells wi' mah nam' in it. A man's reputation is a thing tae bank wi'."

"I'd do sae gladly, for the sake of my honor and yours and this lady's livelihood," Wat said with genuine sadness. "But my ain lands have recently been despoiled."

"What? Are the English dogs still at it in your time? And after a' ye wrote aboot me?"

"No, Great-Grandsire, this was fell magic. Not English, nor even Scots."

"Wha'? Outlanders? Despoilin' my descendants?"

"Aye, and burnin' the bukes."

"The bukes aboot mesel'?"

"Amang others. These same folk were chasing us when we met wi' the Widow Hetherton's trod."

"Do ye ken where they might be found?"

Wat consulted Gussie, who told him, "I've a pretty good idea they'll have gone after Faron and Ellie. We can try back at Carrs'."

"Aye," Wat said, and relayed the information to Buccleuch.

Buccleuch slammed his fist onto the table and scared three field mice into flight. "Then wha' dew we dew sittin' aboot! We ride!"

Gussie blurted out again, "But you've been dead three hundred years or better before these people were born."

Jeannie Gordon spoke up in the unmistakable tones of Willie MacKai, "Then we'll haunt the living shit out of the sorry sons of bitches!"

CHAPTER XXVII

▲▲▲

Though Giorgio had been the worst of his tribe, he was by no means the only rotten apple in the barrel, and his henchmen kept Faron and Ellie captive while they looted Janet Carr's estate in their search for the banjo. Giorgio's wife and uncle remained aloof, indifferent to the search, the uncle playing on his violin, lost in the world of the music, and the wife, as if in a trance, held the phone, through which the banjo kept playing.

This was the stage in the movies or in books, Ellie thought, where the good guys tried to talk the bad guys out of their evil deeds or at least get a long drawn-out explanation from them of why they were perpetrating their crimes. Meanwhile, of course, the good guys were either taping the explanation as a confession or there was a handy police official in the wings, who was listening and taking it all down in shorthand.

Ellie didn't expect rescue. She did ask Giorgio's wife what had become of Gussie, but the woman just shrugged and flipped a cigar butt at her.

"Don't you know those things are bad for you?" Faron asked, but the woman was again engrossed in the music coming from the telephone and from her uncle's hands. Ellie thought that she looked like a woman who was using the music to have a long, hard talk with herself. She was still young and she looked plenty tough, but her nose had been broken and her eyebrows and upper lip were split in more than one place. Two of her teeth were patched with gold.

The banjo began a song Ellie didn't remember and Faron only knew slightly. " 'The Flowers of the Forest,' " he said. "Sort of an elegy for the men lost at Flodden, especially those from the Ettrick Forest. I didn't recognize it at first because it's being played in march time."

Uncle Theo manfully filled in with all sorts of violin ornamentation, though it was plain that he was a fine violinist of the concert type and not much for doing Scottish folk music in the normal course of things. But he had been deprived of playing since his nephew forbade it, and now he played as if anyone who tried to take his fiddle from him again would have to pry it, as the NRA slogan went, from his cold, dead fingers.

"Someone should teach him 'MacPherson's Lament,' " Faron remarked.

"Do I know that one?"

"About the famous fiddler who was going to be hanged, and when people came from all around to see the execution, hoping to buy his fiddle after he was dead, he broke the fiddle instead of parting with it."

"Good for MacPherson and good for you, honey," Ellie said. "I think the old fiddler just helped you recover another song. But I also don't think he would have given you his violin if he didn't have more respect for musical instruments than that."

But as they listened to the music, the swish of tires through mud and the rumbling of an engine announced the arrival of another car, which parked in front of the cottage.

A tall, gray-haired man unfolded himself from the driver's seat and an elfish dark-haired woman popped out of the passenger seat, followed by a very black man in a Polar Circalen sweatshirt and a Laplander hat in blue and red with white rickrack trim. From the backseat, another black man, a black woman, and three smallish blond people clad alike in jeans and ice-blue and purple anoraks stepped out onto the gravel driveway.

"Wow, great!" said Dan, who was, of course, the tall,

gray-haired man. "They're having a party and it looks like they've already made friends with some Gypsies. This is going to be super!"

He rushed into the cottage while Terry and the new-comers began unloading instruments from the boot of the car.

"Hey, gang!" Dan yelled from the doorway, then saw Uncle Theo in the middle of the room playing. "Oops," he said in a whisper, and grinned at Giorgio's wife and whispered to Faron and Ellie, "You're going to love these guys we've brought back from Norway and Iceland. Gachero and his friends know more of the Icelandic songs than the Torun, Solveg, and Soren do."

One of the Gypsy men emerged from the bedroom with an armload of clothing. Giorgio's wife, who snapped out of her trance when the newcomers arrived, set the banjo-broadcasting phone thoughtfully down on the win-dowsill and withdrew her dagger from her sash, fingering the blade and flashing a wide golden smile at Dan. "Hel-*lo*," she said.

"Hi, there. I haven't met you before but I'm Dan. What do you play? Wait till you see what these guys who came with us do. You're going to love it."

"Call me Rosa," Giorgio's widow said, arching her neck coquettishly.

"Hi, I'm Terry," the dark woman said, linking her arm with Dan's as she dropped an African drum on his foot.

But Dan picked the instrument up and walked over to Theo, where he could better hear the interplay between the telephone-amplified banjo and the violin. "Cool," he said, and began pounding out a march rhythm on the African drum.

One of the Gypsies who had been searching the house saw the instruments the Africans were piling in the cen-ter of the room and swooped down to scoop up a fine concertina, which he began playing along with Dan's drumming, Uncle Theo's fiddling, and the telephone-transmitted banjo.

The same song played over and over until every Gypsy

and each of the newcomers who didn't have an instrument joined in stamping their feet, swaying from side to
side, clapping their hands, or snapping their fingers to the
music as if compelled by the cellular pied piper. After the
song had repeated enough times, Faron began singing the
lyrics and Ellie and Terry joined in with harmonies. But
when they got to the first refrain, "The flowers of the
forest are a' wede awa'," which Terry hastily whispered
to Ellie meant "weeded out" in Scots, a new instrument
joined the others. Dan looked up from his drumming,
eyes slitted in ecstasy to say, *"Way* cool. I was wondering
how we could get some bagpipes in with this!"

The pipe music skirled closer accompanied by the
sound of hoofbeats. Suddenly the banjo sounded much
louder, much closer. Outside the cottage the setting sun
gleamed saffron and scarlet in the mud puddles along the
road, cloaking the clouds with bold gory glory. Ellie,
standing nearest the open door, felt the wind rise and saw
the trees bow down as if more traffic were coming up the
road, the weeds flattening as if pressed by tires—or
hooves or feet.

The music outdoors grew louder and louder until suddenly the pipes whined to a halt and the door burst open,
admitting a biting cold wind.

Giorgio's wife, Terry and Dan, Uncle Theo and the
Gypsy man with the concertina, Gachero, the other Africans, and the three Norwegians all crowded into the
doorway, their hair whipped across their faces as the
wind forced them back inside.

Ellie hung on to the door frame longer than the others,
restraining her hair with her hands and peering down the
road. Though she saw no pipers or horses, she did seem
to make out, very dimly, the shadowy outline of a small
curly-haired woman carrying a somewhat more distinct
form that looked like—

"Faron, it's Gussie and the banjo. But there's something wrong with them."

A long derisive laugh erupted in Ellie's face and a
slatternly woman with messy red hair and bloodshot eyes
sauntered into the room carrying a bottle of scotch.

"Hail, hail, the gang's all here," she said and added, allowing her tacky faded pink chenille bathrobe to fall open across her thighs as she sat cross-legged on one of the kitchen chairs, "What the hell do we care? What the hell do we care?" To the wind that had just blown in with her, she said, "Well, I'll be blessed if it ain't the Bold Buccleuch. H'lo there, Buck. What are you doing above the dirt at this hour? Did you bring back that banjo just for little old me? Buck, I'm touched that you remembered, after all these years!"

She laughed again. "You know, little dears, I'm almost sorry I got you into this. The boss says I'm washed up, that debauchery is going out of fashion. Oh, don't worry, Rosa, there'll always be a market for the product I've been supplying to your people for distribution."

Rosa glared at her and spat, the glob landing on the bright red lacquer on the nail of Torchy's right big toe. Torchy, unmindful, rubbed it away with the ball of her other foot.

"They say people are going to stop all the freewheeling fucking around I worked so hard to promote and that blessed Pestilence Devil ruined with his nasty little SID plagues. They say all the important people are going to stop doing drugs and drinking so they can concentrate on really serious power mongering. What's going to be left for a poor girl to do? They don't care if I'm left here playing nursemaid to you suckers for the next seven years until time for me to deliver you up to them."

"That wasn't the deal!" Faron said. "Gussie said that if they played by your rules and got back all the songs and the seven songs for every song they lived through, like you said, they could come back and we could try to take the songs home again."

Torchy shrugged. "So I lied. I do that, didn't you notice? It's part of my stock in trade, along with wine, women (or men, depending on your preference—both for that matter), and song. Crap, I don't know why I let the boss talk me into it. I'm not nearly as good a negotiator as those guys, you know? I just want to have a good time and they're always scheming, always playing games. I

must have been stoned to let them talk me into helping
them get rid of music. It was the best part of Fairie and
the *only* thing they let me bring with me. It was"—she
sniffed and sniveled and began to sob—"it was kind of
like my *dowry,* you know? All I had left of my glamor
besides, of course, my incredibly sexy appearance, and
now they're taking it away!"

"Oh, don't cry," Dan said, patting her on the shoulder. "There's always rock and roll."

"Not for long," she sobbed. "That's next. Ummm,
that feels good," she writhed like a cat as he massaged
her shoulders.

"So why don't you just bring everybody back if you
don't want to stick around here?" Dan asked.

"Yeah," Faron said. "If you've got nothing against the
music after all, let us go. All we want is to sing a few
songs and make a few bucks."

Torchy laughed bitterly. "You know there's more to it
than that. Maybe, if you were all mine and only mine, I
could bring them back. But you're not. The music keeps
these poor saps here in this age connected with all that
went before—with Buck here and Sir Walter," she nodded at the shadows, which were assuming ghostly form
now that the sunset was rapidly fading. "It keeps people
human. Hell's bells, it almost keeps *me* human and I'm
not."

"Could we ask the Wizard Michael to bring them
back?" Ellie asked.

Torchy shook her head. "Nope. They're stuck there
the whole seven years and then you can bet my boss will
be here to collect them. And if I don't deliver them, my
ass is in hot lava. Mick the Wiz can't do much of anything without my help. I thought you knew that. His
power was mostly earthly except for a little inspiration
from me. I'm sorry, ladies and gentlemen, but I'm all the
magic you've got and I just can't get involved anymore."
She blew her nose and wiped her eyes. "I just wanted you
to know how rotten I feel about it all."

"What you mean is that you just got snockered and

were feeling maudlin," said Gussie's voice within her now ghosty-looking form.

"That too," Torchy said. "But at least with you and the banjo in never-never land with the ghosties and such, I'm off the hook about bringing you back. And Rosa and her gang can take care of the others, so I guess it's ta for now, luvvies. Pip pip, cheerio, and all that."

"Wait," Dan said. "What if we did have our own magic? Would you let us try to use it without getting in our way?"

"Honey, you got *nothin'* as powerful as me," she said.

"Maybe we do. You said yourself that music was not only some of your strongest stuff, but it was also a force for the other side. Maybe we could use that."

Torchy's eyebrow lifted. "Maybe."

"Would you stand in our way?"

"Depends on what you're going to do."

"Wouldn't it be better for you," Ellie said gently, "if you didn't know and we just sort of snuck one past you?"

"Good point," said Torchy, standing up with her robe's hem daintily held in two fingers and her bottle of scotch clutched in the other. "I'm going to go powder my nose—and throw up. Plot quickly, darlings."

Terry Pruitt's eyes were shining as she looked up at Dan. "Are you thinking what I'm thinking?"

"Yeah, but a lot depends on Brose and Anna Mae and them. How many songs have they gotten back already, Ellie?" he asked.

Faron flipped open a notebook and said, "Counting today? With the primary ballads, variants, seven freebies per each retrieved ballad, and all of the associated songs, five hundred forty-five. Plus three instrumentals I couldn't find any words for."

Rosa asked suspiciously, "What is this? What you doing? You going to call the cops?"

"Of course not, Rosa," Dan said. "Cops don't usually know any magic—or music. But Gachero and his buddies and Torun and her friends taught us this cool custom, something they do in Iceland and in some parts of Scotland. I think it might help. Give me your hand."

"Why? I don't understand."

Gachero said, in an Oxford-educated voice, "You see, Rosa, it is simply a matter of synchronicity. The Icelandic peoples believe that they contact their ancestors by forming a line of life, a sort of a snake dance, and chanting and singing all of their sagas and songs from the beginning of memory. Thus they keep their history, their national personality, their spirits, alive. I see no reason why such a tactic might not be useful here."

"Makes sense to me. You only keep the songs alive by singing them and maybe we can bring Gussie and Willie and the others back by singing the songs they're bringing back to life."

Rosa grabbed Theo's hand and said, "This is sensible. My family, we are great musicians, great menders of musical instruments. Then I marry that Giorgio. I think, poor boy, to be so hurt and I find I am married to a dead man who poisons what he claims to protect. Music doesn't pay so good, but is part of the Gypsy soul."

The Africans, the Gypsies, the Norwegians, Dan, Terry, Faron, and Ellie all formed a line. Ellie was on the end and she felt large, sausage-sized fingers grasp her own, though no one was on that side of her. The fingers let go of hers long enough to slap her on the behind, then rejoined hers innocently, as if it had been one of the Gypsies who had done it. But then, she had not yet been formally introduced to the Bold Buccleuch's ghost.

Theo removed Rosa's hand so that it linked with his belt, and did the same with Torun on the other side, freeing his hands for his violin. On the center of the table, the banjo suddenly appeared, as solid as it ever had been though slightly glowing around the edges.

A bagpipe wheezed into its first groan as Dan, Terry, and Gachero picked up hand drums while the concertina-playing Gypsy also attached himself to the people on either side of him in a way that wouldn't interfere with his playing.

A long sigh of silence throbbed through the cottage, then the banjo chimed the first notes of "The Gypsy Rover" and everyone began to sing, even the Africans and the Norwegians, who watched everybody else's lips. And when all the words were exhausted to the version that Faron and Ellie knew, Gachero sang a similar song in a Kenyan dialect, and an Icelandic one, and Torun and the others sang variants they knew, until the banjo changed tunes again.

For seven nights and seven days they sang and danced, until their limbs were so weary and their throats so raw, their hands so sore, they could barely move, but still they sang the songs and danced, always linked, always following the banjo. The first two nights, the Bold Buccleuch and his men, Gussie and Sir Walter, and Jeannie Gordon, Glenlogie, the Widow Hetherton, and Neighbor Cuddy solidified gradually to be seen dancing among their living partners, though by morning the ghosts faded once more.

But by the third morning, the forms that belonged to Gussie, to Glenlogie, the Widow, and Jock who had spurned the Flower of Northumberland remained visible, though see-throughish and shadowy, in the dim light filtering through the curtains.

Every once in a while someone would detach from the line and get water or drinks or food for the others, to be chewed and swallowed during pauses between songs or phrases. Now and then one dancer would bow out for a brief rest or to massage the limbs of the others, but never more than one at a time broke the line for all the seven days and seven nights.

During some of the wilder murder ballads or drinking songs, a whirling, high-kicking mote of light cavorted in front of them and around them, and a raucous laugh rose over the singing, a familiar voice shouting, "I can't stand still for this, luvvies, but I can sure as hell dance to it!"

And on the seventh night, just as they were about to drop, the banjo played "The Flower of Northumberland," and Jock waved, and twisted his ring three times widdershins on his left finger, and Anna Mae stepped from his shadow and into the room and joined hands with the living. And the banjo played "Glenlogie" and Jeannie Gordon and her love dropped hands, twisted their rings three times widdershins around their fingers and who but Willie MacKai and Julianne Martin should step from their shadows and into the room to join hands with the others? And finally the banjo played the "Borders Gathering Song" or "The Fray of Suport," and the Widow Hetherton gave her ring three fierce yanks around her finger and her shadow swelled and bulked until it solidified into Brose Fairchild, who also joined hands with those beside him, linking the two ends of the snake dance as the banjo played its final tune, "Will the Circle Be Unbroken?"

CHAPTER XXVIII

▲▲▲

The storyteller had been so engrossed in her own story that she barely noticed the shifting movement of the people around her.

Toward morning, when she finished her story, the dawn pierced the fog at the same time a stiff breeze blew away the patch that had veiled the bus and the passengers to reveal that while the storyteller had been engrossed in her own tale, the other passengers and the bus had disappeared except for one lone figure who sat across from her, her sandaled toes touching the storyteller's. As the last scarf of fog blew away, the remaining listener lifted her head, and her broad straw hat with the chili pepper and rattlesnake hide hatband tilted back to reveal unruly flame-red hair and a dopey, irreverent grin.

This last listener clapped three times, slowly. "Well done, Gussie, luv," she said. "But what happened to the others later? I've missed you, you know. I was—called away rather suddenly by the peace crisis in Eastern Europe."

"Well, Torchy, without interference from you, the kids spent the rest of their seven years researching and singing in Ireland, Wales, Cornwall, all of those places where the songs had direct relatives, then on to Germany and France, the rest of Europe, and back through Africa with Gachero. They'll be along directly."

"I know. I can hear the banjo. I suppose you were going to meet them?"

"I was."

"Well, then, I'll just give you a lift—" She indicated a bright red BMW.

"Mighty kind of you to bother, Torchy, and somewhat uncharacteristic," Gussie said, rising to her feet.

"You've quite gotten the gift of gab since I saw you last."

"Wat's legacy."

"How nice," Torchy responded, climbing in the driver's seat. "Buckle up, now, there's a dear," she said, but the seat belt snaked around Gussie like an anaconda, strapping her in chest and waist and padlocking itself at her hip. "Safety first!" Torchy trilled, though she did not buckle her own belt as she gunned the car into a blurring takeoff down the steep mountain highway. "Now then, where are we meeting them?"

"In the desert, by the banks of the Rio Grande," Gussie said. "How have you been, Torchy?"

And the Debauchery Devil's eyes gleamed red, reflecting the dawn burning through her windshield, she said, "Not good, luvvie. In fact, you'll find I've been fully rehabilitated."

ABOUT THE AUTHOR

ELIZABETH SCARBOROUGH won the 1989 Nebula Award for best novel for *The Healer's War,* which was loosely based on her experiences as an Army nurse in Viet Nam. She is also the author of eleven other books, most of them humorous fantasy, and numerous short stories which have appeared in various anthologies. Her interests include weaving, beadworking, and folk music. She is presently at work on her third serious novel as well as The Songkiller Saga. She and her four cats make their home near Seattle, Washington.

Lulubelle Baker—otherwise known as the Debauchery Devil—is up to her old tricks again. In the following scene, she seems to be trying to seduce the very practical Gussie into gambling . . . but only the devil knows what else Lulubelle is planning.

HOME ON THE RANGE

Now fully in Lulubelle Baker persona, the Debauchery Devil drove her red sports car across Nevada so fast even radar couldn't detect it, and screeched to a halt in Las Vegas.

"What are we stopping for?" Gussie asked.

"I'm sorry, sweetie, this is work," Lulubelle apologized. "This is one of my other responsibilities, one I kind of enjoy now that all my other pet projects have been modified to such a borin' extent. Come on in if you want to."

Gussie figured that she was at least three days ahead of time already, since she had originally planned to take the glacially slow Green Turtle bus all the way from Seattle to San Francisco and to switch there to a pickup truck belonging to a friend before driving for another day or so to get close to where she was now. Lulubelle's devilish driving and the little trick with time warping them out of Oregon and into Nevada had put Gussie considerably ahead of schedule.

Night had fallen as they drove toward Las Vegas but now, on the street, it was bright as day from the big lit signs. Gussie lost

Lulubelle while she gawked at the people, some of them in jeans and sweats, some of them in fancy evening dress, milling around the one-armed bandits in one room, waiting for a show to begin in a hallway that looked like grand balls should be given there. In another direction she saw roulette wheels and heard the voices of the dealers, the exclamations of winners, and the swearing of losers, and caught a flash of red hair. There were, of course, a lot of people with red hair there, many of them women, but that particular shade was the one she had been looking at for the last several hundred miles. Sure enough, there was the Debauchery Devil, who, having made a lightning change of clothing into a red-sequined strapless number, was all snuggled up to some boy who didn't look old enough to drink, much less gamble. The boy grinned as he raked in his winnings.

"I didn't think you ever did anything *nice* for anybody," Gussie said to the redhead.

"Why, sure, honey. In this place they call me Lady Luck. Now that I've encouraged that sweet young thing, he's going to be a true love of mine rest of his life. Doubt if he'll ever get over me."

"I see."

"Oh, don't be so prim and schoolmarmish. Honestly, for a bartender you are the awfulest old prude."

"I'm just not sure I believe you," Gussie said. "You do seem to be an awful lot of people."

The redhead deserted the young man with a peck on the cheek. "Okay, I'll show you. What's your pleasure?"

"I don't even play Lotto."

"Well, not *here* you don't, but if you wanted to I could fix it for you. To tell you the truth, I'm partial to poker myself, and the horses. The boss says I'm reactionary—I still kinda like tradition and the cards and I go a long way back, what with tarot and all. You play poker?"

"I don't reckon I have enough to get in a game around here," Gussie said.

"Sure you do, sugar. Whatcha got on you?"

"About twenty-five dollars."

"Get you some quarters and try the one-armed bandits."

"No. I need that money."

"Don't be such a spoilsport. Come on. *One* quarter."

"Okay. Just one," Gussie said grimly and she dropped it in a machine and waited. Lulubelle didn't wait, however. With a bored look on her face she thumped the machine with the heel of her hand and the pictures all came up dollar signs, and the coins came pouring out. "There. Now there's your stake. Let's go play us some poker."

As they passed the line of people dressed in evening wear Gussie couldn't help craning her neck to see who was in the show. "What is it?"

"Just another damn lecture."

"But I can see there's chorus girls or something on the sign, even though I can't see what it says."

"Yeah. Well, it's about how to use sex in advertising."

"No singers or dancers or comedians?"

"Shoot, no. Nobody wants that stuff anymore. Where's the profit? Although they do have some snappy advertising jingles during the lecture, and the chorus girls do lots of high kicks to keep the audience interested. It's all the rage these days to have meaningful, profitable entertainment. Part of what my boss is promotin'. *Now* do you feel like playin' poker with me?"

"I feel more like another tequila sunrise. A *lecture? Really?* What have things come to? That's the most boring damned excuse for a show I ever heard."

"Yeah, they don't pass out programs anymore, just informational pamphlets. Barrel of laughs."

Gussie bought her chips. Feeling totally intimidated in her smelly and soiled pink sweats among all the well-heeled high rollers, she sat at the table Lulubelle chose. The players looked at Gussie like they could smell her too. But when the dealing commenced Lulubelle blew a kiss at the deck and Gussie won without trying—and kept winning. It wasn't even fun, it was so effortless. Evidently Lulubelle felt the same way, because before long she leaned over and gave Gussie a hot buss on the cheek and wandered off.

Gussie cashed in her chips right afterward, much to the disgust of the others. The cashier handed her one hundred thousand dollars and asked if she wouldn't like more chips. She stared at the money and asked if he had traveler's checks, instead. He directed her to an all-night bank in the lobby.

As she walked toward the bank, she kept wondering when it was going to turn into dried leaves or dust, as fairy gold is supposed to. Then she thought, Well, it might disappear, indeed. The IRS could take it out of her account without her knowing about it. If she bought traveler's checks, anybody looking for her could trace her. If she kept it in cash, she'd probably get mugged. Oh well, easy come, easy go. She stepped back out into the night and found an all-night auto dealership. One brown minivan later she was on the road again.

It did cross her mind to wonder why the Debauchery Devil in her Lady Luck guise decided to favor somebody who was supposed to be her opponent. Then again, there was one thing about that redhead: You never could tell what was on her alleged mind.

Gussie was happy with the van. Nobody knew where she'd gone or what she'd bought and that would make it hard finding her again. As soon as she was safely down the highway, she pulled off at a truck stop and climbed into the back on the nice soft, new-smelling cushions to sleep off the tequila sunrises.

Drifting off to sleep, she wondered again about the redheaded devil. The woman had described the other devils—had even blabbed everything she knew about the meetings they held. All presumably while under the influence. Though she had talked drunk, she didn't act any drunker than usual once they got to the casino. And why had she just let Gussie win like that?

The devil woman's fecklessness and unpredictability were oddly familiar to Gussie, putting her in mind of the way certain musicians tended to act. She wondered if Torchy was really as crazy as she seemed, or if she was up to something.

"Dereliction of duty, D.D.," the boss said, leaning back in his swivel chair.

"O contrary, Chair. I have a lot of duties," the Debauchery Devil said, shrugging. "Couldn't pass through Vegas without making a few converts, now, could I?"

"D.D., you have the right attitude, but you're such a flake," the Expediency Devil said. He was a new, improved model over the slightly old-maidish–looking previous Expediency Devil. This one had crisp, dark curly hair and a lean, mean form that, if he had been mortal, would have been the result of meticulous, but efficient, exercise.

"I just think there are more pressing problems these days than a lot of broken-down warblers nobody listened to even before we wiped out their particular kind of—er—act," she said, in deference to the sensibilities of the others. "We have the people pretty well reconditioned now. Nobody's going to listen to a few jerks who haven't been heard from in years and can't even reenter the country legally." She blew a disdainful smoke ring from her Brimstone Light cigarette, the company brand with the forest-fire logo.

"She does have a point, Chair," the Expediency Devil

agreed. "And we have other agendas. Mustn't let this little prejudice of yours stand in the way of—"

"Don't you be telling me my job, X.P.," the Chairdevil snarled. "Fortunately, I have learned never to rely on D.D, and have arranged a reception committee at the border."

"Who's handling it?" X.P. asked.

"Minions who cannot be deterred by the spells in the cursed instrument carried by Mr. Willie MacKai."

"Minions have failed before."

"Ah, but these minions are cottonmouth water moccasins and a flash flood, as well as some very nasty wetback muggers. I don't think a banjo, even a magic one, is going to be much protection."

Long a lover of folk music and a friend to folk musicians, Elizabeth Scarborough at last brings her avocation to her fiction in the rousing tale of *The Songkiller Saga*. Read Volume 3, *Strum Again?* on sale April 1992, wherever Bantam Spectra Books are sold.
